FRESH
BREWED
MURDER

FRESH BREWED MURDER

Emmeline Duncan

KENSINGTON
PUBLISHING CORP.

www.kensingtonbooks.com

KENSINGTON BOOKS are published by

Kensington Publishing Corp.
119 West 40th Street
New York, NY 10018

All Kensington titles, imprints, and distributed lines are available at special quantity discounts for bulk purchases for sales promotion, premiums, fund-raising, educational, or institutional use.

Special book excerpts or customized printings can also be created to fit specific needs. For details, write or phone the office of the Kensington Sales Manager: Kensington Publishing Corp., 119 West 40th Street, New York, NY 10018. Attn. Sales Department. Phone: 1-800-221-2647.

The K logo is a trademark of Kensington Publishing Corp.

ISBN-13: 978-1-4967-3340-5 (ebook)
ISBN-10: 1-4967-3340-1 (ebook)

ISBN-13: 978-1-4967-3339-9
ISBN-10: 1-4967-3339-8

First Kensington Trade Paperback Printing: April 2021

10 9 8 7 6 5 4 3 2 1

Printed in the United States of America

For Nevin
May your coffee cup be ever full

Chapter 1

I'm still waiting for the day when I magically turn into an adult. One day I'll wake up, and my laundry will be washed, dried, folded, and even put away. I'll like smooth jazz, and the thought of a long lease, let alone a mortgage, won't scare me. My wardrobe will be elegant. I'll relish responsibility.

Today was not that day. Although it should be since my fledgling coffee business was scheduled to launch.

The world was my chocolate-covered espresso bean.

Once I made it through today.

I unlocked the gate to the Rail Yard, a food cart pod in inner Southeast Portland. Once a trolley turnaround spot, the lot developed into one of the best food cart destinations in Portland. Eight carts, including my new business, circled a center stage and a decommissioned short school bus converted into a beer stand.

Visions of cold brew danced through my head, but I needed to finish getting the cart ready before I could crack open the fridge and pour a glass. A carafe of house coffee filled the air with the scent of promise as it brewed.

I brewed a double espresso and sampled it, checking the machine's calibration. It was close to perfect, and after a few tweaks, and a few more shots, which I tasted and poured out, the espresso sang. I downed the final shot, hoping the jolt of caffeine would settle the jitters inside me.

Now I needed customers.

I carried a sandwich board out to the sidewalk and stepped back to look it over. The teal GROUND RULES logo was more retro than I'd intended, but it matched the feel of the cart, and it looked throwback hip. I loved the long window running the length of the trailer. An awning unfolded from the side and sheltered the ordering window from sun and rain.

"I didn't know you were here," my first customer said through a yawn as he ordered an Americano.

"We've only been open five minutes," I said. I pulled two shots and mixed them with eight ounces of hot water.

"You're the only shop open this early for blocks."

"Let me know what you think." I handed over his drink while he inserted his credit card into the tablet's chip reader.

"Perfect," he said after trying his coffee. He wandered to the bus stop on the corner.

My business partner, Harley, thought I was bananas for opening at 6:00 a.m. Few local indie shops open so early. But I wanted to catch as much of the morning commuter traffic as possible, even if it meant sacrificing sleep.

As I stood watching orange rays of the sun cut through the early-morning sky, I understood why shops chose to open later, especially in the winter, when the days are gray and drizzly.

Harley and I were doing this. The reality of the business opening hit me, leaving me proud and panicked. A jolt of cold brew steadied me.

A steady stream of customers trickled in. My nerves settled as I fell into the rhythm of pulling shots and bantering with people. Harley showed up at seven thirty and made drinks while I handled the customers. During a lull, I looked over, noting the purple stripes in her long black ponytail.

Harley looked at me and grinned. "Customers showing up on our first day is a good sign," she said in her low, husky voice like she smokes ten packs of cigarettes a day even though she only has a caffeine habit. No nicotine allowed around her since it might affect her ability to smell the coffee she roasts.

"Hallelujah," I said. "The sign on the street is working."

"Along with the social media blasts."

"Who can resist the siren song of coffee?"

Another customer walked up, and since I was in a good mood, I broke out the cold-reading skills my mother had taught me as a child. After all, a cold read pairs well with espresso.

I paused before I handed a mocha to a college-aged girl who'd struggled to make eye contact with me when ordering. "I sense you sometimes feel insecure, especially around people you don't know well."

"How'd you know? Strangers freak me out."

"I'm psychic," I said in an even tone as if I were serious.

"Oh yeah? Where am I going?"

I'd already noticed the PSU Vikings key chain dangling from the zipper of her backpack, and I knew the university had classes all summer. Her fitted V-neck T-shirt had the original cover of *Pride and Prejudice* printed on it. "You're on your way to school, and you're studying English."

"Oh my gosh, you're legit!" She stared at me with wide eyes.

I laughed, ready to confess I was teasing her and using the cold-reading skills used by mentalists, magicians, and con artists when a guy walked up. The girl turned to him. "She's amazing! Awesome coffee and she's psychic."

"Let's see proof."

I tilted my head to the side like I was reading his aura or something, but I analyzed his clothing. Chuck Taylors, quality jeans, and a graphic T-shirt inspired by the video game *Zelda*, or I was misinterpreting the reference.

"You're a kind person, and considerate, but when someone breaks your trust, you feel deep-seated anger. Keep that in mind today when you go to your job as a coder."

He blinked as the words hit home.

I didn't tell him most people would find meaning in the insight I'd busted out. I'd chosen it because it was an easy road to his trust. His profession was a guess, but multiple tech firms had opened in Portland, resulting in programmers roaming around the city, ordering coffee and arguing which brewery in town made the best IPA.

"What kind of drink do you want? Let me guess. House coffee, one sugar."

He blinked again. "Yes, please."

"See? She's amazing," the college girl said. They walked away together, leaning toward each other while talking.

Harley laughed. "What was that?"

I grinned at her. "The guy's drink was a wild guess. I was going to confess I was teasing them, but they seemed interested in each other."

"Now you're going to be known as both the witty and psychic partner in our business." Harley laughed again and started cleaning the espresso machine. But her phone rang, so she stepped outside.

"Well . . ." My words trailed off as I clocked a guy staring at me. He was older than my last two customers.

I analyzed him as he walked up. Stern face like he was angry or permanently unhappy. Hooded eyes. Even features. Button-down shirt, neatly ironed, tucked precisely into designer jeans, but finished with work boots. He'd be handsome if he smiled. I tried a cold reading on him. "You know, I bet you've faced some major problems in your life, but you've always found a way to overcome them."

His expression didn't waver. "Black coffee to go."

I poured his cup quickly and handed it over. He swiped his credit card, tapped the surface of the tablet with a quick slash of his finger, and stalked away, his spine stiff.

Harley bounced back into the cart. "The co-op called me back! We're meeting with them tomorrow at four p.m. Seriously, if they decide to carry our beans, we'll be set!"

"I still think we should set up a coffee club and mail beans monthly to subscribers."

"Like my aunt's farm in Kona."

No customers were in sight, so we poured a couple cups of coffee and sat down at the picnic table next to our cart.

A guy carrying several loaded bags of groceries walking through the entryway to the Rail Yard caught my eye, and his eyes locked onto our cart. His black hair fell into his eyes, giving him a pesky-younger-brother vibe. He detoured in our direction.

"Hello," Harley muttered to me.

"You must be with the new cart," he said.

"We're Ground Rules," Harley said. "We're excited to open!"

She sounded breathless. I hid a grin.

"It's nice to meet you, Ground Rules," he said.

"I'm Sage, and this is Harley."

He offered his hand, and we shook. "Sage is one of my favorite spices. I'm Zarek."

"Most people say Harleys are their favorite ride," Harley said, and I laughed. She blushed. "That came out wrong."

Zarek smiled. It reminded me of a five-year-old getting caught stealing candy. "How'd nice girls like you end up in a place like this?"

"We're starting a coffee-roasting business and needed a place to land," I said.

"Sounds like you were fortunate. You even scored the only spot with plumbed water instead of dealing with tanks."

"We definitely lucked out." Harley still sounded breathless.

"All of the old carts from across the street wanted to move in, but I guess the owner . . ." Zarek's voice trailed off.

"Introduced fresh caffeine?" I said.

Zarek laughed. "Exactly."

"What's happening across the street?" Harley asked. We all turned and looked. I remembered eating at a gyros cart there a few days before I left town last year to volunteer abroad. The old lot was fenced off, along with a couple of decrepit houses. A few people were standing next to the fence.

"The houses are being torn down, and a luxury apartment building will rise from the ashes. Some of the protesters are up in arms because none of the units will be affordable."

"What does that mean?" Harley asked.

"I'm no expert, but some apartment buildings rent a percentage of units below market rate. This building won't."

"I've read about this," I said. "Not this building specifically, but developers can get property-tax abatements if they rent units below market rate."

"How do you know this?" Harley asked.

"I read the paper."

"I've never seen you with a newspaper!"

"They have a website."

Zarek interrupted us. "It was nice meeting you. I'll see you around."

"Do you want a coffee to celebrate our first day in business?" Harley asked.

"I'm vegan, so if you can do a dairy-free cappuccino, I'm down. Or an Americano."

"One oat-milk cappuccino coming right up! I can bring it to your cart if you'd like," Harley said. She bustled off to make the drink while Zarek carried his grocery bags to his cart.

I followed my friend into Ground Rules.

"Way to dominate the conversation, Sage." Harley poured oat milk into a carafe.

"He's all yours," I promised.

"But now he's going to think you're the witty one."

"I'll purposefully say stupid things around him."

Harley laughed and started making the drink. The buzz of the espresso machine was music to my ears.

When the drink was done, Harley said, "I'm going to take this to Zarek. You stay here."

"No problem."

Harley stepped out of Ground Rules and paused as she debated which cart was Zarek's. Eventually, she spotted the partially opened door of the yellow Fala-Awesome cart and walked toward it.

I debated what to do, but I saw an older woman struggling to carry a box and several shopping bags into the Rail Yard. "Can I help you? I'm Sage. You must be a cart owner, so I'm one of your new neighbors."

She let me take one of her bags. A peek inside showed it was full of flour, sugar, and boxes of butter. I wasn't surprised when she led the way to the cart with the numbers 4 and 20 on the side with paintings of birds.

"What does your cart serve?" I asked. Was pot distribution legal from food carts since marijuana was now sold in licensed businesses? The mural of birds on the side of her cart was impressive, with lots of high-drama black-and-white contrast.

"Pie," she said. "You know, 'four and twenty blackbirds'?"

"Oh, the old nursery rhyme." "Sing a Song of Sixpence" was the last thing I'd thought of.

She acted absentminded. Given the vague look in her light blue eyes, she could've been high, except her pupils were wrong for an altered state. Her curly gray hair looked ready to take flight on its own.

But she looked friendly, so I reintroduced myself.

"Oh, where are my manners. I'm Macie. My cart isn't open on Mondays, but I wanted to drop off supplies and feed my babies."

Babies? I blinked as she went inside and put the butter away in the fridge, and the dry goods into a cabinet. A green-checked apron with an embroidered slice of cherry pie caught my attention. It looked handmade, with bright red pockets. It hung on a hook shaped like a curved spoon.

"That's my favorite apron," Macie said when she saw me looking at it. "I made it."

"It's cheerful."

"I sew daily. How many days of the week will you open? Pie goes well with coffee."

"Our current plan is Mondays to Fridays until two p.m."

"Too bad we'll barely overlap. I'm open Tuesdays to Sundays, although I'll take Tuesdays off after Labor Day." Macie grabbed a baggie filled with brown crumbs from the counter. She walked around her cart to the fence behind and tossed a handful of crumbs onto the sidewalk.

Within seconds, the area was full of pigeons.

"Isn't this a dainty feast?" she said as she scattered more crumbs.

I realized the birds must be her babies. There's a phrase the locals like: "Keep Portland weird." This lady was definitely at the forefront of the movement.

I walked back to my business.

My business. Literally. My cart. The words felt strange, but also right. Like I was meant to do this.

Harley was talking with Zarek as he chopped cabbage in his cart.

I paused. "What's the story of the lady with the pigeons?"

"Macie always stops by to feed the birds. Be glad, 'cause it took us months to convince her to feed the birds on the sidewalk instead of inside the Rail Yard. Know what's not fun? Trying to eat with pigeons flying around you."

"Gross," Harley said.

"I'm going to work on the cart for a bit," I told Harley, and she flapped her hands in a shooing motion. I mock-frowned at her and walked back to Ground Rules.

Harley joined me in the cart a few minutes later with a giant smile.

"Have fun chatting up the new neighbor?" I asked.

"Remember I called dibs."

I laughed.

Harley picked up her bag. "I'm off to roast beans unless you need me here?"

"I'll be fine."

Harley hugged me before racing off.

A few customers bought coffee before my brother marched up to the cart. His dark brown hair was damp, and he was dressed in a dark blue suit, so he was on his way to work.

"Pour-over?" I asked as he walked up and a too-rare smile lit his face, like a brief sunburst gone too soon.

"Please." Jackson inspected the exterior of the cart before bounding inside, his dress shoes clattering on the steps.

"Customers stay outside." I pointed to the door. But I couldn't stop myself from grinning.

"I'm not exactly a customer."

"Yeah, your great legal mind reviewed all my contracts." I suspected he saw me as a little kid with a play coffee stand. I'd forever be the obnoxious teenager he'd babysat when he was a college student and my father worked nights.

I handed Jackson his coffee.

"It's nice to have my barista back. How's it going?"

"We've sold a decent amount."

"We? You working with an imaginary friend?"

I flicked a bar towel at Jackson. He dodged it, snagged the end, and pulled it out of my hands.

"You missed Harley. She left a few minutes ago."

"You still sure about all of this?" Jackson motioned at the cart.

My back stiffened. "Yes." While setting up Ground Rules, Jackson had reviewed the business contracts for me. He'd also asked me daily if starting a coffee company in a city full of micro-roasters was the right choice.

"Just checking." Jackson's smile made me realize I should give him a break. In my brother's mind, I'd always be the kid he watched out for. My last job in the nonprofit world hadn't been as risky as starting my own business.

We chatted for a while, and he left, saying he had a long day ahead of him.

"Be sure to eat an actual lunch and not just drink coffee," I told Jackson as he left.

"Make sure you follow your own advice."

Our carafe of house coffee had been sitting for a while. It might be time to dump it and switch to Americanos or pour-overs for the rest of the day. I poured a few ounces and took a sip, tasting the medium roast with notes of dark berries and spiced dates. Dark roast is my jam, but I could almost switch to this daily. Maybe it was the mix of Bourbon and Caturra beans from a Fair Trade co-op in Guatemala. Or it's because Harley's a genius when it comes to roasting coffee beans.

We'd named our house coffee Puddle Jumper, in honor of Portland's Puddletown nickname, 'cause a cup of this in the morning would make you happy enough to face the day, including jumping in puddles during your jaunts around town.

As I sniffed the brew's aroma, I decided it was too old. As I poured the carafe out, I thought about the steps that went into producing a cup of coffee, from growing and harvesting the coffee cherries in areas far from Portland, processing the cherries until only the coffee beans remain, and shipping the green coffee beans all over the world. Would small farmers in Malawi be surprised to find out hipsters in Portland were digging their crops? But perhaps all this means is lots of things wash up in Portland.

Movement caught my attention. A girl in her midteens approached the cart like she was afraid I would chase her off. Her light brown hair was pulled into a greasy ponytail. Both her jeans and backpack were dusty.

"Do you need something?" I asked the girl gently. She still looked like she was debating whether to bolt.

"I was going to ask if you had pastries or drinks you can't sell and want to give away." She looked at the ground. She blushed.

Her words confirmed my suspicions. She had to be homeless. One of many, including kids. My heart twisted.

"You gave me an idea," I said. "I read an article about a shop in the UK with a suspended drink board. Their customers pre-buy a drink or a snack for someone down on their luck. I'll bring a whiteboard and start one."

"So maybe you'll have something tomorrow?"

"For inspiring the idea, you deserve a drink. What do you want? Coffee? Hot chocolate?"

"Iced mocha?"

I hid a smile, wondering if she'd meant to request the most expensive drink on the menu. "Take a seat and I'll bring the mocha out in a moment."

She nodded and sat down at the table by my cart. All of the furniture here was chained to the ground so it wouldn't walk away on its own. But when I came out, carrying my cold brew and her iced mocha, she looked surprised, like she thought I'd been lying to her before.

I handed her the drink, and the last of the scones. Her eyes widened before she whispered thanks. She took a quick bite of the pastry and didn't give herself a chance to chew before tearing into it again.

"Slow down. Choking's not fun."

She blushed and put the scone down.

"I didn't say stop eating."

She picked it back up, but ate more slowly, taking time to chew. She took a long drink of the mocha before biting into the second half of the scone.

"What's your name?" I asked as I worked through different approaches in the back of my brain. But I wanted to be straight, instead of manipulating her as I'd done to the college girl who now thought I was a psychic barista.

"Gabby," she whispered.

"I'm Sage. It's nice to meet you. You live around here?"

She froze for a second. "Why do you want to know?"

"Just trying to meet my neighbors. Besides, you remind me of myself. Except I was a bit younger than you. Thirteen."

She bolted upright. "Thank you for the food." She scurried away, holding the remnants of the scone and coffee.

I took a deep breath, remembering my own time on the street. But I pushed those memories away. I didn't want them to intrude on today.

After the lunch rush, the Rail Yard felt quiet, with only a handful of people eating in the shade. Only two of the carts were open, but both had been busy. I poured my second cold brew of the day

and cracked open a can of sparkling water and stepped outside. I retired to what I now thought of as "my spot": the closest picnic table.

Zarek walked up. "Hi, Spice Girl."

"Hi, Vegan."

He handed me a bowl with two falafel balls on top of a slice of
tomato and a pile of arugula, all drizzled with a green sauce. "For
you. Consider it a thank-you for the coffee earlier."

My stomach growled. "You must have read my mind. I'm fam-
ished. So tell me about your cart."

I took a bite of the falafel Zarek had given me. The zing of the
green sauce tasted like happiness in a bowl.

"Falafel is my specialty, with vegan shawarma fries being a close
second. I make all of the sauces myself, like the zhug sauce you're
trying now."

"It's amazing."

The woman from the jojos cart joined us. Her light brown hair
was pulled back in a high ponytail, and she looked fit. Like she could
cook all day, run a marathon before bed, and be ready to do it all
again tomorrow. Up close, I guessed she was in her midforties.

"I'm Emma." She put a basket of food down next to me. "Free
sample if you'd like to try my specialty."

"I'd love to." I picked up a chicken tender, skinny and long, and
fried golden brown. Zarek glanced at the chicken and looked away.

"The breading is a family recipe."

I took a bite. The batter was light, not quite tempura, but not
heavy, with a tiny kick. Cayenne and paprika. "Awesome."

"I hope your first day is going well." Emma looked at Zarek.
"Any word on where the carts across the street ended up?"

"Last I heard, most are in storage. The retro cart is going to try
being fully mobile. They tweeted they'll be open by Nike's headquarters today."

"I'm going to miss them," Emma said. "It feels like we lost half
of our family."

As they spoke, I took a bite of the jojo, which was also breaded, as is traditional in Oregon, and it tasted like it had been broasted in a pressure fryer as any proper jojo needs to be to deserve the name, versus being a potato wedge. But I felt a note of sadness because the fries were underspiced. They needed more paprika and a pinch of salt.

"I'm sad the breakfast cart left to open a brick-and-mortar shop," Emma said. "Their egg sandwiches made it into all of the 'where to eat in Portland' lists. We need a big draw so we don't lose the community we have left."

"Think of it as an opportunity. At least now, we don't see a cart with an hour wait while we're dead. My business has picked up since they left," Zarek said, and he and Emma talked about the Rail Yard for a while.

I looked across the street, where a crowd of people had gathered, all holding signs. One said NO LUXURY WHILE OTHERS SLEEP ON THE STREET, while another had the word DEVELOPMENT crossed out by a red X. Another sign said NOPE.

Emma noticed where I was looking. "I like those houses," she said. "It's a shame they're being torn down instead of converted into apartments."

The four-square-style houses looked like they hadn't seen a paintbrush for a few decades, and the moss-covered roofs added to the general air of neglect. The black Jolly Roger in the front window in one of the homes didn't help.

"How many apartments are being built?" I asked.

"Seventy-nine, with commercial space on the bottom," Zarek said.

I nodded. The houses, once converted, would've made six to eight units. But I didn't want to debate the logic of seventy-nine versus eight with Emma.

"Do either of you have an extra box cutter? I broke my pocket-knife this morning, and I need to open up another bag of coffee," I said.

Zarek nudged my foot with his. "I can hook you up."

Macie walked up to us. She looked confused as she stared across the street. "Has construction started?"

"Tomorrow," Zarek said. "Macie, were you in your cart all morning? You weren't open."

"I was sewing."

I glanced at Zarek. He was current on development-related issues, and I was going to ask why, but my dad walked through the gate. I grinned.

He wore a navy blazer over khakis, which was either a nod to the chilly July weather, or he was wearing his sidearm. I caught the glint of the gold badge on his belt, so he was on the job. Which didn't keep him from checking up on my first day.

I jumped up and walked to him. "Hi, Dad."

"Hi, Pumpkin." He leaned over to kiss me on the cheek. "So this is the new business."

"I'll give you a tour of Ground Rules." I waved goodbye as I took my father over to the cart, feeling a sense of pride as I showed him the business I'd built. I'd always wanted to help people, put positive energy back into the world, and in a small way my new business could brighten everyone's day. I saw Ground Rules as my future, but it was the first pebble in a rockslide, causing my past to come crashing into my present.

Chapter 2

The protesters returned in time for the Tuesday-morning commute. A few crossed the street and bought coffee, carrying their signs with them.

"It's small businesses like yours we're trying to protect," one of the protesters told me.

"The way Portland keeps bowing to developers, it's going to end up a town of chain coffee joints and ugly apartments," his friend said.

"Good luck," I told them. I admired how passionate the protesters acted.

But the guy behind them, who looked to be in his early thirties, with dreadlocks in his bleached-blond hair, glared at me. His tattered green headscarf made him look like Captain Jack Sparrow, except he wore faded jeans with the knees torn out and a black T-shirt instead of a pirate's outfit. He held a sign, so he was one of the protesters. He turned away and retreated across the street, and the woman behind him stepped up and ordered a cup of chai.

As I sliced open a new bag of cup sleeves, I was thankful for my fellow business owners since I was using the box cutter Zarek had dropped by and told me to keep as long as I needed. The bright orange handle made me happy, even though it was a stupid (but useful) knife.

The protest had grown to about fifty people and—I paused to double-check—one goat, which was standing on top of a *Scooby Doo*–style Mystery Machine.

My uncle Jimmy walking up distracted me. He was Ground Rules' silent partner, providing the financial backing. He also owned the Rail Yard.

My breath in was shallow and I told myself to straighten up. Act professional. Every bit of me, from my purple-painted toenails to the strands of my blond hair wanted to impress him.

Uncle Jimmy studied the menu. "What do you recommend?"

"Since you don't like sweet coffee, I'd go with a pour-over or Americano."

"Dealer's choice as long as it's to go."

"This is one of the best drinks we offer." I set up a pour-over cone, ground coffee, and added exactly twenty-one grams of single-origin beans. Maybe my job title should be caffeine dealer. Better update my business cards.

When the last of the 375 grams of water passed through the beans, I poured it from the glass carafe into a to-go cup, carefully snapped a lid on, and carried it outside. I handed it over.

"The cart looks good, Bug." Uncle Jimmy took the cup from my hands.

"You'll be pleased with our initial numbers tonight."

"Good to hear. I'm on my way to a meeting with the contractor at the Button Building, so I've got to run. See you tonight."

Hearing the name of Uncle Jimmy's new development made my heart pound. If Ground Rules did well in the Rail Yard, he would rent one of his new micro-restaurant spaces to us. Even though we were family, he wouldn't hesitate to tap out and close on our business if we weren't profitable. So I needed to focus on the here and now instead of dreaming of the day when we had a brick-and-mortar shop plus a food cart for events.

As Uncle Jimmy walked away, the guy without a sense of humor from yesterday stood by the Rail Yard entrance, and he stared at my uncle as he walked away. His stern expression slipped into something deeper. Like hatred. But a college-aged girl with sleepy eyes and an almost terminal case of bedhead ordered a caramel mocha, so I focused on her breakfast of sugar while the stern guy walked up to the cart. He stared at me as he ordered a cup of black coffee. His gaze didn't leave my face as I poured his coffee, like he was trying to read something deep inside me.

After I handed his coffee over, he pointed to the small whiteboard I'd propped up on the counter. "What's this?" His voice was more clipped than normal.

"It's our suspended-coffee board. You can prepay for a drink for someone who needs a helping hand."

"Huh." He leaned back.

I crossed my arms over my chest. "It's optional. It's a small way to give back."

He walked away, and I wondered what his deal was. He liked my coffee enough to come back two days in a row, but he looked at me as if I were worthless. My hands balled into fists, but I told myself to chill. Not everyone has to like me. I don't have to like them. But since I'm a professional, I need to hold my temper unless they do something egregious enough to be banned.

My brother walked up to Ground Rules, with his Australian shepherd, Bentley, on a leash. "That's some protest."

I glanced over. Someone had knocked the fence around the site down, and protesters were sitting on the steps of a house.

The goat was on the roof of the house like a cherry on top of a protest sundae.

"I'm still sad the goats down on Belmont moved," I said. Their undeveloped lot was now a grocery store.

"If my backyard was bigger, I'd buy you a goat. I'd never have to mow or weed the yard again."

Bentley sat staring up at me. "Good thing I have dog biscuits in stock," I told him, and reached for my stash of peanut butter treats.

"Actually . . . ," Jackson said, his voice trailing off.

Nothing good ever happens when my brother starts a sentence with *actually*. Although at least he hadn't added *well* to his phased-out thought.

"What do you want?" I let my breath out in a whoosh.

"Bentley's dog walker is sick, so he'll be home alone all day, and I have meetings until late. Can he stay here with you?"

Bentley collapsed on the ground and rested his head on his paws, like the happenings of a coffee cart were boring.

"You didn't think to call or text?" I asked, knowing Jackson had brought him since it would be harder for me to say no with Bentley by his feet.

"He'll love it here."

So I created a spot for Bentley outside the open door of my cart, in the shade with a bowl of water, while Jackson grabbed a coffee to go.

After Jackson left, my photographer friend Erin showed up with a fancy DSLR camera. She stopped in the entrance of the Rail Yard and snapped photos of the cart, then turned and focused on the goat on the roof of the house across the street. I crafted a mocha, forming a symmetrical heart in the foam on top, and handed it to Erin when she walked up.

"The goat is amazing. Thanks, Sage." Erin put the mocha on the counter of the cart, next to our logo, and snapped a few more photos before tasting it. Erin walked around the cart, taking pictures from various angles, and stopped by Bentley for a while to document his nap in the shade. She photographed me as I made a latte for a customer.

"Let's do another. I want to get some great shots of you making latte art," Erin said, so I made a second latte. I drizzled caramel while the camera clicked away.

We sat outside in the shade, sipping our drinks, for a while. Erin scanned through the screen of her camera. "These photos will be phenomenal. You're so photogenic."

"Can I see?"

She shook her head and locked the camera. "Not until I've downloaded them and examined them more closely. I'll send you a link when they're ready. I might have time to process them tonight."

Erin perked up like a prairie dog when several police cars and a riot truck pulled up across the street.

"Gotta go," she said, and ran away with her camera. Erin took photos as police forced the protesters to move. The demonstrators ended up kitty-corner from us. They chanted and booed as the construction workers moved in.

A guy in dusty work boots, clean jeans, and a button-down shirt came over and bought eight house coffees, and as he was walking away, I realized I'd sold coffee to the protesters' enemy, as he carried the drinks across the street to the construction site. I ducked out of view and checked on Bentley in case anyone looked my way. Bentley was snoring in his sleep, unconcerned about my drama.

But I hadn't ducked soon enough. The guy with blond dreads stood outside my cart. If his gaze was fire, my cart would be in massive flames. Perhaps this was his usual expression. Resting glare face.

"Selling out to the people who ruined the pod across the street?" he said. After another look telling me I was the worst, he marched away. He sat down on top of one of the picnic tables with his dirty sneakers on the bench and looked at his phone.

Whatever. I turned and started cleaning the cart, getting it ready for my next customer.

The afternoon was slow but steady. The taco cart owner, Rafael, traded two carne asada tacos for a macchiato. We talked for a while about cortados versus macchiatos, 'cause in Mexico, they're the same drink, but other countries see a cortado as having more milk. After he left, the owners of the farm-to-table sandwich cart, Hangry Hippo, stopped by to chat for a few minutes and dropped off a house-made salted chocolate cookie.

"You sell La Bake pastries. They're my favorite in town," Adam said. His wife, Carolyn, nodded in agreement.

"Me too!" I said.

"He means favorite other than the cookies we bake," Carolyn joked.

The Rail Yard quieted down. I wiped down every surface in the cart, making sure it was squeaky-clean. A voice talking outside my door caught my attention.

"Aren't you a good boy," the voice said. I looked outside to see Gabby petting Bentley.

"Hi, Gabby, how's it going?"

"Good, thanks," she said, but something was bothering her.

I almost asked if she wanted to talk, but I didn't want to scare her off. So I asked, "Did you see my suspended-coffee board? Thanks for inspiring me to start the program."

"I'll tell my friends."

"How's your day?"

Her shoulders were hunched and she hadn't looked my way. Although she still scratched Bentley's favorite spot behind his ears. "Better since I met your dog."

"His name's Bentley."

He flopped over so she could rub his belly, playing his favorite game of not-hard-to-get. After a few minutes, Gabby claimed the steamer made with cart-made bourbon caramel sauce off the suspended-drink board and hunched off.

Finally, 2:00 p.m. hit and I closed the cart, making sure everything was spotless and put away. I put the two leftover pastries in a bag and locked up the booth. I groaned.

I'd biked to work, and there was no way I could fit Bentley into one of my saddlebags even if he was willing to try to wiggle inside.

"Guess we're walking," I told him, and he wagged his tail in response since I'd said the magic word.

I walked my bicycle, and Bentley trotted alongside me. We cut through the lot to avoid the protesters on the sidewalk, so we passed by Macie's 4 and 20 pie truck. Bentley stopped at one of the bowls behind her cart and drank as if he'd never had water, ever, even though he'd snoozed next to a full bowl all day.

"Leave the pigeons' water alone!" Macie scolded us. I pulled Bentley away. He acted like I'd murdered his best friend.

Macie held a sewing project in her hands, spending her downtime between customers making what looked to be a new embroidered skirt.

"I'm sorry, Macie," I said. She glared at us as we left the Rail Yard and started the two-mile walk home.

After taking Bentley to my brother's house—I rent the attic suite—I spent a couple hours in the shade with a giant bottle of water before hopping back on my bike. My eyes took in the sights as I rode across the river in the direction of my meeting. Once a dilapidated industrial area with abandoned warehouses and a rollicking heroin trade, Portland's Pearl District had spiffed itself up into bourgeois heaven. Now it's full of lofts, both converted from actual warehouses and new construction with faux-industrial details. Plus art galleries, boutiques, and a variety of eating establishments from overpriced pizza by the slice to upscale restaurants. Nary a flophouse in sight. Although the homeless have claimed the Park Blocks as their own, not willing to cede their former territory.

But my destination still showed its blue-collar roots. The Tav has, or at least had, a unique name. A few decades of neglect had caused the ERN to burn out of the sign over the door, and the owner, my uncle Jimmy, rolled with it instead of fixing it. Unlike some of the faux–dive bars sprinkled around town, the Tav had earned its grit. Want an on-trend drink of the moment? Go someplace else. But if you want a drink strong enough to peel the paint off your soul, the Tav is for you. In a neighborhood where gentrification is the name of the game, the Tav's continuing existence defied the odds.

My cousin Miles was working behind the bar, another testament to the Tav's ability to act as if it'd been coated in amber and were resistant to time. Miles had managed the bar as long as I could remember, and he'd always felt like a solid anchor in a turbulent world. As he poured me a shot of bourbon, my eyes wandered over to my favorite part of the bar: the series of stained-glass windows on one wall. As we chatted, my gaze wandered to the center pane, which was the largest of the five. A woman with hair like a lion's mane stands in the center. She holds out her hands like she's asking a question.

"Uncle Jimmy's holding court in the side room," Miles told me. I tipped him before striding away.

Uncle Jimmy was studying a notebook as I slid into the booth across from him. Like the Tav, he felt ageless. His hair had always been silver in my world. I pulled out my tablet and launched my business spreadsheet.

Jimmy didn't even look up. "I'm reviewing the numbers from your first few days in business. You're already pulling in better numbers than expected. I'm proud, Bug."

I felt my face flush. Thankfully the bar's lighting was dim, although the light from my tablet was bathing my face, so I probably looked like a fun-house zombie. But I was pleased inside, both with Ground Rules' revenue and my uncle's praise.

Harley slid into the booth next to me. "Here's to another day of success!" She launched into a monologue about the meetings she'd set up with business owners she'd networked with in the past. One of the businesses, a small local chain owned by a former world champion barista, didn't roast their own beans but carried small roasters. They rotated beans regularly, and their drinks were top-notch.

"They'll consider working our coffee into their rotation. Our meeting's in the afternoon so you can be part, Sage. After five minutes with you, they'll order our beans forever."

"It sounds like you're getting excellent wholesale accounts." Uncle Jimmy and Harley talked about the wholesale side of the business while I tried to focus. The half shot of Elijah Craig Barrel Proof bourbon I'd sipped was making me sleepy, so I abandoned the rest.

"You two are off to a great start. You might be positioned to get a spot in the Button Building when it opens," Uncle Jimmy said.

The Button Building. The idea made a mix of happiness and anxiety shiver through me.

"I'm beat. Getting up before five a.m. is harder than I predicted,"

I said, and yawned. It was already 9:00 p.m., and I didn't want to count the diminishing hours until I was scheduled to reopen the cart. Going to bed by nine made me feel old since I should have been able to go hard all night and be perky the next morning, but my body didn't agree. Hopefully, tonight was an aberration, and after a few weeks of this schedule, I wouldn't feel as if I were turning into a pumpkin after 8:00 p.m.

"Go home. We can talk more about this later," Uncle Jimmy said. Harley promised to summarize the potential wholesale accounts and email them to me. I left them talking. I waved goodbye to Miles and headed out to my bike.

I checked my cell phone, which had been quiet all night. It was dead. I closed my eyes. I'd left the charger in the cart. Ground Rules wasn't too far out of my way, so I redirected my bike, even though I wanted to peel off and collapse at home.

The Rail Yard had closed for the night. Only the Fala-Awesome had a light on inside, but its order window was shuttered. A tumble-weed needed to roll by with a few notes played on an ocarina in the background. I unlocked the coffee cart to get my phone charger.

"You brewing coffee at night?"

I jumped when I heard a voice behind me. It was just Zarek. He grinned as I took a deep breath and centered myself.

"I forgot something." I relocked the cart behind me.

Zarek walked next to me, and I stopped when he rolled the large gate into place and padlocked it. The other entrance was already locked.

"Good night tonight?" I asked.

"Slammed until eight, but I had customers until nine. The summer is always hopping. The winter is the problem in this biz. But it works out, since I teach snowboarding lessons during the winter and only operate my cart a few days a week."

"I'm a horrible snowboarder."

"I can help you with that." His accompanying wink made him look like a five-year-old trying to be a pirate.

"See you tomorrow." I swung my leg over my bicycle.

"Do you have time for a drink? The brewery down the street has a mean IPA on tap."

"Rain check, I have to be back here way too early. I should already be in bed." I waited for a half second to see if he offered to help with that too, but he just smiled, making me feel like the only person in the world.

"Tomorrow," he said, and I pedaled away, wondering how annoyed Harley would be if I went out for a drink with Zarek since she'd called dibs.

My phone alarm chirped at 4:30 a.m. and I rolled out of bed, cursing my late night. I forced myself to stumble to the shower and bike to the Rail Yard.

Thankfully the route was mostly flat as I cut through the east side, since my legs felt like they were filled with lead. The sky was starting to turn orange in the distance, and while the air was chilly, it promised to be a warm day. I paused as I pulled up to the Rail Yard. Someone had spray-painted an arrow in the direction of the construction site with the letters DOWN WI after it. Weirdos. That didn't make sense.

The main entrance of the Rail Yard was ajar, and the gate was unlocked. I paused. Zarek had locked it last night. I'd watched him. Nerves jangled inside me as I rolled the gate the rest of the way open and walked into the lot, pushing my bike. But I let go of my bike and it crashed to the ground.

The overly serious man with the hooded eyes and perpetual scowl was sprawled out on the ground.

His days of ordering coffee were over.

Chapter 3

The first patrol officers blocked off the Rail Yard with yellow crime-scene tape, in addition to marking off a smaller square within. A detective showed up, followed by crime-scene techs. One of the police officers brought me a cup of coffee from a chain shop a few blocks away, and even though the morning coolness had burned off with a vengeance, the warmth of the coffee felt good against my hands. I sat at a picnic table in the opposite corner of the Rail Yard, next to the 4 and 20 Blackbirds cart. Too bad the blackbirds weren't painted to look like vultures or a different bird of prey since they would have fit the theme of the day. But I remembered ravens feed on carrion and my stomach roiled again.

A man in a dark suit and gold detective shield on his belt talked with the patrol officer who'd brought me coffee. The detective motioned my way. I turned my gaze, lingering for a moment on the handwritten sign taped to the order window of Emma's PDX Jojos cart. It was closed for a few days. Her leaving town was fortunate timing since none of the carts would be allowed to open for a while. As small businesses operating on slim margins, this was going to hurt all of us. Including my baby business. Although thinking of Ground Rules' future after finding a body made me feel guilty. A man dying should matter more than monetary transactions. Part of me wanted to bike away and never come back, but I also wanted to stay and fight for my business. Why had someone been murdered next to my coffee cart? And even if he'd been arrogant, he'd been a customer. Something about my cart had drawn him back.

The detective in the suit walked over. He was blocky like he mainlined protein powder in a quest to achieve a perfectly rectangular, solidly muscular shape. His face had almost perfect right angles at his temples and chin. Even his chin dimple looked square.

"I'm Detective Will." He stared down at me with a straight expression like he always played the straight man in a farce, but also never saw the jokes.

"I'm Sage." My voice cracked. I cleared my throat.

"Last name?"

"Caplin." Nothing flickered in his expression, so he either didn't know my father, hadn't made the connection, or didn't care my dad was a Portland police detective. Should I name-drop my dad now, even if I hadn't done anything wrong? And it's not like I'd been caught speeding. I was a witness, however remote, to a murder. My lungs felt like I'd quit breathing and I took a quick breath, trying to keep the world from spinning.

"How did you know the victim?"

I took a sip of my coffee, now lukewarm. "I didn't know him. But he stopped by my coffee cart the past two mornings." I motioned in the direction of Ground Rules.

"Do you know his name?"

I shook my head. "Isn't his ID in his wallet?"

"How'd he pay?"

"Credit card." I looked up and made eye contact with Detective Will. "I should be able to look up his transactions on the cart's tablet if you'd like. It should be in our POS system."

"We'll get to that in a moment." He had me recount my morning, from my ride up to the unlocked gate to finding the dead man. My whole body felt exhausted. Rehashing my day felt like it took more energy than I had. Yet I managed to answer the questions without falling over.

"Was the door to the coffee cart open when you arrived?"

"Yes. I noticed it while I was calling 911." An oval pebble was by my left sneaker. It looked like it would skip well across a lake. I should've played hooky today and headed somewhere, anywhere, other than here. But if I had, I would've pushed finding the body off onto someone else. I took a deep breath and squared my shoulders. Dealing with this was my responsibility.

"How long have you been dating the victim?" Detective Will asked.

My ponytail swished against the back of my neck as I turned to stare at him. "As I said before, I didn't know him. He's too old for me, anyway."

The detective grimaced and jotted something in his notebook. Something told me he was testing my reactions, seeing if I'd let something slip if he shocked me. Or he honestly thought I'd killed the dead guy in a lovers' spat. Part of me wondered what sort of role I could play to make the detective believe me. But I went for the truth. Focused on being me. Although the nerves flowing through my body made me want to play a part, become someone else. A person who hadn't discovered a dead body.

After a few more questions, he left me sitting in silence. I debated curling up on the bench of the table and taking a nap, but decided it was too callous. Plus when I shut my eyes, I kept seeing the dead man's face, frozen in an expression of terror, and the slash across his neck. His hands were on top of each other, near his neck, like he'd tried to stop the blood flow. There'd been a can of spray paint next to his shoulder.

Detective Will walked back. "There's no tablet in the coffee cart. We'll need you to look inside the cart and tell us if anything's missing."

I patted my messenger bag. "I have the tablet. I don't leave it in the cart overnight. Although the coffee equipment is more expensive than the tablet."

I asked myself why I was rambling on like I'd downed six shots of espresso and couldn't stay quiet. At least I didn't blather on to the detective about stopping by the bank after closing the cart to deposit money when we had enough cash to make it worthwhile.

"Can you look up his name?"

I pulled the tablet out of my bag and turned it on. My fingers wanted to tremble, but after a few minutes, I'd found a name. I double-checked it against sales from my first day.

"David Stevens. I'm pretty sure he's David Stevens," I said. The name made a bell ring in the back of my mind, but I couldn't figure out why.

"How long has your cart been here?"

"Today would've been our third day open for business."

The detective left and came back less than a minute later. "I'd like you to tell me if anything in the cart is missing."

We took a path around the crime-scene techs, along the perimeter of the Rail Yard, and approached the open door of the cart.

My heart started pounding. We had more than thirty grand of equipment in the cart, not to mention the time we'd invested in calibrating the machines.

I relaxed a little when I walked inside, feeling guilty because my untouched gear was replaceable. But the man outside must've had a family who cared about him, not to mention a life cut shorter than anyone expected.

"I don't leave money in the cart overnight, and the cashbox is still here." I pointed it out. It was on the shelf beneath the window.

My eyes scanned the French presses, two Baratza grinders, kitchen scales for weighing coffee, and the espresso machine, which I examined twice. The other ways to make specialty coffee, like a Chemex and a pile of Kalita Wave filters for pour-overs, a few inversion filters, along with glass carafes and a pour-over stand, also looked normal. All clean and ready to be used.

I shuffled across the cart. The stockpile of coffee beans looked untouched, as did the contents of both fridges. The storage unit filled with sleeves of cups, lids, swizzle sticks, and other odds and ends looked like it should. All of the cleaning supplies were in place.

"The only thing I've seen out of place is the door to the cart, since it was open when I arrived," I said. But a quick examination showed the door wasn't damaged. Had someone picked the lock? I'd left it securely bolted last night. I'd double-checked while Zarek waited for me.

We stepped back outside, and the detective left for a moment and came back, carrying something in his hands. He showed me a box cutter in an evidence bag.

My heart fell to my feet. The box cutter had an orange handle. The blade was out and covered in dried blood.

"You recognize this." His words were a flat statement. I didn't even consider denying the truth in them.

"Yes, I think so. Last time I saw it, it was in my cart."

My heart started to beat as if I'd downed a couple of double shots of espresso on an empty stomach. Someone had used the box cutter from my cart to kill David Stevens.

No wonder the detective was staring at me like I was a murderer.

Chapter 4

One of the police officers led me out of the Rail Yard with my bike. A crowd watched as we started to walk to his police SUV. I'd tried to refuse a ride home, but the detective had insisted. I was secretly glad.

"Sage, what's going on?" Macie's hands twitched like she needed something to do with them. I glanced at my watch: ten thirty.

Shoot. I needed to call Uncle Jimmy. He had the contact info for all of the other cart owners, and he could notify them about the closure. He'd also be annoyed I hadn't called him already to tell him about today. I paused and looked at Macie, who stared at me with wide eyes.

"I doubt anyone will be able to open today. Maybe tomorrow, but I don't feel hopeful." What would this do to the Rail Yard?

"What's going on?" Macie grabbed my arm. I froze and looked at her. She removed her hand and stepped back. "What's happening? I need to get to my cart."

Zarek joined us. He carried two reusable shopping bags, and lettuce peeked out of the top of one. "I heard a group of teens committed suicide in the Rail Yard?"

"What? No." They both looked at me.

Macie's voice crackled with annoyance when she said, "Sage

won't give me any details. But she thinks we'll be closed today." She twitched like she wanted to force her way through the fence to her cart, Kool-Aid Man–style.

Zarek's eyes darted to the police in the lot. All of his muscles were tense, causing a blood vein to pop out on his forearm. "I just went grocery shopping. I can't afford for this to go to waste."

The ripples of the investigation would catch all of the carts and threaten to drown our companies. How would this affect my coffee cart? Ground Rules had started to feel like an extension of me. I couldn't let it fail. And we needed to do well here at the Rail Yard to get a spot in Uncle Jimmy's new development. And I couldn't let my uncle down. He'd loaned me the start-up capital. He'd believed in me.

Disappointing him wasn't an option.

Macie stamped her foot beside me. "It's not fair to be kept away from my cart."

I noticed Detective Will looking our way. I waved him to the fence and motioned for Zarek and Macie to follow me. "Detective, Zarek and Macie are food cart owners. They'd love to find out more about what happened and answer your questions." I walked away, still pushing my bike, as Macie sputtered behind me.

I pulled out my phone and texted Uncle Jimmy we needed to talk ASAP. I started to put my phone away and paused. There was someone else I needed to contact.

But the patrol officer was looking at me, so I rushed over. We wedged my bike into his official police SUV, and I climbed into the passenger seat.

After thanking the police officer for the ride home, I stowed my bicycle in the garage and trudged inside. Bentley met me at the door and wagged his tail a few times before collapsing on his dog bed.

"I don't blame you," I said, and face-planted on the couch. Maybe I could go to sleep, and when I woke up, I'd find out this morning had been a dream. I hadn't found a dead body. But David's face filled my vision, even though my eyes were closed, so I rolled over and stared at the ceiling.

My phone rang. I answered it without looking at the screen. About time Uncle Jimmy called me back. My body froze when a voice said hello. For a moment, I couldn't breathe.

Today, of all days? Thanks, world.

"Sage, we need to talk."

I forced myself to speak. "Yeah."

"You mean, 'Yes, Mother,'" my mom said like she thought I needed to be corrected like a small child. I should hang up the phone. Hit end on the call like I'd tried to do to our relationship. Nothing good ever happened when she called.

"Why'd you call?" I made my voice sound bored. Not like hearing from her caused all sorts of emotions to well up. Not hinting this was the worst time for her to call since I was already feeling fragile. I made myself sit up. Straighten my shoulders. Scowl. Pull the lingering anger in my brain together to form a titanium shell.

"We haven't talked for over a year, and I wanted to hear your voice. How was your trip to Bali? Did you take up surfing again? You loved catching waves when you were nine."

I snorted. My emotional control was sliding as if I were reverting to being a child.

"I guess you don't want to tell me about your life." My mother sounded disappointed, and I reminded myself it was an act to prey on my emotions.

"And give you ammunition?"

"I'm wounded. You know I care about you."

I let the silence on the airwaves between us speak for me, barely stopping myself from saying, "Yeah, you care about finding out how you can manipulate me." If I said it, she'd know she'd gotten under my skin. She'd know she was winning this talk. Because all of life is a game to my mother, and she always wins.

"Since you don't feel like catching up, there is something we need to talk about."

If I wasn't feeling communicative, why would she think I'd discuss anything with her? "About time you got to the point."

"I heard about your new business venture."

My body stiffened again. "Okay."

"Do you need an investor?"

I barely stopped myself from laughing. Did she need a way to launder money? "No, we're good."

"Many small businesses fail their first year. Extra income will help."

"I'd rather fail on my own than accept money from you."

"You're my daughter and you shouldn't waste your talents. Letting me help you will be good for both of us. Besides, you don't want to know the consequences if you refuse."

"The opposite is true. I'd love to know the consequences. Because nothing you can say will make me say yes."

She chuckled. "Such bravado. I taught you well."

She hung up.

My hand wanted to chuck my phone across the room, but I needed it to talk with people. Uncle Jimmy. Harley. My dad. He'd want to know about this call. Try to track it. Although when I looked back at my call log, she'd called from a private number. As always.

My phone rang again. I checked the caller ID before answering. Uncle Jimmy.

"Bug, what's going on?"

Some of the tension inside relaxed. Uncle Jimmy would know how to handle this. I told him about my morning, including the call from my mother. My anxiety flipped back into overdrive when he said, "Sage, this is serious. I'm driving over now. We need to talk."

He hung up. I stared at my phone, trying not to tremble. He'd called me Sage. He never called me by my real name unless I was in trouble, or something serious was going down.

Footsteps on the stairs caught both my and Bentley's attention, followed by a ringing doorbell. Bentley barked twice, then sat down next to the door.

"How'd Uncle Jimmy get here so soon?" I asked Bentley.

But it wasn't my uncle.

Chapter 5

Two police officers stood on the front porch. I stepped outside, shutting the door behind me, keeping Bentley inside. I slid on the mantle of bravado I'd created when I talked to my mother, although my heart raced.

"Sage Caplin?" one of the officers asked, and I nodded. "I'd like you to accompany us down to the precinct. We have questions for you about the death of David Stevens."

"I already talked to a detective about finding the body."

"We have additional questions and need you to make a formal statement," she said. The taller of the two officers shifted. I inched backward, wishing I hadn't shut the door. What would they do if I went inside and hid under the covers of my bed? Which would only delay this conversation. I let out a deep breath.

"Am I under arrest?"

"Not yet."

"One moment." I called my dad, who didn't answer. So I called Jackson while the police officers watched me, looking like they wanted to frog-march me to their squad car.

"Police officers want me to go with them to their precinct to answer questions," I said when Jackson answered.

"Which precinct?" Props to my brother for rolling with this. So

I asked the officer, who looked annoyed as she told me the Central Precinct.

"I'm on my way there. Don't say anything until I get there, you understand me?" Jackson said.

"Yes."

"Seriously, not a word. No matter what anyone says to you."

"I dig." My voice sounded casual like this happened daily. But my stomach felt nauseous like I'd drunk a week's worth of straight espressos at once.

I hung up and told the officers to give me a minute to get ready. I went inside and grabbed my bag, taking a moment to pet Bentley and ask him to keep his paws crossed for me, before walking back outside and following the officers to their police car.

The police officers drove me to the police station in downtown Portland. One of the officers stood by the door of an interview room while I sat, waiting for a detective to make an appearance. I glanced at my watch, willing to wait five minutes. Anything longer, and I'd leave. I wasn't under arrest. My mother would have told me I was stupid for going with them without a warrant. But she always had something to hide. I didn't.

Jackson was in full-on lawyer mode when he arrived. Charcoal suit today, with the vest underneath I'd convinced him would look sharp and I was sure must be miserable in the hot weather. "I'd like to talk to my client alone," he said as he entered the room.

"Your client," I said after the officer left.

"If the police charge you, I'll call in a favor and get you an actual criminal attorney. You'll want independent counsel experienced with criminal cases for adults."

The seriousness of his words reverberated through me, causing my fake-tough exterior to crack a little bit. I took a deep breath and willed it back into place. I couldn't break now. Not here.

"What happened?" Jackson asked, and I told him the story, from finding the body to police showing up on the doorstep of his house.

"How're you holding up?" My brother sounded sincere. Part of me wanted to burst into tears. I told myself to get a grip and focus.

"I'm okay." But I didn't sound like I was telling the truth.

Jackson patted my shoulder. He glanced at his watch.

"You need to be somewhere?"

He shook his head. "If they make us wait much longer, I'll tell them to make an appointment to meet us at my office. It's a power play."

Jackson turned to me. He looked me straight in the eye. "When, and if, they show up, defer to me before you answer any questions." He went into a full-on didactic mode about how being asked to come to the station wasn't a good sign. His intensity didn't help the nerves in my stomach.

The door opened. Jackson's face slid into a mask of himself. Detective Will strode in, along with a woman in a dark suit. They both carried manila file folders. Everyone here wore suits, except me. I glanced down at my COFFEE IS FOR CLOSERS T-shirt and jean shorts with a three-inch inseam. Someone here was not like the others.

"Jackson Hennessey, Ms. Caplin's attorney."

Detective Will returned the gesture and introduced the woman, Detective Jenkins. Her hair was pulled back into a severe bun, giving her the air of someone who didn't abide by any nonsense. I felt like I'd been dragged to the principal's office for ignoring a rule I didn't care to follow. I told myself to be serious and thought of the man I'd found today. His family deserved answers, and the sooner the police realized I didn't have any, the better for all of us.

My thoughts sobered, and part of me wondered why my emotions were yo-yoing around, making me feel out of control. I liked to see myself as steady; unflappable. I felt anything but calm. I needed to find my inner balance, pronto.

"We'd like you to take us through your morning," Detective Will said.

It felt like I'd tell this story, on repeat, for the rest of my life, like an endless Groundhog Day. But after receiving a nod from my brother, I told my story yet again.

"You said you don't know David Stevens. You claim you didn't know his name until you looked it up in your point-of-sale system," Detective Will said.

Jackson nodded for me to answer, so I said, "That's correct."

"Why are you lying?" Detective Will asked.

I stared at him, trying to analyze his face. He looked like he was telling the truth, unless he was an Oscar-worthy actor. But his gaze was steady, and his intensity felt honest. He eyed me back like he was trying to get my measure. I wondered what he saw.

More important, why did I care?

"When's the last time you saw your mother?"

I felt like I'd been punched. What'd she have to do with this? I glanced at Jackson and saw the same glimmer of apprehension behind his eyes, despite his poker face. He looked at me and nodded.

I chose my words carefully. "I haven't seen my mother since I was thirteen. So fourteen years ago, give or take a few months."

"You expect us to believe that?" Detective Jenkins said. Her voice was hoarse, like she had a cold.

"It's the truth." I heard the honesty in my words, but both detectives looked like they wanted to chant, "Liar, liar, pants on fire," at me.

Detective Will pulled a photo out of a folder and put it down in front of me. Jackson picked it up. We looked at it together.

My mother's face caught my attention. Her golden blond hair was like mine, as were her downturned blue eyes and heart-shaped face. She laughed like she didn't have a care in the world. The man in the photo gazed down at her in adoration.

I knew his face, although he'd never looked happy the few times I'd seen him. Since I'd found his body this morning, I'd never see him smile in real life. I swallowed hard.

"Do you still claim you didn't know the deceased?"

"I hadn't met him until this week."

"So you claim you don't know your mother conned David Stevens out of one hundred thousand dollars."

"What? When?" My voice was starting to turn shrill.

Jackson leaned into me, and I tilted my head as he spoke into my ear. "Let them show their hand," he whispered. I nodded and he leaned back.

We both faced forward, looking at the detectives, who stared back, entering into a silent contest. I wondered who'd be the first to blink, but I knew part of the answer: it wouldn't be Jackson. Even though it rankled, I followed my brother's lead.

Seconds slunk into minutes, which felt like they stretched into hours and days. Detective Will broke the silence.

"Stevens filed a criminal complaint against your mother thirteen years ago."

My shoulder muscles relaxed. My mother had scammed him after we'd parted ways. I knew I hadn't known Stevens, but I was relieved I hadn't been lying, even unintentionally. It also meant I hadn't been a pawn in the grift.

"You're not the only law enforcement agency looking for Saffron Jones," Jackson said. I blinked when he used our mother's legal name like they weren't related. But pretending this was an intellectual matter made sense. Create emotional distance. Stay focused.

"This conversation is over," Jackson said. "Ms. Caplin isn't responsible for anything Saffron Jones may, or may not, have done. We're leaving." Jackson stood up. I followed his lead, my body feeling looser than when I'd entered the room. But the detectives remained seated.

"So it's chance your client's fingerprints are on the murder weapon, and the victim was the main witness in a case against her mother. A case that's heating up."

Her mother. The detective hadn't figured out my relationship to Jackson. We had different last names, but the same address. Something told me the detectives saw our relationship as something different from the truth. We had an angle to work.

I told myself to focus on the truth. Playing the angles was a path to trouble. And what did he mean by "heating up"? Did he say it to get a rise out of me? Or was it the truth? Had my mother made a misstep and the police were narrowing in on her? Not being able to tell made me feel like a thousand bees were buzzing around my head, getting ready to sting.

Jackson's eyes narrowed. "The box cutter was in the coffee cart. Of course my client's fingerprints are on it. We both know the presence of fingerprints doesn't indicate guilt."

Part of me wanted to point out I was smart enough to wipe a murder weapon clean. But offering that tidbit wouldn't help, so I stayed silent, trying not to vibrate in place.

"Is it also chance the door was open, but not broken?" Detective Will asked.

"Someone jimmied or picked the lock. I'm going to advise my client to get a sturdier door and better-quality lock. Any last question before we leave?"

The female detective opened a folder, and Jackson paused. She put a photo on the table, and I stepped forward to examine it.

Gabby stared at me from the photo. She looked clean, and her smile was bright. The photo looked like a school picture, given the blue background. I had similar images at home from my teenage years, except my eyes had never been as innocent.

"Do you know this girl?" Detective Jenkins asked.

"There are lots of girls running around. You'd be surprised how many teenagers stop by my cart for iced mochas. They seem young for a regular coffee habit, but, hey, caffeine stunting growth is an old wives' tale."

"This girl is the niece of the victim, and we found her fingerprints at the scene. She's a runaway and considered endangered, so we need to find her."

"What's her name, and how old is she?" Jackson's voice was less clipped. Softer.

"Gabrielle Blake, age fourteen," Detective Jenkins said. "She ran away from her parents' home in Seattle last spring. This is the first trace we've found of her."

I looked the detective in the eyes. "I hope you find her. It's tough for kids on the street." I followed my brother out of the room, wondering if I'd made the right call.

Chapter 6

As we walked outside, I said, "I can take the bus home."

"I'll drive you. We need to talk." I followed Jackson to the parking garage down the block from the Central Precinct. We didn't say anything as we climbed three flights of stairs and maneuvered to Jackson's hybrid SUV.

"You knew the girl," Jackson said as he pulled out of the parking lot. My back muscles unknotted as I leaned back against the seat. A wave of exhaustion slammed into my brain, making my thoughts fuzzy. I adjusted the air-conditioning to blow my way, hoping the icy air would keep me awake.

"I've seen her around."

"Why didn't you mention her to the police?"

I looked out the window. "Instinct. Gabby reminds me of my teenage self."

I wondered again what the police thought when they saw us, or at least me if they hadn't figured out Jackson was my brother. Did they think I was a grifter, a diseased branch on my family tree?

Growing up, I'd played so many parts it was easy to slip into another role. Becoming whoever would be easiest at any moment in time called me with a siren song of temptation. But that part of my life was over. I was afraid if I kept playing parts, I'd disappear.

Jackson's phone rang, and he clicked a button on his steering wheel to answer it. Uncle Jimmy's voice filled the air. My back muscles clenched up again. What if he blamed me for the trouble falling on his doorstep?

"Sage is with me. We're on our way home," Jackson told him.

"Good. I have to take care of something, but, Sage, we need to talk later today."

"How about early this evening?" I shouted at the microphone on the driver's side of the car. Jackson motioned for me to lower my voice.

"I'll call you. Gotta go." Uncle Jimmy disconnected.

Jackson glanced at me but returned his gaze to the road. We turned into our neighborhood. "Are you sure this coffee business is for you? You'd always talked about nonprofit development before."

"Didn't we debate this to death when you helped me with the contract?" I muttered.

"It's not too late to get out."

"I know you don't see it as important work, like yours, but I'm good at it." So much of the business came naturally to me: handling customers, crafting coffee drinks complete with latte art. The cart already felt like home. Quitting now felt like giving up on myself. Plus it would gut Harley. The more Jackson questioned me, the stronger my desire surged to make Grand Rules a success, both because of the passion I felt for the business and to show my brother he was wrong.

We turned onto our street. When he saw the street in front of the house, Jackson swore loudly.

My heart sank.

Two police cars and a boring tan sedan were parked in front of the house. Jackson parallel parked behind them. He took a deep breath and looked at me. "You don't have anything illegal in the house, right?"

"No. Do you even have to ask?"

"Follow my lead."

A sedan pulled up behind us, making me feel boxed in.

Jackson opened the driver's-side door, and I waited for him to start walking around the hood of the car before I followed suit. The sunshine hit me, causing the last cold molecules from the car's air-conditioning to steam off my skin.

Detective Will climbed out of the car behind us, along with another man in a suit. Two uniformed officers stood on the porch of the house.

I stuck close to my brother as we walked up the front walkway. "Why are you on my property?" Jackson asked the police officers.

A voice behind us answered, "We have a warrant to search the residence of Sage Caplin."

Detective Will held out a sheet of paper, which Jackson snatched from him and reviewed. My throat tightened like I couldn't swallow.

Jackson's expression was impassive as he looked up. "Sage rents the third floor. You can see the rental contract. You're only welcome to look in the areas she legally rents, and the communal areas, meaning the kitchen, living room, and the basement laundry room."

Jackson handed the search warrant over to me. A quick scan told me the police were looking for clothing and shoes with traces of blood on them.

"You're honestly claiming she doesn't have access to other rooms in the building, like your bedroom?"

Several emotions dueled through me. The first was disgust. The second was amusement, since Detective Will still hadn't figured out my relationship to Jackson. Last was the concern the detective was supposed to solve a murder, but was spending his time investigating me. The thought of the double injustice bothered me. David Stevens's family deserved more. I didn't deserve the scrutiny, although I didn't have any choice but to bear it. Maybe I'd fake a grin.

"That's exactly what I'm saying. Are you ready to have all of the nonevidence you find thrown out?" Jackson said. My brother didn't show any emotion, even when the detective stepped closer and stared down at him. Like he was trying to rile Jackson up.

Having my brother on my side made me feel relieved until I remembered I'd need to retain a non–family member if the detective arrested me. But Jackson would know who I should hire. My pulse slowed a fraction.

"I'll be back in a minute." Detective Will pulled out his phone as he walked away. I suspected he was checking out Jackson's claim and asking if evidence would be thrown out if they searched the whole house and, however improbably, found something. I was going to ask my brother why the police were limited to only searching my legal residence, but he shook his head at me, telling me to be silent for now. I held back my questions, although I'd pin him down later. Metaphorically, of course. I was glad the detective hadn't heard the thought because he'd take it in a dirtier direction. I winced.

Detective Will was too far away for me to overhear his call, but he looked annoyed when he shoved his phone into his suit pocket and stalked back to us.

"Only search the third floor and communal areas," the detective barked at the other officers. He turned to Jackson. "I need to see this alleged rental agreement."

"Did you lock the door to the attic this morning, sweetheart?" Jackson asked me. His choice of endearment threw me for about a fourth of a second until I guessed he was messing with Detective Will.

I shook my head no. Jackson put his arm around my shoulder and pulled me to him. He rested his chin on top of my head like he'd done a few times when I was thirteen, and it still annoyed me. But I played along, even though I itched to punch him in the stomach. Something else I hadn't done since I was a kid. He smelled like Altoids.

"Go ahead and search, but remember the limits of your warrant," Jackson said. "There's a copy of the rental agreement inside."

One of the uniformed officers moved from his spot by the front door to stand close to my brother. "We need to pat you down."

Jackson stepped from me and opened his arms. "Sage, they're making sure we're not armed."

The officer patted Jackson down while his uniformed female

coworker did the honors for me. The process made me feel violated, and the faint glimmer of amusement over Jackson's messing with the detective faded away.

Jackson unlocked the door and took Bentley to the backyard before showing Detective Will to his home office off the foyer. I followed, still feeling like the world beneath me was shifting. Jackson pulled out the rental agreement I'd signed when I moved in three years ago and renewed after my time abroad. The detective read it with a straight, borderline-angry face and handed it back to my brother. Jackson made a copy of the contract for the detective and filed the original, and we went to the living room while the officers spread out and did their thing. My whole body buzzed.

We sat on the couch with an officer standing across from us. Jackson picked up a magazine from the coffee table and pretended to read, but his eyes weren't zeroing in on the words. I tried to follow his lead and ended up looking at the photos in an issue of the *Atlantic*. My eyes couldn't focus long enough to take in the text.

Jackson's phone beeped a couple of times, and he answered a few texts. He resumed his magazine like he had all of the time in the world. This was the longest I'd ever seen my brother sit still.

Ages later—in reality about an hour, but it felt like eons had passed—Detective Will showed up in the living room again.

The detective paused and scanned the photos on the mantel. He passed by the one of Jackson and his dad at Jackson's law school graduation, and another of my brother, age five, along with the paternal grandparents who raised him, sitting in front of a Christmas tree. The detective stopped by the next photo.

A few years ago, while trawling through a thrift store, I'd found a cheesy "brother and sister" picture frame covered in platitudes, like "two peas in a pod" and "no stronger bond." The creator had been too energetic with a glue gun and attached several messy glittery hearts and stars to the frame. The pull of the frame's ridiculousness was too much for me, and it'd gone home with me. I'd inserted a photo from the first time Jackson dragged me on a hike when I was thirteen. Jackson's hair flopped in his eyes, much longer than his current close crop, and I looked like a kid, despite only being an inch shorter than I am now. But it was clearly both of us. Mount Hood filled the background.

Jackson had laughed when he unwrapped the frame on his birthday. Then he put it on the mantel and refused to move it, saying he liked it. Even though I'd intended it as a gag gift.

The detective's eyes went to the next photo, a non-Pinterest-fail framed picture of us with my dad from my high school graduation, and Detective Will closed his eyes for a moment.

"You're not going to find bloody clothes on the mantel," Jackson said.

The detective held up a bag. "I'll leave an inventory of everything we're taking to run tests on."

I groaned when I saw the white T-shirt covered in brown blotches in the bag. "Those are coffee stains. I dumped a carafe of French press on myself in the warehouse a few days ago."

The detective still took the shirt with him, along with the sneakers I'd worn during my impromptu coffee bath.

At this rate, David Stevens's murder was never going to be solved.

Chapter 7

Jackson went back to his office after the police left, with instructions to call him if the cops came back or wanted to ask me more questions.

Bentley insisted we go for a walk, so we did our usual route around the neighborhood. The activity didn't slow the momentum of my thoughts, which continued to swirl.

My phone dinged while we'd stopped at one of the neighborhood gardens where several streets came together. A yellow rosebush smelled especially fascinating to Bentley. I scoped out the area, feeling like passersby should be staring, asking me what had happened. I pulled my phone out of my pocket.

Harley: *Police stopped by the warehouse. We need to talk.*

I replied: *Okay. When and where?*

Harley lived a block off trendy Northwest Twenty-Third Avenue, across the river from me, so we agreed to meet at the Tav in an hour. It was between us, even if it was closer to her. The thought of the bike ride called to the restlessness inside me. Like I should start pedaling and never stop. After dropping Bentley off at home, and grabbing my bike, I took a longer route than I needed to.

My pedals stopped midway over Tilikum Crossing, one of the bridges connecting the east and west sides of Portland. The view always calls to me. I stood and looked at downtown Portland on the west side of the river. Tilikum means "people" in Chinook Wawa, a language that developed between traders and the Natives of the Pacific Northwest. One of the local tribes still teaches it to their children. The bridge doesn't allow cars, only pedestrians, bicyclists, and the light-rail train, making it a true bridge of the people. I forced myself to move on. I didn't want to be late.

A woman worked behind the counter of the Tav instead of Miles. As I waited for her to pour a glass of iced tea, my eyes focused on the stained-glass windows. The middle left panel shows a man staring straight forward.

Great. Even the windows feel like they're judging me today.

I took my drink to the far back and settled in. We had a history, me and this booth. Miles had reupholstered any furniture with cloth in the bar after the indoor-smoking ban had gone into effect, but the vintage dark wood was the same. So it'd changed a bit over time, like me, but kept the same structure.

While I waited for Harley, I scanned the local news on my phone. Portland's stations had covered the protest, with special attention focused on the goat on top of the house, but they were quiet about the murder. The news mentioned a suspicious death, but only said the police weren't releasing any details until they had notified the deceased's family. The thought of seeing the news of the tragedy, but not knowing it was connected to me until police knocked on the door, made me shiver. A wave of compassion for David Stevens's family flowed through me.

Harley slid into the booth across from me. She looked like she'd downed too many shots of espresso to sit still. "Sage, the police stopped by the warehouse and interviewed me. You seriously found a body?"

"Yep." I looked down at the slice of lemon floating in my iced tea. I stabbed it with my straw, watching a piece of pulp bob.

"You didn't think to tell me? I'm your business partner. You should call me when you find dead bodies at the cart."

Harley's hands fidgeted with the paper menus left on the edge of the table. I took a deep breath. "I said I'd explain later. I'm sorry I didn't call you earlier, but I dealt with the police all morning. I'm sorry, honestly. You should've been one of my first calls when I was finally free."

"The detectives asked me a lot of questions about you. Is your mother—for real—a wanted criminal?"

"Yes. But my dad's a cop, so the two even out." Sometimes I felt like I was pretending the old wounds in my soul were scars when they were scabs ready to bleed again at the slightest nudge. My mother's call had picked at a few. I should be beyond her ability to hurt.

"Be serious. I knew your mother was out of the picture, but is she a con artist? The detective who interviewed me acted like I shouldn't trust you."

It was my turn to fidget with the collection of condiments left at the table in an old cardboard beer six-pack holder. "It's a long story. Did I ever mention I was born in Germany?"

"You're German? What else haven't you told me?" Harley leaned back and folded her arms across her chest. But she quickly straightened her arms and leaned forward again when I started to talk.

"I'm American. I was born on an army base. My mother was in trouble and needed to get out of town, and she convinced my dad to marry her. They'd known each other in high school, and he'd always thought she'd gotten a raw deal. She had Jackson when she was fifteen, and his paternal grandparents raised him. She convinced my dad she wanted to run away and start a family with him. He fell for her lies. In his defense, she excels at getting men to do what she wants."

"Okay." Harley stared at me without blinking. She'd quit fidgeting as she focused on my words. "It sounds like a movie."

I took a deep breath and tamped down my desire to embellish the story, make it sound even more like a cinematic crime heist than it was. "It's not a two-hour respite from life, like a movie. Real people have been hurt. It's not the story of an evil person robbed by a merry band of Robin Hoods. The should-be Robin Hoods of the story are unrepentant villains."

"So your mom has two kids, and at some point, she stole money."

"When my mother left with my father, she barely escaped being arrested for fencing stolen artwork. One of her go-betweens took the fall and ended up in jail. My parents had me about a year after they were married."

"How'd you end up with your dad? You've always been close." Harley looked like she was trying to figure out if I was for real, or if I was making this up. If she decided this was all a lie, I wouldn't blame her.

"She left my dad when I was two. Took me and split. But when I was thirteen, she dumped me in Portland and disappeared. I haven't seen her since." I filled in the rest of the details, telling Harley about how all those years ago, the bus ride to Portland had felt like it was taking forever. My mother had been anxious, and her fidgeting made me restless. I'd had multiple passports by that point, with different names, and we'd flown all over the world. But I'd never traveled days by bus, and my mother had never before acted worried. She was always in control, looking forward a few steps, analyzing the odds, and maneuvering her pieces of the chessboard into checkmate. So I'd been freaked-out the whole ride.

After the bus ride, we went to a Portland homeless shelter for women and children. My mother had charmed the shelter workers and women around us, who fell for her story. When I'd woken up the next morning, she was gone. She'd left me a business card for the Tav. I'd snuck out of the shelter. A few days later, with the help of a boy slightly older than me and his mom, I'd ended up at the Tav, my stomach growling since I hadn't eaten all day. Miles set me up in the back booth with a grilled cheese sandwich and lemonade. I'd fallen asleep and woke up with Miles's flannel shirt covering me like a blanket, with Uncle Jimmy sitting across from me.

"Uncle Jimmy called my dad. When my father left the army, he started working for the Portland police. He searched when he had time off, and he hired a PI for a while." I left chunks of the story out. Like acclimating to living in one place with a stranger who called himself my father. Somehow, my father had managed to be patient with me. It'd taken time, and counseling, for me to start to trust him. It might have been easier if I'd remembered him, and in retrospect, it'd been hard for me to trust anyone at thirteen, let alone after being abandoned. But he'd kept chipping away at me, even as I tried to build a metaphorical wall between me and everyone around me, since I was sure my mother would come back and I'd leave. She never showed, but my dad was there every day.

"PI?" Harley asked, bringing me back to the present.

"Private investigator. But my mother is a hard person to find. She's legendary." Although *notorious* might be the better description, or *mythical* in an antihero sort of way. She'd never be the hero who completed a quest, but she'd be the princess who manipulated the hero to face monsters to get what she wanted.

As we talked, I realized I needed to tell my dad about the woman who stopped by the cart, and my mother's phone call. And let him know the police thought I was a murderer. Yet another worry trying to tear apart at my nerves and pull me out of the life I was trying to build.

Uncle Jimmy slid into the booth next to me. He studied me for a moment. I could read sympathy intertwined with concern in his eyes.

"You okay, Bug?"

He'd gone back to my nickname. One of the threads of tension pulling on my spine relaxed. But it was ready to be stretched taut again.

"Sage was telling me about ending up here as a teen," Harley said.

"Bug looked about eleven. I found her sleeping in this booth," Uncle Jimmy said. "I knew who she was as soon as I laid eyes on her. She looked like her mom did at that age, and I'd seen photos."

"Photos?" I looked at Uncle Jimmy.

"Your mom sent me photos and called occasionally, but she never told me where you two were. I never knew what phone number or email address she'd use next. She was always in her zone, a few steps ahead of everyone, including me." The note of frustration in the depths of my uncle's voice made me wonder if there was something I didn't know, like if she'd scammed him too.

"The police say the guy who died, David Stevens, was one of her victims," I said.

"He was, and when he found out your mom was my niece, he went ballistic—"

"You call him uncle," Harley interrupted. The simmering frustration was back in her eyes and in the deep undercurrent of her voice.

"It's easier to say than Great-Uncle Jimmy," I said, and Harley chilled a tenth of a degree. Uncle Jimmy was only eleven years older than his niece, and he'd told me once my mom had always felt more like a little sister.

Uncle Jimmy continued, "David Stevens threatened to sue me and accused me of being in league with your mother to defraud him. Her theft stopped him from acquiring a piece of property he wanted, and I bought. But I didn't know she was in the city, let alone collaborating with her on some con. But he's held a grudge against me ever since."

"He stopped by the coffee stand twice," I said. "I wonder why."

"You're across the street from one of his properties, so maybe it was convenient. He's been after me to sell the Rail Yard, but he can't approach me directly because he swore he'd never do business with me. He tried using a shell company to buy it, and I called him out on it. He might have been scoping out the situation. Or we're over-thinking it and he wanted a cup of coffee." Uncle Jimmy's facial expression tightened, like the situation bothered him, but I knew nothing threw him off his game. "You still look like your mom. Seeing you might have thrown him off."

"Maybe." Had my presence been enough to draw him back to the Rail Yard multiple times? But the coffee cart closed in the afternoon, so why would he visit at night? Let alone after the carts shut down for the evening?

Or he'd run into one of my fellow cart owners as they were closing. The idea made me shiver.

There had to be a reason. Maybe it didn't have anything to do with me. But that might be wishing for something impossible.

Harley and I switched topics and made plans to work on marketing to wholesale accounts for the next few days until the Rail Yard could reopen.

"We're bleeding revenue with the cart closed," I said.

"We didn't plan for the cart to break even for six months, so don't worry about it," Uncle Jimmy said. "Focus on the wholesale accounts."

"Everyone at the Rail Yard is suffering from the closure," I said, remembering Zarek and Macie. They'd been frustrated when they'd heard their carts wouldn't be allowed to open. The frantic look in Zarek's eyes made me think he was desperately clinging to the ledge between stability and failure.

"Let them worry about their businesses," Uncle Jimmy said.

The idea made me feel cold. I wanted to help in some way, but how? Feeling powerless made a new surge of frustration flow through me.

"There has to be something we can do," I said.

"If the Rail Yard is closed for an extended time, I'll give cart owners a break on their rent," Uncle Jimmy said. But I thought of the food Zarek had bought. Hopefully, he'd find a way to use it before it spoiled.

After a while, Harley stood up to leave since she had plans to meet up with a guy at a pub by her house. "But he's not as cute as Zarek," Harley said.

"Don't worry, he's all yours," I promised as she left. What would Zarek have said if he'd heard me? I smothered one of my few smiles of the day.

Once Harley walked out the front door, Uncle Jimmy turned to me. We were still sharing the same side of a booth, and I felt trapped against the wall. I braced myself to hear whatever he wanted to tell me.

"David Stevens's body being dumped by your cart bothers me. I wish I knew if this was a fluke, or if someone is sending a message to your mother."

I froze. "What do you mean?"

"One of her marks ends up dead next to her daughter's business, and on a property I own? What's the odds of that being a coincidence? But is the message for her, or me?"

"Good point." I hadn't explored this avenue, which is why Uncle Jimmy is the mastermind, and I'm one of his many puppets. The meaning settled on me, along with a few flickers of fear. If someone was sending a message to my mother, he might decide one of her old marks wasn't a strong enough signal. But her daughter? Even one she hadn't seen for over a decade?

I shivered.

Uncle Jimmy put his hand on mine. "Be cautious, but we don't need to freak out yet. If you were their target, they wouldn't have gone after David Stevens."

"Should we warn Jackson?"

"Jackson and I talked earlier about the murder. He asked most of the same questions I did."

I half smiled. Of course Uncle Jimmy talked with Jackson first. Our family saw my brother as the adult and me as a perpetual kid.

"Be aware of your surroundings for the next few weeks. Vary your commute to work and all of your routines. Check to see if anyone is following you. Note if anyone seems to be hanging around you, wants to talk to you too much, keeps showing up."

"In short, acting like a customer," I said. We wanted people to drop by the coffee cart daily. Conversations were part of the reason people came since they wanted to feel like family. Like friends. But faking brand loyalty could be a good way to keep an eye on me.

"Trust your instincts. They're solid. Keep your phone on you. Check in with me. Miles will stop by occasionally."

"Okay." The weight of the day pressed down on me. All I could think of was retreating home and finally taking the nap I'd daydreamed about. "I'll keep this in mind. I'll even vary my bike ride home."

"Jackson said he'd pick you up."

My breath caught, and I felt even more trapped between my uncle and the wall. Maybe I could slide and crawl out from under the table. Uncle Jimmy straightened his legs out as if he knew what I was thinking.

"It's getting late," Uncle Jimmy said. "You hungry? Or want something other than iced tea?"

I bowed to the inevitable and waited for my brother to pick me up. If any day deserved corn dog nuggets, it was today. With a side of fresh-cut french fries.

Chapter 8

A day later, the Rail Yard was cleared to reopen. My day away from the cart with Harley had been profitable, since we'd signed agreements to provide beans to two different cafés, with leads on more. A local food co-op was stocking our Puddle Jumper and would offer free brewed samples to their customers as a test, with the promise of keeping us in their rotation if the beans in stock sold briskly. We'd restocked the cart early yesterday evening with fresh milk and ready-to-grind beans once we'd gotten the all clear to go back on-site, but none of the carts had opened.

We'd see if people were willing to eat at the site of a murder. Butterflies jittered in my stomach as I locked the gate behind me, and I hurried past the spot on the ground where I'd found David's body.

Every noise made me jump and caused my heart to start pounding as I puttered around, getting the cart ready to open. I should've made Harley help me so I wouldn't have to be alone. She'd join me in an hour and a half, but that felt like too long.

When I left the cart to open the gate to the Rail Yard and invite customers inside, it felt like an act of faith. I should have made a sign listing the "ground rules for being my customer." But putting "don't get murdered next to the cart" or, even better, "please dump bodies elsewhere" might put people off the coffee.

"Stop being heartless," I muttered to myself, even though I knew I was trying to cope by making myself laugh. But it wasn't helping. Maybe I'd lost my ability to make a joke when I'd found the body. I'd never be funny again.

"I heard about a homeless guy OD'ing in the Rail Yard," my first customer of the day said. "I hope being shut for a few days didn't wreck your business. I heard a lot of you food carts run pretty close to the line."

I forced myself to smile as I steamed milk for his cappuccino, wondering if he thought I'd want to talk about the finances of the business with some random guy I didn't know.

"Thanks for supporting us," I said as I handed over his drink, making eye contact like his support shook me to the core. After he'd left, I saw he'd tipped $3 on a $2.50 drink, making me feel guilty I'd sent snarky thoughts his direction.

Most of the usual morning commuters came in and ordered coffee and asked about what happened.

"I heard it was a gang thing," one of my customers told the two people waiting behind her in line. "It was unlucky to happen here."

Gangs. Overdoses. Where were these stories coming from? I'd have to check the local news sites.

"I'm sorry I don't know the details of what happened," I practically shouted as I handed over a latte to the woman talking about gangs in the city. "But thanks so much for stopping by today."

"Let us know what you hear. I'm fascinated. True-crime books are my favorite, and this is the closest I've been to an Ann Rule book in real life," the first woman said, making my smile falter as her words creeped me out. The man behind her eagerly ordered a house coffee and a cream-cheese Danish, so I turned away, using the moment to take a deep breath and then paste a smile on my face. Harley poured the coffee while I snagged the pastry. Our forced days off, and the bombshells I'd dropped about my family life, hadn't messed up our ability to work as a team.

After 9:00 a.m., cart traffic slowed down, and Harley split for the warehouse. A guy walked up, around his early thirties with a full beard, short-sleeve plaid shirt, and cutoff shorts. Hiking boots like he was taking a long trek through the city or loves the feel of sweaty feet during the summer.

"I'm excited to try you out," he said. "Harley and I go way back, so I had to stop by. How's she as a boss?"

"We're co-owners," I said, keeping the smile on my face.

"Sorry, I didn't mean to offend you. I hope I didn't knock you off of your coffee game."

"No worries. Harley's a coffee rock star."

"Everyone knows Harley. Everyone will want to meet you when they hear she has a business partner. Although it makes sense, since I wondered how she'd made the jump on her own. She was broke the whole time we dated."

What was with it with people bringing up my company financials today? And this dude had dated Harley? He didn't look familiar. A lifetime of training kept a bland smile on my face as he debated what to order, finally settling on a macchiato.

"Good choice. It's one of my favorites." I foamed milk before pulling a shot of espresso and carefully pouring it into a ceramic cup, even though I had four-ounce paper cups in case someone was serious about taking espresso to go. But a real aficionado—or *snob*, as I suspected was the appropriate term in this case—would want their espresso served in ceramic. Or glass if it was a latte macchiato, which I halfway hoped he'd order since it's one of my favorite drinks to make. After carefully "staining" the espresso with a small amount of milk, the macchiato was ready.

He stared at the macchiato, as if he were analyzing it with X-ray vision, before taking a sip.

"Dang, this has a rounded taste. Nice cherry notes on the forefront, and toffee at the end." He took another sip. "Good job foaming the milk too. And thanks for not adding too much. Some people act like they're making a cappuccino and use way too much milk. I mean, I'd order a café latte or latte macchiato if I wanted to drown the taste of the espresso. . . ."

As the coffee snob rambled on about his all-time best espresso experiences, I noticed a kid watching us from the street. Maybe sixteen. Gangly, like he'd grown a lot and his weight hadn't caught up.

"How about a pour-over to follow this?" coffee dude asked.

"Guatemala or Ethiopia?" I asked, referencing the single-origin beans we were offering today.

"What's your recommendation?"

"Guatemala, but truthfully, Ethiopian coffees aren't for me. They're too cloying. I want to adore them, but something about the taste puts me off. But many aficionados think they're the best in the world, so it's a personal preference."

"I dig. Guatemala has a cleaner aftertaste, while naturally processed Ethiopian coffee is rather syrupy with a sweet berry flavor." He started reciting coffee-growing facts.

My eyes were drawn to the kid again, who wanted to come to the cart, but every time he took a step past the gate, he stopped and backed up. The coffee snob continued to spout off knowledge, as if he were proving his worthiness to order from Ground Rules.

The coffee dude observed as I set the gooseneck kettle to boil and set about making his pour-over, from washing the filter before adding twenty-one grams of freshly ground Ethiopian beans, to slowly adding water with a slow spiral pour. The guy analyzed each step, waiting for me to make a mistake.

Hopefully, having people staring at me, ready to pounce on stupid mistakes, wasn't my new MO.

Three minutes after I started, I had three hundred milliliters of coffee. I poured it into a to-go cup. "Ta-da," I said, and handed it over.

As the guy sipped his coffee, I scanned for the kid again. He was staring at me through the fence about ten feet to the side of the gate. I motioned for the kid to come and he looked tentative, so I waved again. He slowly started making his way back to the entrance.

"I'd love to get your photo," the coffee dude said.

"Why?"

"My blog, of course, and my social media feeds."

My photo being splashed around online made the butterflies in my stomach take flight again, but I smiled and let him take a snap of me with his phone. He paid and waved as he left. "Harley's not the only rock star in town," he said. He had to intend it as a compliment to my barista skills. Or he hadn't liked the coffee and was going to order more from a real coffee superstar. But I'd read his face. He'd been impressed.

Now that I was alone, the kid's steps were quick as he approached the cart.

"Can I help you with something?" I asked.

"I heard you sometimes give away food and stuff." The kid stared at the ground.

I motioned to the board and told him about the suspended coffees. "How about a hot chocolate?" I offered, even though it wasn't on the board.

"Do you have anything to eat?"

"How about I add a buckwheat fig scone," I said, which was on the board.

His back straightened. He smiled at me and made eye contact for a second, then stared at the ground again.

After I made his hot chocolate, I pulled a protein bar out of my bag and handed it over along with the scone and the drink.

"Do you know Gabby?" I asked.

He looked at me with narrowed eyes, and his shoulders slumped. "Why do you want to know?"

"She's stopped by a few times. I'm worried about her." I grabbed one of my business cards and handed it over. "Ask her to call me if she can't stop by."

"What's in it for me?"

Seriously, kid? I shot him a glance to get real. "Another hot chocolate. A muffin."

"Whatever. No one cares about us."

"I care, as does my brother. He's a lawyer who specializes in child advocacy. He's helped a lot of teens in bad situations." I should snag some of Jackson's business cards and keep them around.

"What's child advocacy?" the kid asked in a quiet voice.

"In a nutshell, my brother represents the interest of kids whenever, and wherever, they need a lawyer. The long version talks about the juvenile court system, divorce proceedings, abuse investigations, foster care, and more."

"I might pass on your message," the kid said, and skedaddled.

Zarek stopped by on his way to his cart, carrying grocery bags. "Was that kid hassling you?"

"Nah." I leaned against the counter, feeling exhausted all of a sudden as I thought of all of the teens on the streets.

"Not everyone's happy you're giving away free drinks to the homeless." It was Zarek's turn to get a look that said "seriously."

"So Macie can feed her 'babies,' but you have issues with a few cups of free coffee?" I massaged my temples against the headache threatening to invade my thoughts. My jaw was tight, so I forced it to relax instead of letting it remain jutted out.

"What you're doing is noble and I won't have a problem with it as long as people grab their drinks and split. But if people who don't have anywhere else to go start hanging out all day, hogging the picnic tables and running off paying customers, it'll be a problem for all of us."

Part of me felt as if I were back in high school. "If anyone has a problem with it, they can talk to me directly."

Zarek grinned. "I'll pass along your feelings. Hopefully, the people you're feeding will treat the Rail Yard with respect. You know we've had our power lines cut before, right? Tweakers sell the cut lines for scrap. They hit the carts twice last spring, and it sucked."

"Sounds frustrating." I nodded along, creating a sense of boring unity.

He leaned in toward me. "It's too expensive to replace the cords weekly. . . ." I zoned out as Zarek talked, until he said, "How about an iced oat-milk latte? I'll drop something by later in trade."

I resumed making coffee, and he took his latte to his cart.

Miles stopped by midmorning and bought an Americano. He hung out for a bit but waved goodbye when the college girl I'd cold read a few days ago dropped by. "Do you have any advice for me today?" she asked.

I thought as I made her mocha. She was taking classes downtown at Portland State, which ran year-round, although some students took the summer off. She was probably close to being done with college, and serious about finishing, but stressed. I remembered how stressed I'd felt my final year of college. I'd give anything to be that carefree again.

As I handed over her drink, I said, "I sense you need to focus on something now and give it everything you've got. But you feel like you've spread yourself thin. Step back and reassess your goals. What's the primary goal you want to achieve? Focus on that, and things will fall into place."

"Oh, you're totally right, my capstone adviser said . . ." She was off and told me about the service-based project she needed to complete to earn her bachelor's in English with a minor in philosophy.

After a while, I said, "Remember, anyone who is a real friend will understand you're busy with school right now. Be honest about what matters most to you: going to a party like every other you've attended in the past year, or buckling down and finishing this project since it means a lot to you?"

She glowed. "You're right. I'm so glad I stopped by. You're a lifesaver. I wish I didn't have to catch my bus so we could talk longer."

She started to leave but paused. "You know the guy I met here the other day? The computer programmer?"

"Yes?" I tried not to smile since I knew where this was going.

"Do we, like, have a future together? We're supposed to get coffee. But he's given me an out, 'cause he knows school keeps me busy."

"Only time will tell if you're meant to be, but go for it. Remember, one cup of coffee doesn't have to lead to anything more unless you want it to."

I waved as she ran to catch the bus to downtown. Hopefully, I hadn't convinced her psychics were real, as she was now primed and ready to be a mark.

But I didn't have long to worry about college students who believe in the supernatural due to my ability to cold read the gullible. A man in a slouchy black T-shirt and faded jeans walked up to my cart, making notes of anxiety flit through my hands. But I told myself to chill and steeled my face into an indifferent expression.

"It's Sage, isn't it?" But I'd clocked the look in his eyes. He'd recognized me as he'd walked up.

"Hi, Mark." I eyed my former boss from my college job at Left Coast Grinds. I'd worked for him when he was opening his first shop after winning both the Northwest Brewers competition and the Brewers division of the US Coffee Championships in the same year, making him a superstar in the coffee world.

He eyed our menu. "So you and little Harley are playing at being coffee roasters. When you get tired of playing, you can ask for your old job back, although Harley will have to grovel."

In my mind, I snorted. Harley deserved an award for the number of years she'd worked for Mark, including as a coffee roaster, which told me how much my friend appreciated Mark's coffee since the man was sleazy with a side of arrogance. I continued staring at him, stone-faced as if he weren't worthy of the energy it would take to form words.

Mark finally said, "I'll have a shot of the Kenyan."

So I set about pulling his shot of espresso, even though I'd have preferred to dump the drink over his head. But I took care as I made it because I wanted to show him we could match him at his own game. I handed it over, along with a small glass of sparkling water.

He took a sip of the espresso and frowned. "You still have a way to go. I heard a man died here, but I wouldn't have guessed the coffee was that bad."

His words made me smirk. He wouldn't be a jerk if our coffee hadn't impressed him. More things to add to my list of "ground rules for being my customer": "Don't come if your only goal is to be a prick."

"Hopefully you won't succumb to the same fate," I said. "Two dead bodies would be a problem."

His eyes darted up and pierced me. I covered a smile. I picked up my water bottle and took a sip, trying to keep my posture from puffing up. Although I should have felt guilty, making a death the punch line of a joke. My eyes narrowed.

Mark finished his shot.

"Come back anytime!" I said in a sweet voice as he left.

The construction project across the street from the Rail Yard began in earnest again after lunchtime as workers began carrying anything salvageable out of the houses. They'd erected a sign about how they were taking the buildings apart responsibly and would donate anything, like sinks and cabinetry, that could be used again to the ReClaimed Goods Center and would recycle as much as possible.

The protesters chanted for a few minutes but faded away. Part of me was sad to see the goat leave, although I still wasn't sure why someone had brought it in the first place. Maybe it was an emotional-support goat.

The first news crew pulled up about thirty minutes before I was scheduled to close the cart. They set up and filmed the construction site before turning their cameras toward the Rail Yard. A woman talked in front of her news crew, pointing in the direction of my cart.

I snuck out of Ground Rules and headed farther into the Rail Yard, hoping to stay out of sight of the cameras.

"Isn't a junkie overdosing three days ago old in the news cycle?" Emma asked when, still watching the news crew, I paused by her cart.

I glanced at her, shocked at her callousness, and also curious. Was she the person telling customers the death was an overdose? "Where did you hear that?"

"Some rando died here. What else could've happened?" Emma asked, but she looked away like she was lying.

Macie joined us and said, "If they're going to scare away customers, at least they could buy food."

Zarek ditched his falafel cart and ambled up to us. "Have you guys seen the breaking news about the death at the Rail Yard?"

We swiveled to him as one.

"I'm guessing no." He held up his phone. "The identity of the dead guy was announced. It's big. Although the police showed me his picture, so it's not like it's a surprise."

Interesting. So I wasn't the only one who knew. Did this mean Zarek had recognized David Stevens's photo? Had he seen David visit the coffee cart? Did they know each other? My eyes narrowed.

"What do you mean?" Emma asked. She looked over, then away, like she didn't have the energy to be invested in the conversation.

"Didn't the police interview you?" Zarek asked. "They stopped by my apartment and asked a bunch of questions."

Emma shook her head. "I went backpacking on the Oregon Coast Trail and had my phone powered off the whole time. I'll have to ask my daughter if anyone stopped by."

I glanced at Emma, noting again how in shape she looked, like she went backpacking often or worked out regularly.

"I wonder if that was the person who knocked on my door yesterday," Macie said. "Someone stopped by a few times, but I was busy sewing. I make quilts for babies, you know."

Human babies or pigeons? I wanted to ask, but I eyed Emma and Macie instead. They acted weirdly unconcerned about the murder.

Zarek shook his head at them, looking as disturbed as I felt inside. "You should pay attention to this case," he told them.

"Why should I care about a rando addict?" Emma asked.

"Because it wasn't an addict. The developer of the building across the street dying in our community is bad news for all of us."

Emma burst into tears.

Chapter 9

All three of us stared at Emma for a moment. Macie put her arm around Emma's shoulders and squeezed. Macie pulled a fabric square out of her apron pocket and started to hand it to Emma but said, "Wait, not this one," and put it back in her pocket. She produced a paper napkin and gave it to Emma instead.

"Did you know David Stevens?" I asked. Emma wiped her eyes and took a deep breath, like she was trying to stop crying, and hiccuped.

"Everyone knew him." Emma's eyes darted away from all of us. "I hadn't thought a real person died here. It hit me that it could have been any of us."

I knew Emma was lying, but given the way Macie was rubbing circles on Emma's back while making cooing noises, it wasn't the right time to call her out.

"Do you think this will affect the building across the street?" Macie asked. "Maybe the old carts can come back."

"It looks like the new building is moving along," Zarek said. "Whoever is second-in-command must have decided to continue the project since they'd already started. The business probably has investors and money tied up in it."

Second-in-command. The idea captured my attention and demanded I look into it. Who benefited from David's death? Just because I'd found his body here didn't mean any of the businesses had anything to do with it, including mine. Maybe I could save my business—and all of our carts—if I figured out what was going on.

Zarek studied me. "David stopped by your cart, didn't he?"

"He bought coffee a few times."

A kid, about nineteen or twenty, walked up. From his ripped jeans, Chuck Taylors, and slouch, I knew his type. Starts with a capital *T*, and it doesn't rhyme with *pool*. Rather, *trouble*. If I'd been a decade younger, I'd already have been in lust.

"Aunt Macie," he said. "What do you need me to do?"

I raised my eyebrows at Zarek as Macie led the kid to her cart, and Emma retreated to the bathroom. "Macie's nephew," Zarek said. "If I heard right, the kid's parents only pay for art school if he helps out at the cart a few days a week."

"Art school?"

"He painted her truck."

My gaze swiveled to the image of the birds and the 4 and 20 on Macie's pie cart. It was beautiful—striking, with high contrast in the design of the birds—but it still didn't remind me of the nursery rhyme.

"He's talented. He was in a show last winter, and I stopped by 'cause Macie handed out invitations."

"A love of arts and crafts must run in their family," I said, remembering Macie's sewing in slow times between customers.

"What runs in your family?" Zarek asked me. Little danger warnings flickered in my brain, although he was most likely making small talk. But his voice had taken on a flirtatious note, and something told me to pay attention to him.

"Other than extreme height?" I joked.

"You're fun-size." I pretended I didn't know what he was talking about, and he tripped over his next words. "You know, like the small candy bars people give out on Halloween? They're labeled fun-size."

"I know. The joke quit being funny years ago. Along with jokes about me fitting into pockets." I smiled.

He relaxed when he realized I'd been teasing him. "Gotcha. The ability to put our foot in our mouths runs in my family. It's a well-honed gift requiring perfect timing and years of practice."

He felt sincere, so I told myself to lighten up. "Both my father and brother are outdoorsy. My brother dragged me hiking all the time when I was a teen. My father's into cycling."

"You have a brother? My older brother keeps bugging me to sell my cart and get a real job."

"Is he vegan too?"

"Not even a little bit. You're lucky your family is into fitness. I'm the odd one out. I played soccer growing up, but now I run, and snowboard in the winter."

"You know, my business partner, Harley, plays a lot of soccer. You guys should talk about that. I usually get my workouts on my bike."

"I noticed you never drive here."

"I don't own a car." My lack of automotive transport made getting supplies to the cart difficult, so someday I'd have to buy a car. Harley and I had talked about getting a vehicle, like a small van, for the business, so I could commandeer it. If Ground Rules survived a murder happening at the foot of the cart. A mass of pain and unease settled in my abdomen again.

"Why'd you decide to start a falafel stand?" I asked.

"Long story." Zarek looked toward the entrance of the Rail Yard.

"Sounds like a good one," I joked. The guy with blond dreadlocks walked into the lot.

"I'll tell you sometime over a drink. You know, I have to check on something." Zarek bolted back to his cart. The guy in dreadlocks glared at me as he made his way over to Zarek's falafel cart.

Instead of returning to Ground Rules, I detoured to the women's bathroom. "You okay, Emma?" I asked as I walked in. The middle stall door was locked, so Emma must be hidden inside.

"I'm fine. I'll be out in a few minutes."

The note of dismissal in her voice told me she wanted to be alone, as did the follow-up hiccup. So I headed back to the picnic table by Ground Rules and sat down on top, debating if I should close a few minutes early today. But part of me wanted to see Emma when she came out, even if it took her hours to leave the bathroom. Something was off with her.

Macie walked by, swinging a patchwork purse with a green starburst button on the front flap. "My nephew's taking care of the cart for the rest of the day."

"How'd you become a food cart owner, Macie?"

"I owned a button store for a long time, but the building my shop was in was torn down. The lease on the new storefronts in the neighborhood was too expensive, and I gave up my shop. My family and friends have always loved my pie. So I switched to baking, and my sister helped me get my cart up and running. I have to do something, you know."

"Gotcha."

"I need to buy navy thread." Macie ambled away, swinging her bag.

As I closed up the coffee cart, I watched a twentysomething kid stride through the lot and stop at Macie's 4 and 20 Blackbirds cart. The kid talked with Macie's nephew for a moment. The kid handed over money and received something in return.

Based on the way the kid tucked his purchase into his pocket, he hadn't bought a slice of pie.

After closing the cart, I biked over to our warehouse space in inner Southeast Portland. We had a small office and warehouse space with a loading dock, next door to a place called Grumpy Sasquatch Productions, which had posters of video games in their entryway, with a wood-furniture builder on our other side. The hallway next to our office echoed with snippets of music from the fitness studio in the back of the building.

Harley was in love with our ten-kilogram coffee roaster (which weighed over nine hundred pounds or, as Harley joked, nine of me).

"Sage," Harley said, sounding breathless. Like she was close to panicking.

"Oh no, what went wrong?" I rushed to her side. She was staring at the bag of beans that had been degassing for a week and were ready to grind. After roasting, coffee beans need time to release the CO_2 that builds up during roasting. Had something gotten into the beans? Did we now have highly caffeinated mice running around?

But everything looked fine.

"What if I messed up? What if I over-roasted the beans and they're terrible?"

I patted her shoulder. "Harley, you're awesome. And if the beans aren't exactly what you want them to be, that's okay. It can take a while to get the new roasts dialed in." It had taken a few weeks to get a product worth selling, but Harley was a professional. "You know your beans will be magic eventually, even if it takes a few tweaks."

It took a few minutes, but I finally talked Harley down, and after a few deep breaths, she ground the first batch of the blend of blond and dark roast she'd created. Harley had been playing around with the combination at home, and this was the first time she'd made it on industrial equipment.

During my previous years working in coffee, I'd often assisted with coffee cuppings, and setting one up now was second nature. We set up several clear eight-ounce glasses and added grounds and fresh hot water from the electric kettle set at the perfect temperature for coffee, just below boiling. We let the coffee bloom in the cups and leaned over to sniff the aroma. As a comparison, we also cupped coffee from Left Coast Grinds along with a couple of our new roasts, both a single-origin from Guatemala and a blend. Harley would want to know Mark, our former boss, stopped by the cart, but I couldn't tell her now. Not when I'd finally calmed her down.

I examined one of the cups of the new blend, looking at it in the light, before sniffing it again. I took a sip.

The mix of dark and blond beans was perfectly balanced. I glanced at Harley. "What'd I tell you? Magic."

She let out a deep breath. "This is the flavor profile I'm going for." She took a sip. "I'm not sure how we should market it."

"It has some of the characteristics of a dark blend, but the higher caffeine of a light roast, right?" Counterintuitively, blond coffees are more caffeinated since roasting leaches caffeine from the beans.

We talked about names as I ground and brewed the beans in a variety of methods—espresso, pour-over, French press—and we agreed the blend was too light for espresso, which is usually a dark roast, but perfect for pour-overs and French press. I even broke out the industrial drip coffee maker, and we made a batch large enough for an army.

"Still good," Harley said as she tasted it. She wrote down a handful of potential names on our whiteboard, adding to the two I'd already listed.

"What should we do with the extra?" Harley pointed to the mostly full carafe of drip coffee.

"I can offer it to the grumpy sasquatches next door." I loaded up a reusable grocery bag with cups, sugar, and swizzle sticks and hooked it over my arm. I carried the stainless steel carafe in my hands and headed next door.

Two women and three men were sitting on the couches in the front of the studio, all holding laptops or tablets. They looked up as I entered. All looked exhausted.

"Hi, I'm from the roaster next door. Would you like some coffee? We brewed way more than we can drink."

"You're an angel," one of the guys said. "We've been here since six a.m. yesterday."

He put his tablet down and looked stiff as he stood up and ran his hand over his short brown hair, making it stand on end. But he grinned at me. His smile transformed his face like the sun coming out on a rainy day. "Let me grab some cups," he said.

"I have paper cups," I said, but he walked into a kitchen off the open-floor-plan office.

His coworkers put their computers or tablets down, all looking like they'd gone a few too many rounds. One of the women rubbed her eyes. "Even when I close my eyes, all I see is this stupid game."

"The end is in sight," someone else said.

"Yes, because I'm going to die before this launches."

"Relax, the coffee will help," the first guy said as he returned carrying a collection of mugs, which he put on the edge of the coffee table. I poured, careful to not spill any coffee on their electronics. I handed the first cup to the guy who'd brought the cups.

"I'm Bax," he said as he took the cup. He offered me his left hand since the right was holding the mug, and we shook awkwardly. He grinned again, making me feel like I'd been sprinkled with pixie dust. I smiled in response.

"Sage."

"You cycle here, right? I've seen you rolling by on your road bike. Cannondale?" When I nodded, he said, "We have weekly lunch rides on Fridays if you ever want to join us."

"Sounds fun, but I manage our coffee cart on Fridays." I held back a grin when I pictured the sasquatches decked out in spandex and helmets, riding in a row. But Bax looked like he'd spent a lot of time on a bike, with the low body fat of someone who rides often, but he was bulkier than your average elite cyclist.

There was a mix of happy groans and primal noises as the sasquatches took their first sips of the coffee.

"What'd I tell you? She's a coffee angel," Bax said.

There was a skip in my step when I walked back into the warehouse. I hummed as I packed up a few bags of beans to pass along to Uncle Jimmy and a handful of businesses we'd agreed to give samples to.

Chapter 10

I stopped at the grocery store on my ride home and picked up a basket of groceries and stored them in the saddlebags of my bike. After taking Bentley for a walk, and reading outside in the shade with him as the afternoon faded into evening, I fired up Jackson's grill.

"The roommate I had while you were gallivanting around the world never made me dinner," Jackson said when he came home. He dropped his laptop bag next to me and collapsed on the chair across the patio table. He picked up the glass of ice water I'd set out for him and held it to his forehead. The beer-can chicken I'd grilled only had a few more minutes to rest, and the caprese salad and corn on the cob were ready to go.

"I thought my room was empty the whole time?" I asked. Other than being a bit stuffy and dusty, it felt the same as when I'd left for my year in Bali, not like someone had lived there for a few months. Had Jackson let someone live in my room, with my stuff, while I was volunteering abroad? I leaned back in my chair and crossed my arms.

"I rented one of the bedrooms on the second floor for two months, but it didn't work out. I'll go get the carving knife." He grabbed a mozzarella ball out of the salad and rushed inside, unable to sit still, doing nothing, for long. I decided to let him tackle the chicken even though I'm more than capable of carving it.

Jackson came back a while later, having ditched his suit for cargo shorts and a Portland Timbers T-shirt. He carried a carving knife and a fork.

As we ate, he told me about his day, since he'd spent most of it on an emergency child-custody hearing after a mother was arrested for DUI with her four-year-old in the car.

"The judge granted temporary custody to the child's grand-mother until the father can fly home from a business trip overseas." Jackson seemed satisfied on one level but frustrated on another. Par for the course for my brother ninety percent of the time.

After eating, Jackson pulled a law journal out of his bag. The sun was starting to set, so I switched on the patio's light. The July days were long this time of the year with sunset around 9:00 p.m.

"Can I borrow your laptop?" I asked.

"Go ahead."

I dug through his laptop bag and pulled out his computer.

"Don't you have your own?" He glanced over the magazine for a second.

"It's all the way upstairs, and it's acting weird." I logged on to the guest account on my brother's laptop and googled David Stevens's business.

"Bring it to the office, and I can ask my IT contractor to fix it." Jackson returned to his reading.

It didn't take me long to learn Stevens Homes Inc. was family owned. David was the CEO, and his son, Arthur, was general man-ager. I studied Arthur's photo for a moment. The same face shape as his dad, but he looked friendlier. Like he'd say hi to the person mak-ing his coffee. Even thank them.

Their company had built apartment buildings and homes all over the Portland metro area for the past thirty years, along with offices and mixed-use buildings.

"Is there a way to find out the content of someone's will?" I asked Jackson.

"Do I want to know what you're doing?" Jackson looked up from the journal.

"You asking as my lawyer or my brother?"

"Both."

I turned the laptop and showed him the screen. "I'm curious who had a reason to want David Stevens out of the picture."

Jackson moved his bag and slid into the chair closest to me. He scanned the "About Me" page of Stevens Homes Inc. It gave me a flashback of life after I moved in with my dad and Jackson was in college, followed by law school. Jackson would stay over when my father worked nights and badger me to finish my homework. We'd end up hitting the books together at the dining room table. I'd been annoyed my father didn't trust me to stay home alone, but secretly glad to have Jackson around, even if he'd taken it as the opportunity to check my homework and order me to go to bed at 10:00 p.m.

Some things hadn't changed much in the past fourteen years. Although I was prepared to remind my brother he couldn't ground me if I didn't let him order me around.

"You want details about David Stevens's estate," Jackson said. "Tread carefully. His will should go into probate eventually, which will turn it into a public record. Did anything specific make you wonder about this?"

I told him about my day at the food cart, including Emma's weird reaction to the news. "There has to be something I can do to protect Ground Rules and the Rail Yard."

"As long as this stays academic and you don't do anything stupid or dangerous, I'll help." Jackson logged out of the computer's guest account and into his own and, within a few minutes, was searching a state business database, looking into Stevens Homes Inc.

"Looks like their board of directors was David, his sister Mary, and an attorney named Grayson Jade. I wonder how their shares are broken down . . . ," Jackson muttered as he dug through state records.

Since Jackson had commandeered the laptop, I used my phone's browser to search David's name. I ignored the articles I'd seen earlier about his death and opened up an in-depth profile on the local Business Gazette's site.

David talked about his desire to shape Portland's future. One of his proposals was for a large-scale homeless shelter using land the city owned but wasn't currently using. He wanted to integrate everything, from different social service organizations, including satellite offices of a few local nonprofits, addiction-treatment options, lockers, showers, a place to sleep, job center, shelter section with family rooms, and more, in one central location.

"A center like this would help my downtown tenants, who deal with the homeless day in and day out, while also providing the assistance the most vulnerable of our society desperately need," David said about his idea. "We need to take proactive action based on sound economics and addiction research instead of wringing our hands."

The article also talked about the changing face of downtown, about how multiple lots that currently house food carts and parking are scheduled to be redeveloped in the next five years into apartments and office space. The incentive to move into Uncle Jimmy's new brick-and-mortar development felt like the difference between long-term success and failure. I felt for all of the small businesses that'd be affected at some point. From what I'd seen at the Rail Yard, my fellow food cart owners were passionate about their companies and worked long hours. While the coffee cart was doing well, keeping it profitable for a long time—especially when the rain came—was a definite question mark that worried me in the middle of the night. I turned my thoughts back to the matter at hand.

This research could be pointless. David's background, including his passions and plans, could be irrelevant if he was a warning to my mother. Only his history with her mattered if that was the case. Or he'd rubbed someone the wrong way with his desire to shape the landscape of the city, and somehow it had led to David's being murdered next to my food cart. Maybe his history with my mother was a coincidence.

I rubbed my forehead, wishing I'd known David was the victim when my mother called since I could have asked her. Not that I could've trusted her answer.

Wait. David had seen my uncle the morning he'd stopped by.

He'd glared at Uncle Jimmy. But there's no reason David and my uncle would've ended up at the lot together in the middle of the night.

"What's on your mind?" Jackson asked, but it was more of a demand.

I shook my head.

"Seriously, spill. I know you've thought of something." Jackson's eyes flashed with anger; he clenched his teeth to not snap at me.

So I told him about our mother's phone call.

He took a deep breath and let it out. "She called you, and you didn't tell me? Our mother contacting you is serious, Sage. Plus you lied to the police."

"No, I didn't," I snapped back. "The detective asked if I'd seen her. Not if I'd talked to her."

Jackson rubbed his hand over his hair. "I saw her last year."

My body froze. "What?"

"I went to a convention in Washington, DC. My final day there, I went out by myself for dinner, and she showed up. She sat down across from me."

A thousand questions flew through my mind. I settled on a basic one instead of pointing out Jackson hadn't told me about it, so why was he annoyed I hadn't run to him when she called? "What'd she say?"

"Our mother said I looked good. She'd heard I'd done well for myself and wanted to see me since it'd been a few decades. She asked about you, said she'd done her best to train you, and she was glad we were close."

My whole body wanted to freak out, and my heart started pounding, making my hands shake.

Jackson's eyes looked distant. "I hadn't seen her since I was sixteen and she dropped by unannounced. She told me about you. She wanted me to know I had a little sister."

"There's something I always wondered." I debated if I'd regret bringing this up. Jackson motioned for me to continue. "Why'd she keep me? She left you with your dad and grandparents. She could have left me with a neighbor until my dad came home and gone her merry way, unencumbered by a toddler."

Jackson looked away from me, toward the lantern hanging off the porch. "Why does our mother do anything?"

I looked at him, trying to read his face to see why he'd answered my question with another one.

Jackson caught me looking at him. "I have an idea why she kept you, but I'm not sure you want to hear it." He picked up his now-empty water glass and looked into it.

"Tell me. The truth is always better." I sat up straight, ready to take a blow, but I was telling the truth, and from the way Jackson looked at me, he believed me.

"I've tracked several of our mother's heists and probable crimes. She"—Jackson's voice trailed off for a moment, and he took a breath like he was steeling himself to finish—"used you in some of the early ones. I've only seen pictures, but you were an adorable child. I'm speculating, but I'd guess a pretty woman with a small child seems like someone you'd want to help. Having a child breaks down defenses and probably made her more believable. She could play on her mark's desire to protect not just her, but an innocent kid."

"She made me call a guy Daddy. I was five? I always guessed she stole something from him." He'd bought me books and offered me cookies during afternoon tea. Once in a park we'd played with a soccer ball, and he'd smiled and felt like a happier person.

"Jewelry," Jackson said. "I bet he was the diamond merchant in London. She ditched him after their engagement party, meaning, he gave her an expensive gift and she was gone a few mornings later with a big shipment of diamonds."

"He gave me a necklace too, a heart with a green stone dangling inside. But I didn't have it for long. Our mother took it." I'd loved the necklace and remembered bawling when she'd taken it away. But she promised me something better and ordered me to forget about the man who'd given it to me. I'd gone on an airplane with one of her friends, a man whose name I couldn't remember but I was also told to call Daddy while we were together, and we'd met up with my mom a month later. The guy had taken me to the beach daily. Fellow customers of the resort had raved about how charming my "father" was.

"She went to ground for a while after that, before stealing artwork in Australia."

"Melbourne," I said.

"That's right. Miami was next."

I shook my head as memory flashes filtered through my mind. "We went to someplace else for a while before that. Buenos Aires?"

"I don't know about that. She barely escaped a grift in Chicago after Miami. She nearly walked away with a cool half million, but the guy wised up, and the FBI barely missed both of you. I saw one of the photos. You were about ten."

"Chicago. I remember going to a Cubs game with a guy. He paid for me to have the Cubs logo painted on my cheek, and we'd sat with baseball gloves even though we were in a box seat, far away from any potential foul balls or home runs."

"What did you think at the time? Did you have any idea what was going on?"

"I thought we were playing a game. It's all I knew—traveling around. Our mother made me learn my new name and backstory every time we moved."

"It's a miracle you ever learned to read."

A few forgotten memories showed up in the foreground of my mind. "Homeschool, and a handful of private schools for a few months at a time. She had me do all sorts of memory games too. She called them skills I needed to survive. One of her friends was a former college professor, I think, and he taught me if we were together. Especially math. He turned algebra into puzzles." I'd been ahead in both math and English when I'd started regular middle school, although I'd felt like I'd come from a different planet.

Jackson stared at me. "What friend?"

I closed my eyes, trying to remember. "A man. Around her age? Dark brown hair, but he bleached it a few times. Hazel eyes. He joked he could play any role and said he should have been an actor even though he was good with computers. She left me with him a few times. Looking back, she trusted him more than anyone else."

Jackson let out a deep breath. "Keep your eyes open. If you see him or anyone you recognize from that time, call me. And get out of the situation."

"Trust me; I don't want to get involved."

I yawned, and Jackson half smiled. "I'm heading in to sleep myself in a few minutes. Thanks for dinner, and I'll see what I can dig up about David Stevens's business tomorrow."

"Night." Jackson went upstairs, and I knew I should shut off my phone and do the same. But I decided to search Ground Rules online, curious if any reviews had trickled in, and found my photo on the *All Wired Up in Little Bay Root* blog, along with a review of the macchiato and pour-over I'd made.

I sent the link to Harley.

She texted back immediately in all caps, *OMG, YOU SERIOUSLY FLIRTED WITH MY EX?*

What? I replied.

He never likes anything, but he raved about you. Did you slip him Valium or something? What drug makes people happy?

I texted back a row of *????* Followed by *people skillz.*

Partnering with you is the best idea I've ever had, she replied.

My whole soul sighed and hoped she still felt that way once the police finished the murder investigation.

Chapter 11

Jackson stopped by the coffee cart on his way to work the next morning, blatantly checking up on me.

"You'll never turn a profit if you give away free coffee," he said, and shoved $4 for his cappuccino along the counter at me. "See you tonight." I got my own petty revenge and added a cappuccino to the suspended-coffee board, funded by Jackson's contribution.

The rush of customers passing through should've made me feel cheerful. I played a happy part, ignoring the nerves that bubbled up and told me to view everyone who approached as a potential threat. Harley's morning help was useful as always during the rush, and we made arrangements for me to visit the warehouse once I closed the cart.

During a lull, I started a pour-over for myself, trying to ground myself in the pattern of making the drink. After it brewed, I took it to the table outside. As I took a sip, I told myself to be in the moment. Focus on what I needed to do now, who I was. Sage Caplin. Age twenty-seven. Coffee shop owner, unflappable. I suddenly remembered this was the way my mother had coached me as a kid before she introduced me to a person she was, I now knew in retrospect, scamming. I put the coffee down, feeling sick.

A woman I didn't recognize entered the Rail Yard. Her hands

were clasped together and her posture was slumped. She stood for a moment, looking around. She headed to Ground Rules.

"Can I help you?" I asked gently from my seat on top of the picnic table. I kept my voice soft, instinctively knowing she'd spook if I was too loud.

"Do you know . . ." Her voice trailed off. I scoped her out again. Around fifty. Understated luxury purse. Her dark jeans and an elbow-length cardigan over a modest tank continued the elegant but low-key vibe. Nordstrom shopper, I guessed. Or similar upscale department store.

I stood up, but I didn't say anything.

She paused for a second before saying, "This will sound morbid, but my brother died here. I want to visit the spot."

"You're David Stevens's sister." She didn't look like her brother, and I was willing to bet her medium brown hair with natural-looking highlights came from a chichi salon. But she felt like a person feeling a life's worth of pain.

She looked me in the eyes. "Yes."

"I'm Sage." I offered her my hand, and she shook it. Her hand felt brittle, like it'd be easy to crush into a fine powder. Her nails were painted the same dusty pink as her lipstick.

"Mary."

I motioned to a spot on the ground on the opposite side of the cart. "There. I'm sorry for your loss."

Tears leaked from Mary's eyes, but she looked stoic as she looked at the spot. It wasn't much. No one would guess someone would die in that few square feet of pavement. Grief hit me again, even if I hadn't known David or liked him. His sister cared, and that counted for something.

"Can I get you a cup of coffee?"

"You know, I'd like that," Mary said, sounding surprised, so I went to the cart and poured her a cup of house coffee and brought out the sugar and the half-and-half pitcher to the picnic table.

"You found David." She looked at me for a moment before adding a splash of half-and-half to her coffee and replacing the lid.

"Yes."

"That must have been awful. Thank you for the coffee," Mary said, but she hadn't taken a sip yet. "The past six months have been the worst of my life."

"I'm sorry."

"First, my daughter ran away, now my brother died."

"Your daughter?"

Mary looked up at me and her gaze sharpened. She reached into her purse and pulled out a five-by-seven envelope. She slid a couple of photos out and handed them to me. "Have you seen her around? She goes by Gabby. The police say they found her fingerprints here."

My breath caught as I looked at the same school photo the police had shown me, along with a snapshot of Gabby dressed in a muddy soccer uniform, holding a water bottle, grinning at the camera. She looked happy, not like the girl I'd seen skulking around the Rail Yard.

"What happened to Gabby?" I asked. Kids end up on the street for all sorts of reasons, but going from a soccer-playing, affluent teen to runaway in less than a year was extreme. But all sorts of bad things happen behind closed doors, no matter the zip code.

"It's stupid. We never told Gabby she was adopted. My husband and I couldn't have children, and when my brother's girlfriend became pregnant, we agreed to take the baby. My brother didn't want Gabby to know he was her biological father."

"Your brother? You mean . . ."

"David." Mary nodded. She squeezed her eyes shut. "But my husband and I went through a bad patch last year and filed for divorce. Gabby found out she was adopted. She was furious and ran off." Mary shook her head. "Gabby must have contacted David. A normal guy would've kept Gabby until I could pick her up. But David's relationship with Gabby's mom ended badly, and he was never willing to look past it and forgive his daughter for existing. I'm sure he was cruel to Gabby when she showed up on his doorstep."

"Poor girl." Gabby must have felt unmoored. Angry because the people she called Mom and Dad had lied to her. Had she ridden that anger until she found herself out on the street, until she was lost to everyone, even herself? She hadn't called home. If Mary was telling the truth—and she felt mostly honest, although she could be showing herself in a better light than she deserved—Gabby would've been welcomed if she came home. More than welcome, given the waves of pain flowing off Mary when she talked about Gabby.

"The police found Gabby's fingerprints here. . . ." Mary's voice trailed off. She stared at the cup of coffee in her hands.

"Where did they find them?" Mary had been so forthcoming, maybe she'd tell me. Was this the reason the police brought Gabby's photo to my interview?

"On a can of spray paint."

I paused, remembering the spray-paint canister next to David's body. The cap was red.

Red like the partially written graffiti in the street by David Stevens's new development the morning I found his body. Could Gabby have killed her father? The thought made me feel nauseous.

"Do you know anything about what happened here?"

"Only that the situation is sad," I lied.

She looked like she didn't believe me. She sipped her coffee. "This is excellent, by the way."

"Your brother stopped by a few times."

"Coffee snobbery runs in my family. I'm sure David loved your cart. Before coffee went upscale, my father would have beans flown in from South America, and he'd roast it himself. It was one of his favorite hobbies." Mary looked lost in her thoughts, and I left her there for a moment.

Did she wonder if her daughter murdered her biological father? Had the thought even crossed her mind? Or were the signs of stress appropriate to everything she'd gone through without that question, which would make anyone feel frazzled to the tenth degree?

"I can't believe I told you all of the troubles in my life." Mary straightened up and laughed sarcastically. "Want to hear about how my husband and I never signed our divorce decree? We stayed together. If we'd made the decision earlier, Gabby never would've found out she was adopted. She wouldn't have run away."

"Or she would have found out some other way. Secrets never stay hidden."

"Maybe." Mary still looked like she wanted to rewrite the past year.

"If I see Gabby, I'll try to get her to talk to you." Mary loved her daughter, and maybe I could make Gabby see that.

"Thanks." Mary looked stiffer, as if her spine were turning to steel. As if she was getting uncomfortable around me. But she looked over my shoulder, and her eyes narrowed.

I turned and saw Emma pushing a load of boxes and bags into the lot on a rolling cart. Emma blushed when she saw Mary and rushed past us.

When I turned back around, Mary was staring at a man entering the Rail Yard.

"Aunt Mary," he said, and I recognized Arthur from the Stevens Homes Inc. site. He was shorter than his father and looked softer. Less stern. Like he was made from a malleable rock while his father had been one hundred percent granite.

Mary stood, and they hugged.

"Why did you want to meet here? It's morbid," Arthur said.

"Gabby was here." The undercurrent of desperation in Mary's voice tugged at my heart. There had to be a way for me to help.

I stood, telling myself I should go back to my cart. But I stayed and eavesdropped.

"Did you hire an investigator as I suggested?" Arthur asked.

"Yes, but he didn't find her." Unshed tears were gathering in Mary's already-red-from-crying eyes. She was ready to crumble.

I retreated to the cart, saddened by her story. When I'd briefly ended up on the streets, it would have been easy to have slid through the cracks and disappeared. Become one of the faceless, forgotten street kids. But I'd been lucky and made two friends, fourteen-year-old Manny and his mother, who'd looked out for me. I'd only been homeless for three days, and most of that time had been with them. They couldn't go into shelters since they would've been separated, since teen boys have to go with the men. So the three of us slept in their car. Each night had been like a week as the hours ticked by. The feeling that had permeated my mind, giving thirteen-year-old me a sense of fear that had lingered for months, had invaded the foundation of my life. It'd always be a part of me.

Arthur came up a few minutes later and ordered an oat-milk mocha. "My aunt said your coffee's excellent."

I started to steam the oat milk. "It must be a hard time for you, with your father's death and your little sister missing—"

"She's not my sister," Arthur interrupted.

"Biological half sister and adopted cousin, then," I said, a tart note coming out in my voice. I turned to focus on the drink, crafting an image in the microfoam and dusting it with sweetened cocoa before handing it over. Maybe the heart in the foam would remind him to feel compassion for the girl who was his sister, whether or not he wanted to claim her.

Arthur took his drink and stalked off.

Poor Gabby. Maybe she had good reason to disappear.

Chapter 12

Macie and Zarek walked up as I was locking up my cart after closing. The lunch rush had long faded, and multiple carts had up signs saying they'd reopen at five.

"The old sandwich cart organized the music here at the Rail Yard," Zarek said. "We're starting that up again. I'm going to take the lead on the music schedule unless one of the other carts has an objection."

"Fine by me," I said. That explained why the Rail Yard's calendar of events had ended two weeks ago.

Macie said, "I want to bring in the cat rapper. Have you seen him? He's delightful."

"Don't cats eat pigeons?" I asked.

Zarek covered his mouth, trying not to laugh.

Macie frowned. "Good point. I'll make sure he doesn't bring his actual cats with him when he performs."

"So are you down if we start scheduling music?" Zarek asked me.

"For sure."

"I'll put out a call for bands on Wednesdays and one weekend night, as we did before," Zarek said. "The construction should be quiet at those times. We had several regular local bands, so I might be able to get one scheduled for next week."

I glanced across the street, where the houses were still being dismantled. Macie shook her head as she looked at the construction site with her lips pressed into a tight line. She turned and walked back to her cart.

"Any chance you want to help me with this?" Zarek asked. "I'm taking the lead because someone needs to do it, but the thought's already stressing me out."

"Is music that big of a deal?"

"It completely transforms the Rail Yard. We draw bigger crowds, and the fans of the bands buy food. It keeps us in everyone's minds, especially when we make the lists of happenings around town in the local papers. So, yes, it's a big deal. Sales have gone down since we stopped hosting music."

Did I have the bandwidth to take over the music project? And if I did, should I make sure Ground Rules was open when the bands played? If David's death tied back to my mother, even though it wasn't my fault, I should say yes. Since the death must have had a more significant impact on sales than no music. I took a deep breath.

"Tell you what, let's schedule the first band or two and see how it goes. I might be terrible at it."

Zarek laughed. "I bet you'll be amazing. You doing anything fun?"

I looked up from unlocking my bike. "Meeting up with Harley. We might have an appointment to do a cupping of our beans for a hotel downtown." Or maybe that was next week.

"Sounds like you two have a pretty serious business plan."

"The cart is our first step in world domination." I swung my messenger bag over my shoulder.

"Good for you. I need to figure out a long-term strategy, especially if, or rather when, this lot's redeveloped."

"You think that's going to happen?" I asked, wondering about my uncle's plans for the lot. He'd refused one sale, but it was to David Stevens. Maybe he'd sell to someone else or develop it himself. The Button Building wasn't his only active construction project.

"It's too prime of a location to remain a food cart lot, and let's be honest: it's underutilized now. I heard the Rail Yard owner has a few micro-restaurant developments in the works. I should schedule a time to meet with him and get him to lease space to me. Food carts are on the way out. There will always be some around town, but the heyday has passed."

His words struck me. Either he didn't know I was related to Uncle Jimmy, or Zarek was making a sideways approach.

Zarek looked like overstewed coffee that's sat around too long. His eyes stared at the construction. "I don't want to be like Foster, who is struggling now that he lost his lease across the street."

"Has he moved someplace else?"

"No. Foster's job hunting and put his cart up for sale. I can offer him a few hours a week at my cart, but not as many as he needs to live. I wish I could bring him on full-time."

"I'm sorry."

"If I can open a café, I can offer him a job."

Part of me felt guilty since if my business failed, I wouldn't be homeless, although I'd feel like I'd lost part of myself. While Zarek and his friend had most likely built their carts from scratch. "My fingers are crossed for you and Foster," I said.

"Good luck with your cupping. Knock their socks off."

"Thanks. One question."

Zarek turned back to face me.

"There's a blond guy with dreads who shows up, but I've never seen him buy anything."

"That's Foster. If you need any help at your cart, he's reliable."

"He always looks grumpy."

"Like I said, he's stressed."

We said our goodbyes, and Zarek looked solemn as I rode away. I wondered if he was trying to convince me to put in a good word with Uncle Jimmy without directly asking. Or was he talking to a sympathetic ear because he was worried?

My phone rang after I'd biked a few blocks. I pulled over, realizing it wasn't Harley. It was a local number.

"Hello?" I asked, wondering if the caller could hear the tentative note in my voice. My last unknown caller hadn't been a happy conversation.

"I heard you were looking for me," a girl's voice said.

"Gabby?"

"What if it is?"

I almost snorted. Because if it was Gabby, I had a lot of questions. Like, did you kill your father? But I didn't want to scare her off. I forced myself to smile so it would come through in my voice and kept my tone gentle.

"If this is Gabby, I want to make sure you're okay. And I'd want to tell you your mother stopped by my cart. She's looking for you."

"My mom . . ." Gabby sounded younger than she had when she first called, as if my words had shattered up the glass shell she'd been hiding behind.

"If you stop by the cart, I can help you."

"You're trying to trick me. You want to set me up."

"We can meet elsewhere—"

"Whatever." Gabby disconnected, and I stared at my phone. She had tried to sound tough, but underneath, she was terrified. Of her mother? Of me? I took a deep breath and put my phone away. For now, I needed to focus on Ground Rules. I'd worry about Gabby later.

The charming guy from the Grumpy Sasquatch studio, Bax, was outside his office, taking a breather. So I stopped and said hi. He grinned when he saw me and subtly moved into my path. Not so far in the way to be annoying or threatening, or to stop me from walking by, but enough to catch my attention.

"Long story why, but we ended up with a metric ton of chocolate. Want to trade coffee beans for a few boxes of truffles?" Bax asked.

I tilted my head when I looked at him. "What type of coffee do you like?"

"Anything in a dark roast, although most of my employees simply want caffeine."

I nodded. "Sure, I'll bring some by in a few minutes."

"Awesome. I'll put several boxes aside with your name on it."

I was still smiling as I walked into the building to reach the Ground Rules front door. The front office was tiny and decorated with a desk holding up a pyramid of fake bags of coffee. I passed through into the warehouse.

"You're finally here." Harley was practically hyperventilating.

"Wow, chill. I said I'd be here by three and it's only two fifty." I held my hands in a calming gesture. "Do we need to leave for the coffee cupping with the hotel?"

"No, that's next week." Harley sat down, but she tapped her foot and couldn't decide what to do with her hands. She popped back up and started pacing.

"How much coffee have you downed today?"

"That's not it. There's this guy, Tanner. We used to play soccer together. We always talked a lot about coffee, and I gave him some tips for a coffee gravy he was playing around with."

Coffee gravy sounded delicious, but that didn't explain why Harley was vibrating while digging her fingernails into the palms of her hands. I motioned for Harley to continue her story.

"Tanner heard about our new business, and he's getting ready to open his own restaurant."

"Is he interested in carrying our beans?"

"More than that. Tanner's café will be open from breakfast through dinner, and he wants us to come up with a specialty coffee-drink menu, both cocktails and nonalcoholic. Plus he wants us to train his staff on how to make coffee properly. He'll buy our beans, of course."

"At least we'll know they'll do justice to our coffee if we train them." Ideas started firing through my brain. We needed to find out what kind of food Tanner was planning to offer so we could pair our drinks with his menu.

Harley started pacing again. "We need to come up with something amazing. Revolutionary. No basic espresso martinis or drinks other bars offer."

"Plus a few classics so we don't alienate reluctant eaters. But with a twist. Plus a few creative options."

"They're going to install an espresso machine, so we should consider basing any cocktails around that, so it'll always be fresh. We should recommend an immersion dripper or clever coffee maker for their evening service for the same reason."

"Good idea. That's a good way to make sure the coffee's fresh. They could offer a light, medium, or dark roast, prepared to order." My words briefly kept pace with my brain as I thought out loud. I could see where Harley was going with this. An immersion dripper would be less labor-intensive than pour-overs and easier to clean quickly. "Maybe a few cold brew cocktails too."

"We need a plan and coffee cocktails recipes. But I've never worked in a bar." Harley continued to pace.

I shut my eyes to think. "We'll need to see sample menus from his restaurant. I already have a few ideas." I opened my eyes and glanced around the warehouse. We could brew a bazillion different types of coffee, but we didn't have any alcohol. "If I give you a list of liquors and mixers, will you pick them up? They're too heavy to bring here by bike, else I'd do it."

"Sure."

I pulled a pad of paper out of my desk and made a list. Bourbon, gin, applejacks, Chambord, Grand Marnier. I thought for a moment before adding Irish whiskey, Frangelico, and Bénédictine.

Harley looked over my shoulder. "What are you thinking?"

"Cold brew, or iced espresso, pairs well with Bénédictine and cream for an easy after-dinner drink. But I have some ideas for unique cocktails."

I started writing down drink ideas on a separate sheet of paper while Harley read over my shoulder.

"We can't taste-test all of these by ourselves," Harley said.

"Not without dying of alcohol poisoning." I handed her the shopping list. "We should invite friends over to help. I have ideas of good taste testers." Like my cousin Miles.

Harley picked up her purse. "This qualifies as a business expense, right?"

"As long as you document it properly. Enter it into the expenses spreadsheet the accountant set up." I walked over to the coffee Harley had roasted last week and weighed out a two-pound bag of our Twelve Bridge Racer espresso roast and a one-pound bag of our Puddle Jumper. I smelled them, picturing how they'd taste in mixed drinks.

"What're you doing?"

"The sasquatches next door offered me chocolate in exchange for coffee, so I'm playing nice with the neighbors." Plus the siren song of truffles sounded perfect, especially with this new stress.

"Didn't you think you should check in with me first? What if I'm not okay with you giving out product?" She sounded frustrated.

"I'm going to share the chocolate, and you're forgetting something." I made my voice calm, hoping the notes would chill out the tension vibrating through Harley. Since telling her Tanner's new project wasn't as big of a deal as she was making it out to be wouldn't help.

"You'll have to be more specific."

"The studio next door has a coffee station. If we play our cards right, they'll serve our beans full-time. Or they'll keep passing along free chocolates and gifts."

"What if I want chocolate too?"

"I already said I intend to share, and I'm sure they would've of- fered the same to you, except Bax saw me first. You know, we should invite them over for the cocktail tasting. I have no idea if they have good palates, but they're in the 'goes out to brunch' demographic Tanner must want to reach."

"I can't believe you're worried about the guys next door when we have so much to do." Harley ran her hands through her hair again, flipping one of the purple streaks to the front.

I held out my hands in a calming gesture. "We've got this. Luckily I've worked in a bar, and between the two of us we'll come up with drinks that'll knock your friend's socks off."

"We better."

We decided to host a small cocktail-sampling party in two days and invite both our business neighbors and friends over. I texted Miles and begged him to come since he'd been pouring shots as long as I remembered.

"I've never done a proposal like this," Harley said, still carrying her keys, which she jangled.

I guided her to the door. "Neither have I. I'm doing what feels right. It'll be fine."

Harley finally left to run to the liquor store. I stood for a moment, taking a series of deep breaths and letting them out, feeling my fingers relax, followed by the muscles of my arms, leading to my back. Once I felt normal, I snagged the bags of coffee and headed next door.

Bax and one of his coworkers were sitting on the couch in the front of the office, studying something on a tablet. I held up the bags of coffee.

Bax jumped up when he saw me. "Fantastic." He took the bags from me.

"I have a small favor to ask."

He looked wary, and I smiled to disarm him. His face relaxed.

"We're working on coffee cocktails recipes for a potential client, and we need guinea pigs. So if you and your coworkers are up for it, we'd love to invite you to the taste-testing party we're hosting."

"Inviting us over to drink isn't a favor." Bax laughed. "I'll share your invite with my staff. Some of us should be able to make it."

"Awesome." I handed him a note with the party details, and he gave me several boxes of chocolates from a local specialty shop, bound together by string. The sticky note on top said *Coffee Angel*.

I laughed.

Chapter 13

Two days later, after locking up the cart, I hustled to the warehouse. Harley was parking her Subaru as I biked up, so I helped her carry in bags of groceries and party supplies. We had three hours before our cocktail-sampling party started.

Harley washed our new glassware, and I assembled platters of appetizers and stored them in our fridge. We were focusing on cheese and charcuterie, plus salads I'd assembled in four-ounce mason jars, as well as vegetable platters. After making a few wraps and cutting them into rounds, we had enough food to accompany the drinks, and if needed, we'd order pizza. My stomach growled at the thought, so I made another wrap and practically inhaled it. The turkey settled my stomach.

I strained the cold brew I'd made last night and tasted it. It was strong, which wasn't a surprise as it had brewed for about twenty hours. If I'd wanted a lighter taste, I would've asked Harley to strain it this morning when it hit the twelve-hour mark. Or I could've used a light roast.

By 6:00 p.m., we'd set up a couple of tables to serve as a bar, complete with the new glassware, and I was ready to take my place behind it as bartender. A purple cloth covered the table laden with the platters of foods. Harley set up borrowed chairs around a couple of round tables, although we'd arranged the layout to encourage our attendees to mingle. With each drink, I'd hand out a short survey on an index card.

The sasquatches from next door showed up first. They started out with a gin-espresso-Chambord cocktail and took their cards and made notes about the scent and taste of the drinks. Each received a mini-version, so they wouldn't be tanked by their second cocktail.

"Told you they'd be helpful," I murmured to Harley, who stood next to the bar, ready to wash dishes and help out.

"A tad more Chambord would make it awesome," Bax said. He dropped a filled-out index card into our comment basket. He put his dirty glass in a bus bin and grabbed a can of sparkling water. He stood next to the makeshift bar and we chatted.

"The studio has been here four years. I started the business with my friend, and we've grown enough that we've considered moving to a bigger space, but we're getting ready to launch a new game and . . ."

A while later, the door to the warehouse was open again. Zarek walked in. He beelined in my direction.

"You designed the branding for Grizzly Brewing? I love their logo," I said to Bax.

"Yep. I have a small side hustle doing design work for breweries. It's a break from video games."

Zarek walked up. I'd invited all of the food cart owners from the Rail Yard, and he'd been the most excited.

"Hi!" Harley stepped forward and cut Zarek off. Her voice had gone extra-smoky.

"Hey, Harley-Girl."

"Here's our cocktail list. Tell me what you want, and Sage will make it for you." Harley motioned to the chalkboard we'd set up. She rested her hand on Zarek's arm. "Let me know if you have any questions."

"What do you recommend, Sage?" he asked.

Harley's face fell for a half second, then she blurted out, "I recommend the Bénédictine cocktail."

I glanced at Harley and back to Zarek. "Bénédictine has honey, so it's not vegan."

"Some vegans eat honey," Harley interrupted.

"But not all. It's controversial," I said.

Harley scowled and her eyes narrowed a fraction.

"But the drink with Frangelico is vegan. Does that sound good?" I looked at Zarek.

Zarek nodded. "I love Frangelico."

As I started making Zarek's drink, Harley talked to him, and he'd turned to face her. Bax grinned at me. "Make one of those for me?"

"Of course!" I mixed an ounce of Frangelico with an ounce of vodka along with three-fourths of an ounce of cold espresso and mixed it before pouring it into four waiting rocks glasses.

"Is your cart closed?" Harley's voice carried over the growing din of conversation.

"Foster agreed to cover my cart tonight. He works for me off and on. . . ."

"So what exactly do you do, other than 'design'?" I asked Bax. He'd started telling me the video games they'd launched and the new one in development when a new voice interrupted us.

"Aw, it's nice to have Bug make me drinks instead of the reverse."

Miles. I couldn't help myself and answered sweetly, "Aw, you can go bite yourself."

"I'm wounded. Is this any way to treat customers? Worst bar ever."

I laughed. "Bax, this is my cousin Miles. Miles, Bax is the owner of Sasquatch studio next door."

"Hopefully Bug is an okay neighbor," Miles said.

"We love having them next door. When I officially met Sage, we'd pulled an all-nighter, and she showed up carrying a full carafe of coffee like an angel from coffee heaven."

"I've never seen Bug as an angel." Miles winked at me.

I handed them each a Frangelico cocktail, and as they walked away, Miles asked Bax if he designed sasquatches all day. Zarek eagerly took the third cocktail. One of the sasquatch staff claimed the fourth, and I made another round as more people arrived. I made a pitcher of cold brew with balsamic vinegar and apricot juice for a handful of people who weren't drinking and poured a rocks glass's worth for me.

My friend Erin wandered around with her camera, taking photos of me bartending and of our guests drinking.

"Are you a professional photographer?" one of the sasquatches asked Erin.

She blushed and stammered, "I have to take care of something," and scurried away.

He looked at me. "Did I say something wrong?"

"She's shy. She's only fearless behind the camera." I made the sasquatch another drink. The owners of the Hangry Hippo sandwich cart, Adam and Carolyn, walked into the warehouse and looked around. Adam lit up when he saw me. Carolyn followed him over.

"Thank you for inviting us," Adam said.

"I'm happy you came! Can I make you a drink?"

As I measured out shots of Frangelico, vodka, and cold espresso for another round of coffee-truffle cocktails, Carolyn asked, "How's business going for you at the Rail Yard? The murder made our business fall way off, especially during dinner."

I paused with the cocktail shaker in my hands. "I'm sorry to hear that."

"How's your business been?" Adam asked.

"It's growing, but we started from zero. Zarek and I are planning to bring music back two nights a week. Do you think that would help?"

"Perhaps," Carolyn said, and took a sip of the cocktail I'd handed her. They wandered off.

If David's murder kept customers from visiting the Rail Yard, it would affect all of us. Especially the innocent.

One of the sasquatches who had been hovering over to the side asked, "Your cart is at the Rail Yard, right?" He looked young, about twenty-three, with black hair pulled back in braids. He held one of the alcohol-free cold brew mocktails, although he'd had one of the Chambord drinks to start.

"That's right." I eyed him. Was he about to pump me for information? Call me a murderer?

"My sister's been obsessing over David Stevens's death."

"That's . . . interesting."

"She works for the Regional Housing Alliance and argued with him the day before he died, so she feels guilty."

"Why did the RHA and David Stevens argue?" I hoped the sasquatch wouldn't ask for inside info about David's death.

"Stevens's company refused to offer any apartments to low-income residents. They only do market rate, and he wanted to keep his buildings exclusive. I think my sister quoted him as saying he only wanted 'top-notch' clients. Like renting a unit to someone working hard for thirty thousand a year would ruin the ambience of his building." The sasquatch snorted. "It's not like they tried to turn his buildings into transitional housing."

"Which is also sorely needed."

"For sure. It's hard enough for people with full-time jobs to find a decent place."

A couple of the sasquatches walked up and claimed the final two truffle cocktails, and the guy with braids walked away.

Everything I'd learned about David's life made him feel more and more complicated to me. The article where he proposed a multilevel approach to dealing with homeless had been thoughtful, as if he'd spent time outlining his plan before talking about it. But he'd been cruel to Gabby when she showed up on his doorstep.

And once, he'd looked at my mother with adoration.

Why had someone attacked David? I wish I knew. Not knowing made my hands want to shake. So I searched for Harley and saw she was still talking with Zarek. I hid a smile as I grabbed the bus bin full of glassware. I loaded the glassware in the dishwasher and set it to run. Thankfully we still had plenty of clean glasses. I should find something to do and try not to obsess over the fate of the Rail Yard and other things I couldn't control.

"I could use a couple of these recipes at the Tav," Miles said when he came over for another round. "Good job."

"If Tanner passes on the recipes, you can have them." Exhaustion flowed through me, and I was on the verge of laughing at everything, no matter how ridiculous.

"You're welcome to pick up shifts at the Tav if you want. You inherited the bartending gene."

"Yeah, I learned when I barbacked for you." I handed over a drink to Miles.

"Good point. I taught you everything you know."

I rolled my eyes.

"What's this?" Zarek asked. Harley must have relinquished him. Then I saw the swish of her ponytail as she entered the bathroom.

"Just talking about how Bug owes her success in life to me, and my teachings," Miles said.

Zarek glanced from Miles to me.

"We're cousins," I said.

Zarek's face relaxed. "Why do you call her Bug?"

I closed my eyes.

"Because she's as cute as one."

Zarek laughed, and Miles left and headed in Bax's direction.

"Do you have plans for Sunday?" Zarek asked me. "'Cause I have an extra ticket to the Timbers game if you want to go."

Thank heavens he was inviting me to a game and not some big romantic evening. "I'm a fan of the team."

"I noticed your Timbers shirt a while back," Zarek said.

I laughed and forced myself to take a deep breath. "And I noticed your Timbers Army shirt."

"So what do you say?"

I closed my eyes, picturing my calendar. I opened them and looked into Zarek's hopeful brown eyes. "I should be free. Can I text you tonight to confirm once I have a chance to catch my breath?"

"Perfect."

Harley walked up as I was handing over Zarek's next drink sample. She moved possessively close to him.

"It's vegan, right?" she asked me.

"Of course."

I spun back to Zarek. "We need to talk about the logistics of holding music at the Rail Yard. Let's get something scheduled sooner than later."

"I'll send you a link to the online doc I started. I have a band for this coming weekend."

"You moved fast."

"They've been playing monthly at the Rail Yard for years and assumed they were still playing. I'm glad I emailed, since they would've shown up anyway."

He smiled my way as he and Harley moved over to a table on the side of the warehouse.

The angel on my shoulder told me to turn down Zarek on Harley's behalf. But going to the game sounded fun, and from Zarek's posture, he wasn't interested in Harley, let alone planning to ask her out. But preserving peace with my business partner mattered more in the long run than a Timbers game, so I'd talk to her later.

The party slowed down after 8:00 p.m. We were all getting old. When I was younger, things didn't even get started until after nine at the earliest. But I heard murmurs about spouses, girlfriends and boyfriends, kids, testing the user interface of the video game again, and sleep. The usual.

Bax walked up. "Looks like your party was a success. The drinks were excellent."

"Glad you liked them."

"What do you have on tap for next week?" Bax asked.

My heart started beating faster. "Other than coffee domination?"

"Like Wednesday night. Do you have an opening in your dance card to meet up for a beer, or will you be focused on grinding the rest of the coffee roasters into bitter pulp?"

My heart smiled, but I kept my face serious. "I suppose I can take one evening off."

"My buddy opened a new taproom, and I designed his logo and signage. Now that it's up and running, I want to float by and scope it out. I'll buy you a beer if you keep me company."

"What time are you thinking?"

"How about seven? Give me your number and I'll text you the details. I can pick you up too, if you'd like."

"Text me." I handed my business card over.

Bax tucked it into the chest pocket of his shirt and tapped it. "Talk soon." He walked away with two of his coworkers, and I wanted to dance a jig.

After the last of our partygoers left, I put the filled-out surveys in a safe spot in the top drawer of my desk before tackling the party cleanup.

"Want a drink?" I asked Harley as I wiped off the bottles and got ready to store them in a kitchen cupboard.

"Yes, please, but nothing with coffee."

"Maybe I should keep downing shots and work straight through my shift tomorrow before collapsing into a jittery, overtired mess." There's no way I'd be able to fall asleep tonight after all of the coffee I'd drunk during the party.

After mixing a couple of nightcaps, I stashed the alcohol away while Harley finished packing away the clean glassware while the final load ran in the dishwasher. Since we didn't need the glasses most of the time, we'd box them and store them until our next function, where we'd wash them all over again before using them. But we'd left a selection of specialty glassware in our kitchen just in case. You never know when you'll need an emergency cocktail.

As I handed Harley a Chambord gin fizz, I said, "I have something to tell you."

"Zarek asked you out, huh?" She took a sip of her drink. "Not bad. I've never had raspberry with gin before, but it works."

"Yes, Zarek did, but I didn't commit. I wanted to talk to you first."

Harley looked away from me. Her shoulders were hunched. "You should go out with him."

"You sure? You staked your claim ages ago."

Harley's smile only lifted the left side of her mouth. "But we're not simpatico. Zarek asked questions about you all night, so it was clear which direction the wind was blowing. Will you say yes?"

"I'm tempted. Zarek has tickets to a Timbers game this Sunday."

She groaned. "I can't believe I already gave my blessing. I'm jealous. They're playing New York, and they're amazing."

"We'll figure out a time to go to a game together. A friend has two Timbers Army tickets, but she can't make every game. I'm sure she'll offer the tickets to me sometime soon."

Harley clinked her glass against mine. "I'll drink to that."

She pulled chairs over, and we both sat down. My leg muscles felt tense, and I massaged my left calf.

"I thought Bax was scoping you out." Harley's voice turned overly airy. "His eyes followed you around the room."

I laughed.

She groaned. "Two in one night?"

"He invited me to check out a new taproom with him. It's not a big, romantic date. His friend owns it. Bax designed their logo and stuff."

"Please, that's the perfect casual date. You can go out to dinner afterward or call it a night after a pint if it's a dud. It's perfect."

My face felt hot.

"Look at you. Asked out on two dates in one evening."

"It's not like it means anything. My relationships never last long.

One in college lasted six weeks, but he went home for a month 'cause of winter break in the middle of it."

Harley half smiled and looked at her drink. "The right guys will come along eventually. We have each other until they do."

"True dat."

We drank silently for a moment, then finished cleaning the warehouse. We had a future to meet.

Chapter 14

On Saturday afternoon, I jumped out of my friend Erin's van, holding the hem of a slinky wedding dress, and grabbed my bike and bag. My messenger bag didn't match the embroidery on the front of the dress, but I couldn't care. Although my feet screamed at me. Don't worry, I told them, I'd change before biking home. Comfortable shoes were high on my list of priorities.

"The dress!" Erin called from the driver's seat.

"Come by my house tomorrow." My voice sounded grumpy.

Erin nodded, and she looked exhausted. I'd modeled for her before, but today had been a challenge for both of us. I knew she'd ask me to pose for her again, but I knew she'd never, ever, again ask my groom-for-the-day to be in a photo shoot. My fake groom put stereotypical bridezillas to shame, acting overly demanding and snarky all day. Worse, he'd implied multiple times that not only did Erin not know what she was doing, but that she didn't know how to operate her camera. Erin might be quiet, and more likely to roll her eyes than argue with someone, but she's a phenomenal photographer and knows it.

The Rail Yard was bustling, full of groups enjoying the perfect summer evening. Eighty degrees, sunny, golden. Fala-Awesome had a line, so it was good I'd shown up to help with the music.

Even if I looked like a cake topper.

I locked my bike to the back of Ground Rules and rustled in my bag for my keys.

"Are you having your reception here?" a woman asked. "That's so Portland."

"Nah, I'm here to work." I clocked her double take with a smirk.

I closed the door of Ground Rules behind me so I could change into my usual shorts, T-shirt, and sneakers. The cart was stuffy and mostly dark, but being alone was a relief. My updo wasn't my usual cart-style, but after pulling a few fake-pearl bobby pins out of my hair and pulling it back into a ponytail, I was ready. I double-checked my hair using the vanity camera in my phone. Good enough.

The owners of Cartography called me over when I darted outside to open my cart's awning.

"Any chance we can buy a bag of coffee? Preferably whole beans?" the woman who ran the cart, Angela, asked. She eyed my face. I should've scraped off the caked-on makeup.

"For sure. Just give me a minute. Dark or medium?"

"Medium. I have to get up at four a.m. tomorrow. I'll practically need a coffee IV, and we're out of beans." Angela laughed.

"Let me finish my cart's cold brew station. I can bring beans over when I'm done."

"Diego can follow you over." Angela motioned to her husband, who was dropping off food to a table. He wore an Argentina national-team soccer jersey. "Any chance you'd be up for a trade? A cold brew for a couple of alfajores?"

I paused, but Angela started talking before I had a chance to answer. "Alfajores are cookies—"

"Cookie sandwiches with dulce de leche inside?"

"Exactly! You must've had them before. Today's offerings are dulce de leche or strawberry."

I nodded, not wanting to get too into the months I'd spent in

Argentina as a child. But I remembered the food, and part of Cartography's menu had always reminded me of my stay.

"How do you choose which foods you offer?" I glanced at their menu again. They served foods from all over the world. Today's specials were Katong laksa, inspired by Singapore, and tagliata with arugula and garden-fresh tomatoes, based on Italian cuisine.

"My dad was a diplomat, and we moved all over the world, so I try to re-create my favorites from the places I lived. Diego is from Argentina, and he insists we offer empanadas and different desserts. And maté, of course. Diego drinks it by the bucket."

"That's interesting."

"I tried to draw a map of our influences once, which is how I came up with the name Cartography."

"I love it."

Three customers walked up, so I checked on the band, the Glisan Street Duel, who were setting up on the stage. They'd brought their own PA system and said they'd be ready to kick off at seven. A handful of people were starting to settle in at the tables facing the stage, so I hustled back to my cart. I set about opening it with a limited menu of cold brew and cart-made coffee sodas, which I was rolling out for the first time. They were basically sparkling water mixed with housemade vanilla syrup and concentrated cold brew.

More people than I expected stopped by for coffee, living on the edge by drinking caffeine after 6:30 p.m. Although if you're planning to stay out all night, early-evening coffee is a great pick-me-up.

Diego carried a handful of cookies over, along with cash. "You've visited Argentina before?" he asked as I poured a couple of cold brews and handed over a bag of our Puddle Jumper.

"Once, as a kid. I loved Buenos Aires. I was obsessed with the planetarium and the park it's in."

"The Parque Tres de Febrero."

We chatted about Argentina for a while.

"How's business going for you?" I asked.

"It's slow. Hopefully the music brings in customers."

Angela called for Diego, and he hurried away with their coffees and beans. I took a bite of one of the alfajores, enjoying the creaminess of the dulce de leche inside. This would go well with our espresso. In my mind, I could taste it served with a macchiato. We should create a few inter-cart specials, like a cookie-and-espresso combo pairing Cartography and Ground Rules. Or I should stock their cookies in my cart, and also if we eventually opened the shop.

The tables by the Déjà Brew cart were filled with people drinking beer, and Zarek's Fala-Awesome still had a line a few people deep, and the guy with blond dreads, Foster, was helping Zarek. Emma had a teenage girl working with her. The girl ran by with a couple of chicken-and-jojo meals for customers. The Rail Yard was even busier than when I arrived, and I felt like I was glowing as I looked around. This wasn't only a ramshackle lot. It was a community. Being part of it made me feel warm inside. Someone would do a lot to defend such a special place.

The music started, and I sold coffee sodas to two twentysomething girls who wore THE GLISAN STREET DUEL T-shirts. I'd never heard of the band, but they'd brought in a decent group of fans, and the music attracted more people in from the street.

The Rail Yard felt like a different world than it had on Friday morning. Was it the music, or all of the carts being open? Both? Several carts only opened for dinner, and only some of the owners showed up for dinner prep before I left. Maybe Harley and I should find an employee or two and stay open later. The handful of late-night or twenty-four-hour coffee shops I knew in the area did well, but they were an alternative to bars. I doubted we'd attract many customers at 8:00 p.m. on a cold, rainy December day when the sun sets by 5:00 p.m.

A man slunk through the crowd and started rummaging through the recycling next to Cartography. Everything about him said he was homeless, and from the way his hands jerked, he was either high or had a physical impairment.

"Get out of here." Diego held his hands loose at his side, but I could tell he was primed to move quickly.

"Who's going to make me?" the homeless man asked, but his

shoulders were shrunk in, the words thrown out from bravado. He retreated as Diego advanced on him. The homeless man ran, scurrying through the crowd and out the main gate.

"We don't need Diego getting into brawls over recycling again," Emma said, pausing next to me, holding an empty tray against her hip.

"Brawls are a regular problem?" I asked.

"Diego got into a full-on fight when he caught someone stealing from their cart, and he's chased off people going through the recycling before." Emma looked past me. Her eyes widened. "Catch you later." She scurried off.

"Do people try to steal the recycling often?" a deep voice asked. I looked to my left to see Detective Will standing next to my cart.

"Doesn't that happen anywhere with recycling bins? I heard thieves broke into the Rail Yard last winter and stole copper wires from multiple carts. Although I don't know much about that."

"Because you allegedly weren't here."

"I was in Bali, but you don't have to take my word for it. The State Department must have some sort of record. Big Brother is always watching."

"Did you meet up with your mother in Bali and make plans to murder David Stevens?" Detective Will stared at me, his eyes as intense as usual.

"When you were a kid, did you make that face at something, and it froze, and you've never been able to change expressions since?"

"What's that supposed to mean?"

"It means if you have questions, talk to my lawyer."

"If your brother is in on the murder, if you're working together on behalf of your mother, you'll all go down for it."

Inspiration struck. "Did you know that when Renato Bialetti died—you can thank him for the popularity of the Moka pot—his ashes were stored in a Moka pot and buried next to his wife? By his request, not out of some petty revenge by his children."

"What does that story have to do with this situation? Unless you killed him too."

"Bialetti was ninety-three, so I assume he died of old age. I told you to talk to my lawyer, so if you keep asking me questions, I'll throw out random facts."

"Oh?"

Was he hoping to get a rise out of me? Get me so worked up I'd confess my extensive life of (imaginary) crime?

As I let my breath out, I told myself the buzz of annoyance vibrating inside my bones flowed out with it, leaving me centered. Not feeling like a detective-size mosquito was buzzing around me, waiting to strike. "Like if you have four pennies, four dimes, and three quarters in your hand, you'll have a dollar nineteen. Which doesn't sound impressive, except it's the largest amount of coins you can hold without being able to make exact change for a dollar."

When Miles said I'd inherited the bartender gene, he probably meant the ability to distract people with random facts. Although based on the way the detective's eyebrows—rectangular, like the rest of him—had drawn together, I was making him angry. Good. He deserved it since he was hassling me instead of solving a murder.

"Check that out. Your eyebrows moved."

He gave me a final glare before walking in the direction of Cartography. Maybe he thought Diego and David Stevens had gotten into a fight over recycling. If Diego had seen David Stevens skulking around, they might've argued. But it didn't explain how the box cutter from my cart ended up involved.

Foster gave me a Detective Will–like glare as he carried a couple plates of falafel by. Exactly the warmth I needed. The weight of David's death settled on my shoulders, making me feel heavy. The makeup on my face itched. Today was never going to end.

Chapter 15

On Sunday afternoon, I'd arranged to meet Zarek at a café a short walk from the stadium. I left my bike in the storage room of the Tav and strolled to the meeting spot along with a handful of fans also dressed in green jerseys. Although I'd left my official Timbers Army scarf at home, unlike most of the supporters I saw, who didn't let the eighty-five-degree weather stop them from wearing scratchy acrylic around their necks.

The café advertised vegan fare, like açai bowls, along with coffee and fresh smoothies. I could see Zarek opening a similar restaurant, although something told me nothing here matched his falafel or cart-made sauces.

Zarek texted he was running late, so I ordered a smoothie with almond butter and strawberries and grabbed a spot by the window. The smoothie was sweet with a nutty backing.

"I'm sorry I'm late," Zarek said. "Foster is covering my cart, and he was running behind."

"No worries." We had forty minutes to game time.

Zarek went to order a smoothie, and I watched a woman pushing a shopping cart filled with a hodgepodge of boxes and recyclables wander past.

"You'd think the city would figure out a solution." Zarek slid into the seat next to me. His eyes watched the woman with the shopping cart.

"Maybe someday. Hopefully soon."

"Cheers to that. We need better housing options. I'm always afraid I'm going to face a rent increase and end up on the street myself."

As we talked, my eyes strayed to the two teens who'd set up shop next door. The office was closed for the weekend. One teen held a fishing line with a bucket on the end.

"We should walk to the stadium," Zarek said after checking his watch. We threw away our now-empty cups. As we left, I read the sign on the teen's fishing pole: ANGLING FOR CHANGE.

At least he's creative. My heart felt heavy as we walked down the street. A flash of brown hair caught my eye, but my pulse relaxed. It wasn't Gabby, although the girl hustling down the sidewalk was about the same height.

I needed to stop jumping at shadows and enjoy the game.

We joined the mass of bodies streaming out of the stadium after the Timbers and New York drew 2–2.

"I can't fully embrace sports that don't have a winner each game. I know it's a soccer thing, but it drove me crazy when I played when we drew when I wanted to win," Zarek said.

"Draws are beautiful. It adds a layer of complexity to the strategy of the game while adding meaning to each match throughout the season."

"True. But I find it annoying." Zarek laughed. He grabbed my hand as we exited the stadium and weaved through a sheer mass of bodies. I wondered if this is how salmon feel when swimming upstream each year on their way to their deaths.

Once we crossed the street a block from the stadium, the crowd thinned out.

"Do you have plans for the rest of the day?"

"My bicycle is safely stowed in a bar in the Pearl District. I need to pick it up at some point."

"Want to grab a sandwich?"

Smoothies, and now sandwiches from a hole-in-the-wall vegan shop. But the seitan was flavorful, and the store was generous with avocado. Plus the tomatoes were summer fresh, so I couldn't complain.

"Why did you become vegan?" I asked Zarek. He'd gone for a tempeh bowl.

"It was a moral choice for me. I don't like to see other beings suffer."

I had the sense he'd answered this question often. "What will you do if it turns out carrots are sentient?"

"Stop eating carrots." Zarek smiled at me.

"What about honey?" I remembered how it briefly came up at the coffee-cocktail party.

He laughed. "Are you trying to push my buttons? I avoid it, but I'm not adamantly against it. And I debate adding eggs to my diet. They're a cheap source of protein and can be ethically raised."

"You could even raise your own."

"If I had a yard. And the time."

We'd finished eating when Zarek's phone dinged. He closed his eyes after reading the text. "I have to go. As I mentioned, Foster is running my cart. His son might have broken his arm and is going to the ER."

"I hope Foster's son is okay."

We bused our table and walked in the direction of the Pearl District. We stopped by Zarek's car, which turned out to be a small hybrid sedan. Exactly what I would've pegged him as driving.

He stood close beside me. "You want a ride?"

"It's only a few blocks. I'll walk."

"I feel like I should escort you to your bike, or something."

I shook my head. "Go relieve Foster so he can see his son."

"Thanks for understanding." Zarek leaned over and kissed me

briefly on the lips. He smiled softly when he pulled back. "I'll see you tomorrow."

I smiled back, feeling my face blush. "Not if I see you first."

Zarek shook his head with a grin and climbed into his car. I waved as he drove away, and my steps felt light as I walked to the Tav.

Miles was working behind the bar. "You look happy," he said.

"Fun day."

"Can you hang out for a minute?"

"As long as you hook me up with a glass of lemonade."

Miles poured me a pint from a jug in the fridge before disappearing into the back, leaving a female bartender I didn't recognize in charge. Tattoos covered her arms, which were on display under her tank top. She poured a couple of shots and I sipped my lemonade. The mirror behind the bar showed a version of me sitting, looking happier than usual. It didn't feel like a fun-house mirror for once, and I glanced over at the stained-glass windows. The far-left pane showed a crowd of people, and their eyes stare at something outside the window. They were forever transfixed, eternally asking a question that would never be answered. Would anything in my life be momentous enough to inspire someone to make a window?

A man sat down next to me. I caught his reflection in the mirror. Early sixties. Vaguely familiar. Highball glass. Clear contents, so probably a gin and tonic. Or vodka tonic. I didn't want to lean in close enough to sniff and find out.

"Jimmy talks about you all the time," the man said.

"Hmm."

"This business with David Stevens is fascinating. He had it out for your family. Is that why you offed him?"

"Did Uncle Jimmy claim that?" My happiness fizzled away, but I was proud of the calm in my voice, perfectly edged with sarcasm.

"It's the word on the street."

"You guys gossip worse than my friends did when we were in middle school." My eyes moved away from him like he wasn't worth the effort of looking at. But the muscles in my neck and shoulders started tightening. People were gossiping about me. Assuming I was a criminal. Exactly what I'd tried to avoid since understanding the foundation my early childhood had been built on.

Miles returned and tossed the bartender a T-shirt. She looked at him.

"No tank tops, remember? You need to cover your pits when you're at work. House rules."

She rolled her eyes and reluctantly pulled on the T-shirt, which said THE TAV across the front, and I knew the back said IF YOU ASK FOR AN UMBRELLA IN YOUR DRINK, IT BETTER BE RAINING.

No uncovered pits at work. There's a motto for life.

Chapter 16

On Monday morning my thoughts centered around seeing Zarek. Would it be weird? But the cart was slammed all morning. When Harley showed up, she shifted into barista mode without a word, and we worked together to take care of a long line of customers.

"You haven't told me about yesterday," Harley said during a break. She was updating the supply list for the cart, and I read over her shoulder. We had enough milk for the rest of the day, but she'd stop by the grocery wholesaler and bring fresh supplies with her tomorrow morning.

"The Timbers drew with New York," I said.

"Yeah, I watched the game. But that's not what I'm asking, and you know it."

"The date was fun. Zarek's a nice guy."

"Fun? Nice? Blistering recommendation. Guess I dodged a bullet."

I laughed. "I'd consider going out with Zarek again."

"Sounds like the date didn't set your world on fire."

"But there's enough promise for a repeat, but we'll see what happens in the long run."

"What do you think about us making Ground Rules shirts with our logo?" Harley asked. "My sister got into screen printing as a hobby and she's pretty good. She could make us shirts to order."

"What about aprons for the cart? Any chance she can do coffee cups?"

We made plans until Harley left. I made a few drinks for a trickle of customers and noticed Zarek walk through the front gate. He set about refilling his cart's water tanks while I handled a series of customers. It's not like I was watching his every step, I lied to myself. During a break, he ambled over.

"How's Foster's son?" I asked.

Zarek ran his hand through his hair, pushing his bangs back from his eyes. "The poor kid did a number on his arm. He'll be in an elbow cast for the rest of the summer."

"How old is he?"

"Eight. So no more swim lessons for a few months, or soccer."

"Poor kid."

Zarek's phone beeped, and he glanced at it. A timer app flashed on the screen as he said, "I'll drop by later."

"Cheerio."

He hustled back to his cart, and not long after the lunch rush descended in earnest. I was steadily busy, but during a break, a football bounced off the side of my cart. My hands clenched into fists. I looked out to see a couple of kids playing catch in the lot. After a negotiation involving their splitting a cookie, they quit throwing the ball, and nearby customers gave me a round of applause, while the kids' oblivious mother chatted on her phone.

In addition to my cart, the kids had also hit one of the light poles, and something was hanging off it. I borrowed a chair from in front of Emma's cart and climbed it to check out the light.

The hanging white box wasn't part of the light. I looked at it closely, before carefully detaching it. I climbed down.

It looked like a spy camera. I flipped it over in my hands. There wasn't a spot for a memory card, so it had to stream to a nearby device, or the cloud. I shivered. Had someone been watching me? And how had it been attached to the light?

Was the camera filming my cart, or Emma's? And who was looking at the footage?

More important, how long had the camera been here? Could it belong to the police?

I put it in my apron pocket and returned the chair to the table in front of Emma's cart.

My brain waffled over what to do. Call the detective? Track down who had placed this? One of my high school friends was a decent hacker, and I knew she could crack this.

But what if the camera showed David's murder. If it did, and I hacked the footage—or, realistically, had a friend do it—would the video be useless?

I did the next best thing: pulled out my phone and made a call.

My dad was off duty when he biked up to the cart forty minutes later, dressed in spandex like he'd been on a ride. He examined the camera, which I'd wrapped in a baggie and stowed in a paper bag in case it was recording. He looked like he was about to say something, so I held up my hand in a "wait" gesture and rewrapped the camera. I left it on a shelf in the coffee cart. I walked outside, snagging bottles of cold water on my way. I handed one to my dad.

"It might record audio too," I said.

"Pumpkin, if someone is watching the video feed, they'll know you found it." His voice was gentle, but I could hear the skeptical note underneath it, asking if I was losing the plot.

"True." I slumped. I held the bottle of water to my forehead as if the jolt of cold would help.

"You know what you should do."

I looked up and made eye contact with him. He raised his eyebrows at me, and I nodded. Arguing was pointless.

So while he sat next to me, sipping water, I made my next call.

After I hung up, we chatted about the cart, the business, and bicycle maintenance for the twenty minutes it took my next gentleman caller to show up.

Detective Will looked as humorless as ever, but a hint of surprise, possibly annoyance, crossed his face when he saw my dad.

I handed over the camera and again told my story of finding it.

"Is this why you killed David Stevens? Because you caught him putting up surveillance cameras and it made you angry?"

I stared at the detective, positive he was trying to provoke me again. "And waited a few days to tell you about the camera?"

"It's convenient."

"That kids with a football partially knocked it down?"

My father watched both of us impassively. I shot him a "help" look. He grimaced and took a sip of water, but his eyes were wary. I reminded myself he was in my corner.

Detective Will's eyes flicked briefly to my father and back to me. "As I said, convenient."

"Did you look around the Rail Yard for additional cameras?" my father asked me.

"I did a quick walk-through. If there are more cameras, I didn't see them. But this was hidden. A trained observer like, say, a police detective, might have better luck." A thought crossed my mind. Could the cameras belong to Uncle Jimmy? But he would've turned over footage of the murder if they were his. Unless he didn't want the footage to be seen.

"Caplin, go back to cold cases. You shouldn't be involved with this." Detective Will stared at my dad, who looked back impassively.

My hands clenched into fists. The detective treating me like dirt was one thing, but my father deserved respect.

"Sage," my dad said, "call your brother. If Detective Will wants to ask you more questions, you should only do so with a lawyer present."

My dad's words stabbed my heart. He thought I'd killed David Stevens?

"Not that I think you're guilty, Pumpkin. But someone planting a camera here could mean several different things. I'd rather you have Jackson's legal advice protecting you."

My dad must have seen one of the possibilities that had slid through my thoughts, especially if David Stevens's death tied back to my mother. Or Dad was worried the detective believed I was the villain in this situation instead of a pawn caught in the crosshairs of a bigger game.

Detective Will shook his head. "I can't believe you were married to a grifter. Doesn't say much about your detective skills."

"Says the detective wasting time investigating me instead of the real perpetrator," I snapped back.

My father held up his hand in a calming gesture toward me. "Personal attacks aren't going to solve this case." His voice was mild.

"As I said, Caplin, you shouldn't even be here."

"That's fine. Sage can call her attorney, and you can question her later. Do you have your phone handy, Pumpkin?"

I pulled my phone out of my apron pocket and held it up. "I'm sure Jackson will be happy to drive over."

Detective Will looked angry. "No, we're done here." He stalked away.

My father watched him go. "If he asks you to revisit the station or shows up and asks you any questions, call your brother right away. If Jackson's not available, call me. I know a few good defense attorneys."

"I thought they were the enemy?" The bleak note in my voice made the joke fall flat.

My dad mussed my hair like I was a little kid. "We have an adversarial system for a reason. While I'm not enamored with the profession, there are a few defense attorneys I respect."

"For real?" I touched the top of my head. I'd have to redo my ponytail.

My father's smile was grim. "When we solved a case last year—a twenty-year-old murder—the defense attorney tried to get the defendant to explain why he'd killed a young woman. The defendant never opened up. But I believed the attorney tried his best to get answers while never losing sight of his primary job of representing his client."

"That's sad."

"Calling her family and telling them the case was solved was a relief, even if we never learned all of the details behind her death. Knowing we never forgot their daughter meant a lot to them."

Would this be David Stevens's fate? A murder case that would cool off and be relegated to the cold case unit, leaving some of us, like me, under suspicion for the rest of our lives? I shivered.

Emma walked over after my dad biked away. Dark circles were under her eyes, and her ponytail looked messier than usual. The tangles in the long mass made me think she hadn't bothered to brush her hair before pulling it back.

"What's going on?" Emma leaned her elbows against the counter of my coffee cart. Her hands were tense like she was waiting to hear something awful had happened.

"There was a spy camera on one of the light poles." I was scrubbing down the espresso machine, making it gleam. At least this was something I could control.

She paled. "Spy camera? For what?"

My hands stilled as I watched her. Something was going on here, and I knew there was something hinky about her relationship with David Stevens.

"Whose cart was being filmed? Mine?" The pitch of her voice kept rising, making my ears hurt.

"You're acting like someone might have had a reason to record you."

Her whole body went tense like she was suffering from emotional lockjaw.

One of the voices in the back of my mind told me to be kind, but a different one ordered me to go for the jugular. I split the difference and settled on a simple statement of fact. "If I was a suspicious person, I'd wonder about you and David. His sister recognized you." And she was hiding something.

Emma rubbed her watery eyes. "Don't repeat this, but I've been dating him for the past nine months. But I broke up with him and left town the night before he died." A tear flowed from her left eye.

Had David hid the cameras at the Rail Yard to spy on Emma after they broke up? Did a stalker heart hide under his gruff exterior?

Emma wiped her face with a napkin. Her voice was quiet when she started speaking again. "David was getting controlling by the end. It felt like the closer we got, the more he expected me to do something sneaky." Emma threw the napkin away in the garbage can under the counter of my cart.

"Kicking him to the curb sounds like the right call. He sounds scary."

"But when it was good, it was amazing. I hoped David would settle down once he learned he could trust me." Emma rubbed at the skin along one of her nails.

"One of my friends had to make a full-on plan to break up with her ex 'cause he was super possessive, and she was afraid of him," I said. My thoughts raced. If police shows tell the truth, the love interest of the dead person is always the primary suspect. Had Emma followed the cliché and killed her boyfriend?

Emma looked down, and when she looked back up, her eyes were red. I got the sense I was the first person she'd told about any of this. "He wasn't violent. He snapped at me and said I was using him to get one of the spaces in the development across the street. He said it was shortsighted of me to break up with him now. Even though me moving into his new building was his idea. I just wanted to be with him. The jerk." More tears flowed from Emma's eyes.

Emma's words grated against her comments a few days ago. "Wait, I thought you were against the development? I thought you were ready to join the protesters."

The bitter undertone of Emma's laugh made me shiver. "Those houses were a great example of Old Portland four-squares, even in their neglected state. But I want to expand my business. I also promised David I'd keep my ears open over here, since he wanted to build on this lot too."

"How'd a food cart owner and a developer end up meeting, anyway?" David had been a successful businessman visible in the Portland landscape for years, but I didn't know much about Emma's past. How'd she end up starting her own business? I should investigate her background.

"David stopped by when he was scoping out this lot. He said my food reminded him of old-school Portland, since most of the transplants have never heard of a jojo. He asked me out for a beer, and everything clicked from there."

I poured two cups of coffee, and we moved to the picnic table and sat across from each other. Emma looked like talking was a relief. Like the words were severing an anchor that had been threatening to drown her.

"It was fun at first. We went hiking together, and out to hear bands. Everything felt easy for the longest time like we were meant to be together." Emma closed her eyes, and her face was soft like memories were warming her from the inside out. But her expression twisted to grief. "David must have loved your coffee. He was particular, only buying local beans and grinding it fresh. He said he would've preferred to roast his own except he didn't have time."

Part of me smiled, since David's sister, Mary, had said the same thing. "Sounds like you two had a promising start. It's too bad it flipped upside down."

Emma crossed her arms over her chest. One hand clutched her T-shirt. "After the six-month mark, things started to feel more serious between us. I wanted to introduce him to my daughter. When I told David, he freaked out."

There's no way I could tell Emma about my mother's influence on David's life. Did Gabby's showing up on his doorstep coincide with Emma's suggesting introducing her daughter to David? The timing worked out, more or less. Seeing the daughter he rejected might've messed with his head and he freaked out. Sympathy pinged at me. Between a nasty divorce, my mother, and whatever relationship drama surrounded Gabby's birth mother, David hadn't had much luck with women. Maybe my mother had inalterably messed with his head, ruining his ability to form lasting relationships. Plus he'd seen my uncle at the Rail Yard. Had Uncle Jimmy drawn him back, somehow? But my uncle had been at the Tav when David died, at least earlier in the evening. As a sliver of guilt snaked through me, I told it to take a hike. David's death wasn't my fault, but the idea invaded my emotions, making my sense of optimism that life would work out deflate into nothingness.

Chapter 17

After finding the spy camera, and the conversations with Emma and my father that had made my life feel doomed, getting amped up to present coffee-cocktail recipes was hard. So I pulled a double shot of espresso at the warehouse and downed it while Harley and I double-checked our proposal. I yanked a happy persona across my face. I could do this. The drink recipes were solid and our offerings were different without being off-putting.

Plus Erin had texted a photo of me hoisting a cocktail shaker with a big smile across my face. Sage the happy bartender.

After changing from my coffee cart attire into a sheath dress that made me feel like a hipster Audrey Hepburn, we drove across town. I studied the evolving Portland landscape. We were staying on the east side and didn't need any of the bridges. Part of me wished we'd cross the river and see the wild, uncontrolled natural energy it carved through the heart of the city. Instead, we passed new apartment buildings and business complexes interspersed with old, mainly one-story buildings, historic homes, and city parks. There were a few tents and "zombie" RVs, meaning RVs long since on their final wheels.

We met Harley's friend at the space he was remodeling in Northeast. He gave us a quick tour, showing us the dining room and the bar, which featured a lot of industrial lighting juxtaposed against rustic furniture. The minimalist feeling was hip, but not too cold, and reminded me of half of the new restaurants I'd seen around town. Both the restaurant and the bar side had large windows and doors facing the street outside, letting in summer light.

Tanner shook my hand and flashed a charming smile my way. He showed us around the space, pointing out the reclaimed flooring from a high school gym and the custom-made light fixtures. Tanner was close to forty, and he had a collection of scars on his elegant hands. I could see those hands performing kitchen magic.

"We're doing a Southern-inspired menu with a Northwest twist. Ham steaks with coffee gravy, cornmeal waffles, and gumbo and fried chicken for dinner. But we'll also have hazelnut pancakes, and wild-caught salmon, with eclectic rotating specials. We'll be open for breakfast through a late-night dinner menu. I'd love to get people in the bar for coffee during the day and cocktails in the evening, so our coffee menu needs to stand out. You can get a vanilla latte anywhere. I want drinks that no one else in Portland has." Tanner finally paused and looked at us, ready to hear our response.

Harley looked as if a massive wave of stage fright had hit her, turning her into an ice sculpture. So I took over.

"That's good, 'cause we developed ideas focused on unique offerings. Our options pair Ground Rules espresso and cold brew with different alcohols, like gin. We also have plenty of nonalcoholic ideas, both as stand-alone drinks during the day and as an after-dinner dessert."

"I'd love to offer funky breakfast lattes. Plus a few standards." Tanner's words were right up my alley, and my nerves settled from faking calm to feeling in control. The smile filtering across my face was real.

Tanner's eyes lit up as I outlined a few drink ideas, like a s'mores latte made with chocolate sauce, honey, espresso, and steamed milk. "You could put a few marshmallows and a dusting of cinnamon on top, even melt them with a crème brûlée torch. It'll taste like a graham cracker with chocolate and marshmallow. Perfect for dessert."

Harley, ever the coffee purist, shuddered. "That sounds disgust-ingly sweet."

Tanner laughed. "Sage, I'm guessing this is why you deal with customers. Harley wants to convert the masses to black espresso, but coffee drinkers raised on blended coffee drinks expect something sweet."

Harley looked to the side, amusement mixed with an underlying note of hurt on her face, which quickly smoothed off. "I'm lucky to be in business with a people person."

"Do you know any drinks that use sage?" Tanner asked me with an underlying note of challenge.

A memory clicked into place in the front of my mind. I could taste it. "How about a maple-sage latte."

"Tell me about it."

"You'll need to make the maple-sage syrup ahead of time. It's a take on simple syrup, so water boiled with maple syrup, and fresh sage, plus a little brown sugar, then strained. For the drink, you make a latte and use the maple-sage syrup like any flavored syrup. It's a twist on a maple latte."

"I like it. What would you recommend for Harley's namesake drink?"

I glanced at my business partner/friend. She was intense and driven, and always on the go. Without a challenge or something to do, she falls apart. But she's funny and loyal, and more spicy than sweet.

"Have you ever tried a kopi jahe? From Indonesia? It's coffee brewed with ginger. But my favorite version involves brewing the coffee with an infusion of lemongrass, cardamom, cinnamon, ginger, and palm sugar, and serving it black or with coconut milk, although you could offer cream. It's a good house coffee with a kick since it brews best it in large batches."

Tanner's eyes focused on the wall behind me, and I could tell he saw the possibility of the drinks, probably debating whether the fla-vor profiles would clash with or enhance the food. "Any other unique latte ideas?"

"Almond fig," I said. "Or we can turn any seasonal fruit into a syrup. Some, like apples, would pair well with the soft fruit notes of our Central American coffees. That's why we have a cocktail with applejack."

"Anything with blackberries?"

"There's a coffee Chambord on the sample menu." As I spoke, he picked up the packet we'd given him and flipped to the menu. "It's blackberries muddled in gin with Chambord and cold espresso. It would make an excellent brunch drink with hazelnut pancakes. You could substitute marionberries for blackberries in the recipe to make it sound more regional. Chambord's made from a mix of raspberries and blackberries. Since marionberries have both in their family tree, the flavor profile matches."

"Your ideas are perfect. You have the sort of creativity I was looking for."

"We also offer technical expertise in everything from how to pull the perfect shot of espresso, to keeping the equipment in optimal condition."

"So you guys are opening a storefront?"

"Hopefully. Our coffee cart is off to a brisk start, and we're working on a space in a new development scheduled to open next winter." The pride in my voice rang out.

"Too bad, 'cause I would've hired you to manage the coffee program here." Tanner's eyes went back to the proposal we'd prepared. I wondered if he'd meant he would've hired Harley, me, or both of us.

I looked at Harley and gave her a quick "this is going well" eyebrow raise, and she grimaced back. She'd known Tanner for years, so she needed to settle down.

"Which development?" Tanner asked.

"The new Button Building," Harley blurted out.

"Is that one of David Stevens's new developments?" Tanner looked up. "I'd talked to him about space in the building by your coffee cart, but this opened up first. Now I'm glad I'm not across from your cart since I wouldn't want the competition."

"You don't think you'd compare to us, huh?" I laughed.

Tanner grinned. "And I couldn't carry your coffee if I was across the street from you. If the Rail Yard survived, since David wanted to get a mix of restaurants that would've shut you all down."

"I wonder why he disliked the food carts?" I suspected I knew the main reason: Uncle Jimmy owned the lot.

"David said it looked too ramshackle and dirty compared to his new building. I should've asked him if he wanted to destroy everything that makes Portland cool. Although admitting that now sounds thoughtless. He was intense, but an exceptionally alive guy, you know? He had drive. He alienated people, but I respected him." Tanner looked down, like he'd realized he was talking trash about someone who'd been murdered. He looked up suddenly. "Wasn't David found at your food cart lot?"

"Sage found his body," Harley said before I could deflect the question. I swallowed the annoyance that threatened to flash across my face since it was time to act smooth and professional.

"That's horrible." Tanner's look my way was sympathetic.

I remembered the horror I'd felt and let it wash across my face. I dug down deep to sound young, delicate. "It was terrible, like a nightmare. To answer your original question, Stevens Inc. doesn't own the Button Building development."

"Let's talk about something else," Tanner said, and we moved back to solid ground and talked about coffee.

As the meeting progressed, still going well, I thought about how at least one thing in my life looked promising.

Chapter 18

The Wednesday-morning coffee rush fell into its usual swing. After three weeks in business, I knew my regulars, always by order and frequently by name. Falling into the rhythm kept me from looking forward to my plans for the evening, which caused little fluttering butterflies to flit through me whenever I visualized my calendar. I focused on the now: making drinks, keeping the coffee cart clean, and not burning my face off with the steaming wand or something equally brilliant.

Harley came, helped, and was by midmorning getting ready to take off for the warehouse.

"I'll let you know if I hear from Tanner about our proposal." The underlying tension in her voice came through, especially now that she didn't have anything else to focus on.

"If it works out, great, but our business isn't dependent upon one restaurant." I hoped the assurance in my voice would filter through her.

Harley rubbed the back of her neck. "Working with Tanner would be a dream come true. He's legit. Wait until his restaurant opens and you try it. Every element of his place will be scrutinized down to the smallest detail because of his past. If we provide the coffee, it'll end up in the reviews along with the places he sources his ingredients. Some of his glow will reflect on us."

Part of me wondered how much Tanner-the-man factored into the equation. I suspected the answer was somewhere in the middle of the continuum scale of our coffee being in the hippest new restaurant in town and charming restaurateur.

Harley handed me a list. "Let me know if you want to add anything. I'll stop by the grocery warehouse and drop it off tonight."

I studied Harley's loopy handwriting. "Can you pick up the supplies for chocolate syrup? We're good on caramel and vanilla."

She handed me a pen, and I scribbled down the ingredients I'd need to make our dark chocolate syrup. We'd opted to make most of the syrups for our drinks in-house, and the responsibility fell on me to make them in the warehouse's kitchen.

Harley left, and customers came by. During a lull, I pulled out my phone and felt a tad guilty as I searched Zarek's info online. He had a website for his food cart, and his last name, Costas, was on his "About" page. He'd opened his food cart to provide fresh vegan fare to the world. His Instagram account was full of culinary photos from around town mixed in with snaps of his falafel, along with shots of quirky Portland. He balanced the "check out how good my food looks" line perfectly, promoting his cart without verging into over-promotion. Considering the number of hours he worked, he managed to take a ton of photos. But it's not like people's social media accounts offer up a true mirror of their lives. It's a curated reflection of the lives people want the world to see.

"Excuse me." A strident voice interrupted my thoughts, flipping me into work mode.

I looked up with a smile. "Hi there. What can I get for you today?"

"Do you think your boss would appreciate you lounging around, staring at your phone instead of working?"

I motioned to the chalkboard listing today's specials. "Our pour-over bean of the day is spectacular if you're in the mood to have your socks blown off."

She sniffed. "I want a sugar-free hazelnut latte made with skim milk."

"We only have sugar-free vanilla. Is that all right? And what size drink?" I was tempted to make my voice saccharine sweet like sugar-free vanilla syrup, but I kept it light and professional. Even if her entitled tone made me want to tell her to get over herself. Life was too short.

She sighed loudly. "If that's all you have. I should've gone to the shop down the street. They have sugar-free hazelnut."

"I'll make a note to look for sugar-free hazelnut next time I go to our supplier. Would you like a twelve-ounce drink? Sixteen or twenty?" I didn't tell her I made a point of having at least one sugar-free syrup on hand for people that needed, or wanted, it. But offering customers a choice of two flavors was a good idea.

"Sixteen." She still sounded put out as I started to steam the milk.

"Why aren't you making my drink?" she demanded.

"I'm steaming your nonfat milk right now."

"Why're you steaming milk for an iced drink? That sounds disgusting."

Fantastic. I'd broken the number one rule when making coffee in the summer: ask the customer if she wants her drink iced.

"Sorry about that. Iced, nonfat, sugar-free vanilla latte coming right up."

I scooped ice out of our machine and filled her cup and measured in the nonfat milk and sugar-free syrup before pulling the espresso shot and adding it. She stared at me eagle-eyed the whole time as if I were going to spit in her drink.

I stirred the drink and snapped a lid on before handing it over with an unopened straw. "Ta-da! That'll be four fifty."

She handed over her credit card, and I put it in the chip reader and swiveled the cart's tablet around to face her. She sniffed again while tapping the screen.

"Do you have a card for the cart's owner? He should know how lazy his employees are. You'll never be successful without some hustle."

I smiled as I handed her one of my business cards, resisting the urge to tell her I had hustle in spades. "Here you go."

She sniffed and toddled away, iced drink in hand.

I wondered about her. About people who are determined to find fault. Yes, she'd caught me on my phone during a lull in traffic, but as soon as I knew she was there, I'd served her promptly and done my best. I'd even sacrificed milk to the cause, which I poured out, then cleaned the pitcher in preparation for the next customer who ordered a hot drink.

After cleaning, I picked up my phone and searched Zarek's full name and skimmed the results. He'd played soccer over a decade ago for Portland's Jesuit Catholic high school. My friend Erin had also gone there, so I texted her and asked if she'd recognized him from her high school glory days when she saw him at the cocktail party. Zarek followed up high school by playing soccer at the University of Washington. He'd sounded knowledgeable about the game last weekend, but not arrogantly so. It was a good sign he hadn't wanted to lecture me about the ins and outs of soccer minutiae.

The next couple of links for Zarek were reviews of his food cart and interviews with a number of local vegan blogs. Seeing them reminded me of the joke "How do you know if someone is vegan or does CrossFit? Don't worry, he'll tell you." But Zarek had proudly talked about his friend's meat-heavy food cart without sounding sanctimonious, so I couldn't hold his food views against him.

I searched online for Rafael, the owner of the Taco Cat, and I could only find reviews for his cart. He didn't have his own website but linked to a bare-bones social media profile.

Macie, on the other hand, was a social media addict, posting photos of sewing projects, buttons, and craft projects, along with posts about pies. She even updated her accounts daily with specials. I found an old article about the closing of Button Extravaganza, her old shop, which was on a close-in east-side street developed into a hip destination of cafés, boutiques, and apartments. A handful of people missed her business enough to write reviews posted months after the store closed, lamenting the loss. Who would have thought buttons would inspire such a dedicated following.

Emma, meanwhile, had a professional site for PDX JoJos, complete with a page on the history of jojos and how it was a regional food, which I'd already known, although I wasn't sure why. I found an interview that included her last name: Dennison. She'd mentioned a daughter, and after a few clicks, I found her. Tana Dennison looked like a younger version of her mom and was studying ecology at the University of Oregon. Emma had mentioned going backpacking. I wondered if Tana had spent her summers camping in the nearby forests and mountain ranges like both my dad and Jackson loved to do.

My email dinged with a new message, so I opened it and started laughing. The entitled woman from earlier had complained about the inattentive young blond girl who was too focused on her phone to give adequate service.

A glance at the clock told me it had been a while since my last customer. I hoped its being slow wasn't a harbinger of things to come and that our early success wasn't a fluke. But a busload of people taking a beer tour showed up for lunch, and I was hopping busy. I'd need to investigate my fellow cart owners later.

Tonight's scheduled band was a bluegrass-folk hybrid duo, and I set up the stage during the afternoon and waited for Harley to show up at four thirty to take over for the evening. They told me they'd been playing at the Rail Yard regularly for several years, which explained why Zarek had gotten them scheduled so quickly.

As I walked away from the stage, I beelined to the beer cart, which was never open when I was, and met Jeremy, the son of the owner. Jeremy was about twenty-five and had a notebook and several books on literary criticism on the cart's front counter like he was studying between customers.

"Do you brew your own beer?" I asked.

"We always have one or two of our beers on tap, plus other local breweries." Which explained why their tap list showed several local heavy hitters. "My father has always dreamed of opening his own brewery, so he started this when food cart pods started popping up. We have two different beer buses at different food cart lots."

"We're starting as a cart, but we have brick-and-mortar dreams."

"That's my dad's dream too although so many taprooms have opened."

"I take it you're studying English?" I nodded at his books.

"I'm getting my master's."

Rafael, the owner of the Taco Cat, walked up as I talked with Jeremy. "I hope we get a good crowd tonight."

"How'd you come up with the name Taco Cat?" I asked.

"My daughter named my cart. She's obsessed with kitties."

I glanced over at Rafael's cart, where his daughter sat outside, coloring, while his wife worked the window.

"Can I get a pint of lager? I want to use it in a marinade," Rafael said, and traded a plate of carne asada tacos for a pint of beer.

Jeremy and I chatted for a while until a customer showed up at Ground Rules, so I hustled over to make an espresso.

By early evening, Macie's pie cart was happening, and she put up a sign saying she was sold out of both marionberry and bourbon pecan. Her nephew was helping her, and he slouched by Ground Rules a few times as he delivered slices of pie to customers. Could he have snuck into the Rail Yard the night David Stevens was murdered?

I shook my head. Baseless suspicions weren't helping, and I liked my fellow business owners too much to accuse one of murder. Finally Harley showed up at five thirty and apologized for being late. My stomach nerves took flight in full force as I biked away, fueled by two conflicting emotions: one, that I might have left Harley working in the same food cart pod as a murderer. Not knowing who to trust at the Rail Yard was starting to weigh on me. But the second reason soon took over my mind, even though it was sillier: I had a date.

Chapter 19

Bax had offered to pick me up, but I arranged to meet him in the new taproom he wanted to check out. I'd spent a ridiculous amount of time deciding how to dress for tonight. So far, whenever I'd seen Bax, he'd worn jeans and collared shirts, and once I'd caught a brief glimpse of him in a suit like he was on his way to a business meeting. I, meanwhile, had been rocking my usual summer coffee cart uniform: shorts and fitted T-shirts I didn't mind getting soaked in coffee.

Preparing for my date with Zarek hadn't been as nerve-racking. But we'd been heading to a game, which had an unwritten anything-goes dress code. I studied my reflection. The sundress was the right choice and made me look approachable. Date-ready, especially after a dusting of eye shadow, pink lip gloss, and freshly washed hair dried into beach-ready waves. I was tempted to pair the look with confidence-giving combat boots, except the July weather called for sandals.

It was 7:02 when I showed up in the doorway of the Hoptimal Pint Taproom. Two minutes late. Bax was already there, his eyes flicking between the tap list and the door. He was casual in jeans and flip-flops, and a navy T-shirt fitted enough to show off his muscular arms and flat stomach, but not tight enough to be bro.

Bax hugged me. His shirt was buttery soft, and he smelled like sandalwood.

The nerves in my stomach settled. Something told me the date would fulfill its potential.

Bax ushered me to a barstool and, once I was seated, swung into the spot next to me. The bar had an electronic tap list showing the amount of beer left in each of the twenty kegs they had on tap.

"Did you bike over?" Bax asked.

"My bike was calling my name, but I caught a ride instead." Mainly so I wouldn't start out the evening glistening with sweat. Pit stains and this dress weren't a winning combo.

"It's too bad you can't join us for the lunchtime no-drop bike rides."

"My dad's part of a midday cycling group when he can make it." As the words left my mouth, I wondered about the wisdom of mentioning my father on a date. It couldn't be worse than bringing up an ex. Although Bax had said his group didn't drop riders, which is cycling speak for never leaving anyone behind. Did he think I'd be slow?

"So biking is a family thing." Bax leaned in.

"My father was overjoyed when I got into cycling. He's been useful since he's always happy to help me tune my bike, and it's important to keep it in good shape. . . ." Why was I babbling about bicycle maintenance?

But Bax listened as if my conversation were the most fascinating one in the world.

The bartender emerged from the back and made his way over to us at a snail's pace. "What can I get you?"

"I'd like the Wolves and People farmhouse ale on tap. I've wanted to try them for a while," I said.

"I need to see ID first." The bartender's voice held equal notes of disinterest and dismissal, and he barely looked at me as I handed my driver's license over. I was surprised he was even able to grab it without missing since his eyes were focused on a spot a foot above my head.

The bartender glanced at my ID half-heartedly, then did a double take and looked at me again like I was trying to scam him. "Are you honestly twenty-seven?"

"Don't you know it's rude to ask a lady's age? And, yes, I'm twenty-seven."

The bartender didn't ask for Bax's ID as he took his order for a locally brewed IPA and slouched off to pour our beers.

"You do look like jailbait." Bax lightly touched one of the waves of hair brushing my shoulder, making me shiver in the air-conditioned taproom.

"There's no way I look younger than eighteen." I gave him my patented "seriously" look.

"True. But I'm thirty-three and look like I'm on a date with a college kid. But I've talked with you, so I know you have a baby face. Versus being a coed with daddy issues."

"Who says *coed* anymore?"

"Guys feeling nervous on dates, obviously."

"There's no need to be nervous," I said like butterflies hadn't fluttered inside me all day and weren't currently threatening to make me take flight off my barstool.

The bartender dropped beers down in front of us and walked away. I paused and looked at the beers, which were lined up perpendicularly between us. Both were golden, although one was deeper in color.

Bax nudged the lighter pint my way. "Cheers."

We clinked glasses.

I raised my glass and took a sip, resisting the urge to cold-read Bax for fun. I didn't want to create any fake intimacy. If we clicked, it needed to be real.

Citra hops exploded across my tongue. Not a farmhouse ale.

"This is yours."

Bax swapped pints with me. "Sorry."

"Not your fault, and that's an awesome IPA. I'm guessing the bartender isn't your friend who owns this joint?"

"No, and my buddy's going to be pissed to hear about the service when he's not around. Tonight is the first evening he's taken off since opening the taproom."

"I like the logo you designed." I tapped the Hoptimal Pint coaster.

"Thanks. It's nice to take a break and work on small-scale projects, like a logo, instead of an entire game that takes forever."

As we talked and sipped our beers, the bar heated up.

Someone snorted beside me, next to my ear, and I had to hold back a grunt of annoyance after a quick glance his way. Of any bar in Portland, my former boss Mark Jeffries had to show up here? We made brief eye contact, and recognition clocked over his face when he realized I wasn't just a blonde at the bar.

I turned to face Bax, who was talking about his six-year-old son, whom he had joint custody of with his ex. But I could feel Mark behind me. Bax's shoulders stiffened.

I blinked hard. "You still here?" I turned and looked at Mark.

"The service here is a joke. Kind of like the clientele."

The little voice at the back of my mind told me to channel tonight's bartender and show nothing but indifference. So I took a sip of beer and let my eyes wander back to Bax. "So have you ever watched the adult soapbox derby? I always debate entering, but I never do."

"It's not until August. We might have time to throw something together." Bax's eyes glanced over my shoulder a couple of times, so Mark was still hovering behind me. Bax's eyes asked who this guy was, and what our connection was.

"We can't just throw a soapbox derby car together. It has to be awesome. One year, one of the entries looked like a taco cart, and they even handed out tacos on the way down the hill."

"That sounds amazing."

An amplified voice said, "Testing, one, two, three." A woman stood with a microphone in the other room. "Who's ready for open mic night? Portland's best slam poets are ready to go!"

Mark groaned behind me. "Great. Well, tonight's a bust. No service, and now bad poetry?"

Mark left, and the tendrils of tension around my spine relaxed. But Bax hadn't regained his easygoing feeling that Mark's arrival had destroyed.

"Was that an ex, or something?"

"Ex-boss. To make a long story short, Harley worked for him as a roaster until we started Ground Rules. Now he's intimidated by our business and shows it by putting us down."

"He acted like you have a history. He looked at you sort of . . . proprietarily."

"I worked for him as a barista in college for a while. But we never had a personal relationship, if that's what you're asking."

"He acted bitter. As we've talked about, I've done work for a few breweries, and they were all supportive of each other. I would have thought coffee would be the same way."

"There has to be a bad apple or two."

"True. How about we blow this Popsicle joint and get tacos down the street? My treat." Bax rested his hand on top of mine. His pint was empty, but I still had half an inch of beer.

I said yes and downed the last of my farmhouse ale. Bax put his hand on the small of my back, guiding me through the growing crowd. Behind us, a slam poet chanted his mother's pearl necklace was a noose.

"The slam poet sounded interesting," I said.

"I'd come back to listen, but I'd rather spend the evening talking with you."

We talked over al pastor and carne asada tacos, with habanero salsa. Bax was weirdly happy I could handle spicy food. Eventually, he offered me a ride home, and I accepted.

"You live about a mile from me. Easy biking distance," Bax said as he parked outside Jackson's house. Bax hopped out of the car.

I looked at him quizzically as I climbed out.

"Have you forgotten your Emily Post rules of etiquette? I need to escort you to your front door."

"So you're an etiquette devotee?"

"Occasionally."

We chatted up the walkway and continued to talk on the doorstep. The porch light flicked on.

"You don't live with your dad, do you? Or a jealous husband?" Bax looked wary, making me laugh.

"Close. I rent the attic suite from my overprotective big brother." My living situation was one of many things we hadn't talked about, and we could've talked all night.

The door behind us opened. Bentley trotted out first, followed by my brother.

"Sorry," Jackson said as Bentley sniffed me quickly before zeroing in on the new person. Bax knelt down and scratched Bentley's head.

You couldn't wait? I mouthed to Jackson, and he shrugged.

"Jackson, this is Bax. Bax, my brother and his dog, Bentley."

"Hey." Bax stood up. They shook hands, eyeing each other. Thankfully it didn't progress to chest thumps.

"C'mon, Bent," Jackson said. Bentley led the way to the sidewalk.

"I should probably say goodbye." Light disappointment coated Bax's words.

"I have to go to work early tomorrow."

"Let's meet up again. Maybe Saturday? There's a Prohibition-style speakeasy I want to check out. But there's a small chance my ex is going out of town, and I'll pick up my son a few days early, so I'm not sure if I'll be free. I'll text tomorrow afternoon when I know."

"I'll consider clearing my dance card."

He grinned and waited to leave until I was inside. From inside the foyer, I watched Bax trot back to his car, feeling like I was floating in place.

But I knew gravity was going to come calling for me soon.

Chapter 20

The next day, Arthur, the son of the murder victim, showed up a little after 9:30 a.m., not long after the morning rush dwindled and a few minutes after Harley left. He stood next to the window and watched me make his pour-over. With the help of the cart, we were eye level.

"I'm sorry I was rude the last time I ordered coffee," he said.

"It's okay. You were under a lot of stress, and I was out of line." The coffee bloomed in front of me, releasing the fragrance of the blend Arthur had chosen. I could taste the aroma, full body with notes of blackberry and toffee. Harley had wanted to call this roast I'm Your Huckleberry until I pointed out that made it sound like a flavored coffee, which was a giant no in both of our books.

"You made a good point. Gabby is my sister, even if my father didn't acknowledge her."

I slowly added more water to the filter in the all-important circular pattern. "Poor kid."

Arthur nodded. "I should've made a point of being in Gabby's life, even when she thought we were cousins."

"I always wanted a cousin my age growing up."

"My aunt's brilliant too. I wish I'd inherited her business sense."

"I'm sure you're underestimating yourself."

Arthur chuckled, but it was dark sounding, with notes of self-loathing and frustration. "I'm only CFO because I'm family. Nepotism at its finest."

"If you're in charge now, you can always bring your aunt on board, if she's not involved now." The last ounce of water filtered through the coffee grounds, working its way into a glass pitcher. "But have faith in yourself. Don't let fear get in the way of you doing what you need to, whether the decisions are the ones you need to make at work, or building a relationship with Gabby." As the words left my mouth, I realized I sounded like a cross between a greeting card and cliché fortune-teller. Or like I was buttering him up to scam him.

Arthur grunted.

"Sorry, whenever you stop by, I lecture you." I handed his coffee over. "I should focus on my boundaries when you're around."

"I've been thinking about why my father came here. He said something about trying to expose a scam, but I can't imagine what he thought he'd uncover."

"I found a spy camera on one of the light poles."

Arthur squinted at me. "White? About this big?" He motioned with his hands. I nodded. "We have those for construction sites. He took a couple out of our office stock the afternoon before he died. I regret I didn't make him tell me the whole story, but I was on my way to meet up with my wife and didn't take him seriously."

The phrase *honesty is the best policy* echoed in my brain, and I knew what I needed to do. "There's something I should tell you. Let me come out of the cart, and we can talk."

Arthur eyed me as he sipped his coffee. I sat down across from him with a bottle of water.

"There's no easy way to say this, but my mother is Saffron Jones." I took in a deep breath, ready to ask Arthur if he knew about my mom, but based on the way his eyes widened, he knew. I breathed out slowly.

"Are you for real?"

I nodded, feeling embarrassed. "It's not something I brag about."

"So you're related to James Jones." Arthur looked confused, like he was working out how I could be related to the woman who conned his father.

"Great-Uncle Jimmy if you want to get technical."

"I gotta ask. Did your mom scam your dad out of money?" Arthur's eyebrows had raised in a question, and he looked more interested than upset. So he wasn't ready to storm away like my presence would taint him.

I shook my head. "My dad was in the army. Long story."

"So you were a military brat?"

I edited my history on the fly. "My dad's now a detective with the Portland police."

"Thanksgiving must be a hoot."

"That's an understatement. But it's not like my mother stops by for family dinners. She's been underground my whole life."

"Do you think your mom ties back to my dad's death? Are you doing something illegal here?"

I shook my head hard enough my ponytail created a breeze. "No. But your dad might have recognized me 'cause I look like my mother. You know he was dating Emma, the owner of the PDX JoJos cart, right? He could've put the camera up to keep tabs on either of us." But given the timing, and if he put up the camera the night he died, it'd be a safe bet to claim he was checking up on me.

Unless David had come to take the cameras down. After all, Emma had taken off on a solo backpacking trip after a fight, or so she claimed. Unless Emma had lied. Maybe David had broken up with her. She wasn't able to handle the rejection, especially if she thought he'd renege on leasing the retail space he'd promised. But Arthur had mentioned new cameras, so David was more likely setting them up. Wait, *cameras*? Plural? I'd only found one.

Arthur looked thoughtful, and another thought pinged around my brain and bounced out of my mouth before I had a chance to process it. "When you use the cameras on construction sites, how do you access the video feed?"

"We set up the cameras to upload to an account in the cloud." Arthur's eyes scrunched as he looked at me, like he wanted to know why I'd asked.

My heart contracted. "You do realize the camera might have caught your father's death, right?"

Arthur paled. Pointing it out made me feel terrible. But it was important, so I told myself to buck up. My back straightened. I looked him in the eye.

"Should I check the cloud to see if the footage uploaded?" He sounded like he didn't want to see it.

I half smiled at him, hoping he'd feel the compassion I was trying to send his way. "Or help the police access the footage. Let them watch it. There are things you don't need to see."

"I'll look up the name of the detective in charge of my father's case. I've met him, but I must've blocked his name from my memory."

"I have his card." I went back to the cart and pulled Detective Will's business card out of my bag, stopping myself from snorting when I read his first name. William. WILLIAM E. WILL, DETECTIVE. Had a lifetime of being Will E. Will smothered any sense of humor left in his body? I mentally crossed my fingers as I handed the card over to Arthur, hoping the camera had footage that would bring the whole situation to a close. Show I was innocent. Show I wasn't connected to the crime, even unintentionally.

As Arthur stared at the card, like he was gathering up his courage to call, I wondered why David had put cameras up in the Rail Yard. But the more critical question nagged at me: Who had David run into? And was there a second camera here, or had he only set up one?

But there was a different problem I could solve, and I thought of a person who might be able to help. So after Arthur left, I texted a friend and called in a favor.

As long as you provide the usual, he texted back.

I smiled in relief.

"Good news?" a voice asked.

I looked up. Zarek. One of the people I'd sent a quick mid-morning text during a break between customers. Last night, he'd sent me a joke GIF. I'd responded back, *LOL*, a measly thirteen hours after he'd sent it, which I'd followed up with a *Sorry, didn't have my phone on last night*, since I didn't want him to think I'd been ignoring him. Clearly, I was regressing to a teenage state instead of assuming he'd treat my delay like an adult. Just because someone texts me, it doesn't mean I need to respond promptly.

"Well, hello, sailor," I said. "Want a coffee?"

Zarek leaned against the side of my cart. "I'd love an Americano. The Rail Yard was hopping last night, and I was here past midnight cleaning. I need caffeine, stat."

"That's good, right?"

"Best night I've had all summer."

We chatted as I made his drink. His tension melted away as he took a few sips of the coffee I'd taken extra care to make.

After a trip to the warehouse to make some syrups for the cart, followed by a quick trip home to shower and wash off the aroma of coffee, I sat on my front porch. I had a couple of homemade burritos and cans of sparkling water, and I'd pulled on a bright orange T-shirt from the back of my bottom dresser drawer. This particular shirt made a mix of heartbreaking and happy memories flood me.

A bright orange truck pulled up, driven by a guy whose T-shirt matched both the pickup and my shirt. Inner City Assistance takes their color branding seriously.

Manny hopped out of the truck when I approached and gave me a bear hug. "I haven't seen you in forever."

"Thanks for helping me." I handed over one of the burritos and a can of grapefruit sparkling water. Manny took a bite and glanced inside the burrito as he chewed, checking out today's "the usual," which is always a meal, frequently a sandwich, preferably homemade, but he'll accept takeout when needed. Or my "let's toss these ingredients together and call it a burrito" dinner such as tonight.

"Let's eat here so I can listen to your story," he said. So we retired to the front steps, and I gave him the lowdown on Gabby.

He listened carefully, and I studied the side of his face as he stared at the ground, chewing thoughtfully. He swallowed and took a sip of water. "There are a few camps not too far from the Rail Yard. But the settlements are always moving, and there's no promise Gabby's staying in one. If we don't find her today, I can call my friend with the Street Kids Action Team. She has a good rapport with the kids and might be able to work a few leads."

"I thought most of the kids avoid social workers?"

"When word got out we have ways to avoid calling their parents, it helped. They're cautious, but we sometimes get them to trust us."

"What do you mean?"

"If SKAT takes a teen into the shelter, they legally have to notify their guardian. But if there's a reason that's dangerous, like the kid is fleeing abuse, they can notify social services, and there's a process they can follow to get the kid help and even enrolled in school without sending the kid home."

I saw the way the logic played out. "So the state becomes the kid's guardian."

"More or less, complete with a social worker who specializes with former street kids. It's not ideal, but considering some of the situations the kids run from, it's a better choice than sending them back, or leaving them to fend for themselves on the streets." Manny looked troubled and took the final bite of the kidney-bean-and-sweet-potato burrito, flavored with a mustard sauce. He motioned to the plate that used to hold the food. "These were good. Inauthentic, but delicious."

"I thought you'd like them. One of my roommates in Indonesia used to make them."

"You were able to find tortillas there?"

"Not usually, so we subbed roti canai, the local flatbread, in. It was passable. But there was a Mexican restaurant nearby, and the owner would sell us tortillas to take home."

"Was the Mexican food any good?"

"Let's say he did the best he could, given the limitations of what was available." Manny laughed. "The Bali local food was awesome. I miss it."

As Manny drove us to our first stop, his fingers drummed against the steering wheel, keeping time with the rock music playing over the truck stereo. I studied his high-fade haircut, which was like him: precise, orderly, and proud. Even after a day working for Inner City Assistance, helping people in transitional housing find work, get medical and addiction help, and eventually move into their own apartments, he looked put together. His bright orange T-shirt, which told the world he worked with ICA, looked ironed, and his boots were clean. My own feet felt confined in similarly sturdy hiking boots, but closed-toe shoes were part of the dress code. Visiting a homeless camp and stubbing your toe into a used needle was 80 million shades of a bad idea.

Manny parallel parked next to a lot a couple of blocks from the Rail Yard. A handful of tents were under a couple of trees on property with a small neighborhood substation, so it must belong to the local power company.

"I'm surprised they're able to set up here," I said.

"They get run off, but they come back. They move when they have to, but can't stay in one place for long. So they cycle back, and the pattern continues."

"And eventually, there's no place left for them to go." I saw the situation as a deadly form of musical chairs. Whenever the music stopped, there was one less spot, but the person without a place lost more than a game at a birthday party.

"Let's roll." Manny hopped out of the truck.

I followed him to the back tailgate. He pulled out a couple of reusable shopping bags.

Kits of hygiene supplies peeked out of one bag. From past volunteer experience, I knew the packets contained personal-care items, including toothpaste and a toothbrush. I took the second bag and glanced inside, seeing food bags with a bottle of water and an apple, along with a stash of shelf-stable food and a flyer listing the resources Manny's organization offered. The color of the paper matched both the crackers and our T-shirts.

"Hi," Manny said to two women sitting on the curb. Both looked to be in their late thirties, but life had dealt each of them a hard hand. They could've been much younger. My heart twisted.

Manny offered them the hygiene kits, which they accepted. The snack packs made both of them brighten.

After chatting with them for a moment, Manny said, "We're looking for a teenage girl who's been hanging out here. Gabby. Have you seen her?"

"Why you want her?"

"Her mother misses her," I said. "I want to make sure Gabby is safe."

They looked at me warily, so I added, "I won't force her to go home."

One of the women looked down at her feet while the other searched my face for a moment. "Gabby been around. Dunna know where she at."

"Okay." My heart felt like it deflated several inches.

"You should ask Tommy. They were tight."

"Tommy?" My back straightened. I looked at her again.

"Kid, scar like Harry Potter on back of his hand."

"Like a lightning bolt?"

"Yeah, that him."

"Thanks." I could feel their eyes on my back as we walked farther into the lot and handed out our kits. Everyone took them, although some of the recipients refused to look us in the eyes.

The people in this camp were adults, and I wondered if Gabby stuck with kids her age.

I talked with a woman for a few minutes about the services ICA offered. "I want a home again," she told me in a quiet voice. Scabs covered her skinny arms, along with bruises from injection sites. "You're sure they'd help me?"

"Yes. Helping people is their mission." I motioned Manny over, and he explained the process to her. She listened and took one of his business cards.

As we climbed back into Manny's truck, I asked, "Do you think she'll call you?"

"I hope so." I could hear the doubt threaded throughout the undertones of his voice.

We drove to the next camp.

Chapter 21

"Are you going to come back and volunteer with me? Or is this a onetime shot since you're looking for Gabby?" Manny asked as we drove to the next camp.

Since coming home and starting Ground Rules, I hadn't volunteered anywhere. Since the business was up and running, I needed to start giving back. "I will. I haven't started any volunteer gigs yet. I can commit to a weekly session."

"Email me, and we'll set up something official. Although I'll be relieved when you're no longer looking for a lost kid."

"Someone has to find her."

"It has to be messing with your head."

I looked away from Manny, out the window.

"You're going to claim it's not bringing up memories?" Manny asked as he parallel parked.

"Lots of things bring up memories. Looking for one kid isn't going to send me into a downward spiral." But I knew Manny was remembering how we'd met. He'd noticed me hanging out alone during my thankfully brief experience on the streets. He and his mom had taken me under their collective wing and helped me find Uncle Jimmy and the Tav.

As a thank-you, Uncle Jimmy had helped them find a place to live, and Manny's mom had worked at the Tav until she found a job as a law office receptionist. Now she was a paralegal for the same firm. Once his life stabilized, Manny did well in high school and did even better in community college, before transferring to a four-year university to study social work. He'd gone from homeless to high school graduate, to university graduate, and he eventually earned his master's in social work. But he'd never forgotten where he'd come from.

I looked Manny's way, reading the concern on his face. I softened. "I'm okay. I promise. It's been a tough couple of weeks. But I'm doing this because it feels right." And it might help get police pressure off me. Arthur and Mary deserved the chance to reunite with Gabby, which was more important. Although if Gabby had killed her biological father, Mary might regret my bringing her daughter back into the light.

We climbed out of the truck. A couple of kids and a collection of raggedy tents and litter were in an empty lot with NO TRESPASSING signs next to a juice bar. The kids sat huddled together as they watched us approach.

Manny held up his bag so the ICA logo was visible. "We have food and hygiene kits." He'd pitched his tone to sound cheerful, but the kids looked ready to run away.

Manny pulled a handful of snack packs out of his bag and passed them out. I followed his lead and offered the hygiene kits to the teens.

One of the kids was drawing on a dusty sketchpad, but I couldn't make out the image before he tucked it out of sight under his shirt. He stared at me like I was invading his private space.

"Do you know Tommy?" I asked.

"Never heard of him." He looked away from me, obviously lying. But I didn't say anything as I handed out more packs.

A guy, late teens or early twenties, came out of the tent. He squatted and looked over the shoulder of one of the girls, leaning against her as he checked out the hygiene pack. "Useful," he said, and poked the tampon.

She said something to him, and he leaned in closer and whis-

pered in her ear. He was rangy, but his arms had definition under his
tight black T-shirt.

All sorts of warning alarms dinged in my head, but I ignored
him and handed out a few more packs. Manny was kneeling on the
ground and chatting with a trio of kids. He said something about
"SKAT" and "school."

"Give me one of those," the early-twentysomething said. When
he threw out his hand, I noticed the scar shaped like a lightning bolt
on the back.

Tommy.

As I handed him the pack, I made myself sound casual as I asked,
"Have you seen Gabby around?"

His brown eyes scanned me, causing another warning note to
sound in the back of my mind. "Why are you asking about Gabs?"

"I haven't seen her for a while."

"I'll tell her you asked about her. She's busy."

"Will she be here later? I can stop by."

"Don't worry, I'm taking good care of her." A warning came
through in Tommy's voice. Was he protecting Gabby out of altru-
ism, 'cause he thought I wanted something from her, or was he possessive? I suspected the latter.

As I handed out more packs, Tommy's eyes burned through me.
The kids, who had started to talk to us, turned silent.

Afterward, Manny looked at me as we walked back to the truck.
"Want to grab a drink?"

All I could do was nod. I didn't have the energy for anything
else.

We returned the truck to Inner City Assistance's headquarters in
Old Town and hoofed it a few blocks north to the Pearl District.

Even though we discussed continuing to the Belgian-beer bar by
Manny's studio apartment, the siren song of the Tav was too much to
resist. The place was hopping, with the usual barflies, some of whom
waved to me, along with groups of people I'd never before seen.

Miles poured us both pints of IPA. We found a spot on the side of the room, but we kept an eye on what we wanted.

When one of the pool tables opened up, Manny and I commandeered it. I picked out a pool cue that felt perfectly weighted, not too light, but not heavy, with an even distribution.

"I bet you five dollars I'll win," Manny said.

I shook my head at him.

"When's the last time you played?" he asked.

"Over a year ago."

"So it's a fair bet."

"It's your money." I dropped a $5 bill next to my pint of beer. Manny put five ones on top and weighed them down with a saltshaker.

As Manny racked the pool balls, I turned and glanced at the stained-glass windows, my gaze stopping on the center-right panel. In it, a girl kneels in a beam of light streaming from a window in a door. She could be praying. Her hair falls around her like a blanket. She reminded me of my failed mission today, but maybe my hopes would pay off in the long run.

Manny broke but didn't knock any of the pool balls into a pocket. He waved for me to take over the table.

After analyzing the table and looking forward three moves, I knocked in the thirteen, followed by the nine and the eleven. Manny groaned beside me.

"Stripes are lucky," I said.

My phone buzzed as I lined up my next shot. Manny scanned the screen. "Someone named Zarek wants to know if you'd like to get breakfast on Saturday. So he's asking you out to breakfast, and not brunch? I'm guessing he's not a hipster. Wait, his second text says he wants to go to the coffee shop that claims they brought avocado toast to the USA."

"Zarek runs a food cart seven days a week. Saturday morning is probably the only free time he has." I lined my shot up again. Part of me felt touched, especially since I had no idea how Zarek maintained his cart's schedule without tearing his hair out.

My phone buzzed again. Manny burst into a belly laugh. "Bax says he enjoyed last night, Coffee Angel. Seven p.m. next Friday because he has his son this weekend?"

I closed my eyes. "Do you have to keep reading my phone?"

"If it distracts you enough so I can win, of course. Besides, it's fascinating. Two boys are following you around, and you haven't mentioned either of them? Even the one that calls you an angel?"

I put my pool cue down, so the end was on the floor. I stared at Manny. "It's not exciting. And I'm the Coffee Angel, thank you."

"I'll be the judge. Spill."

I refocused on the game, knocked in the ten, and told Manny about going to the Timbers game with Zarek before taking my next shot.

"Timbers fan. That's promising."

"Bax is into biking."

"I bet his bike isn't the only thing he wants to ride."

I missed my shot.

Manny chuckled. "Gotcha."

I shook my head. He knocked in the seven but scratched on his next shot, and I took over again.

"Which boy will you say yes to? Or will you turn down both of them?"

"Maybe I'll say yes to both offers."

I set about winning the game. Manny groaned and asked, "Double or nothing?"

"It's your money." I racked the pool balls.

My head pounded during my bike ride to work the next day from downing too many pints of IPA the night before, followed by fitful sleep as the alcohol burned through me between midnight and 5:00 a.m. Maybe Harley could take over the cart from midmorning on.

As I unlocked the main gate, a crashing noise from the construction site made me wheel around. I clutched the gate as if holding on to something substantial would stop my head from spinning. My stomach needed the same memo.

Several teens sprinted out of the construction site. One, a boy in a red shirt, squeezed through a hole in the fence. Another two, a boy and a girl, climbed it, dropped to the other side, and took off running.

A fourth figure ran out. Tommy. My eyes narrowed.

"Is everyone out?" the boy in the red T-shirt asked.

"Go!" Tommy yelled, and shoved the boy. They ran down the street.

Dark smoke started to waft up from the partially dismantled house. I called 911, but my voice froze as one more teen came running out, as the voice on the other end of the line asked about my emergency.

Gabby. She squeezed through the fence. She held her left eye even though it made her run awkwardly.

"There's smoke at the construction site on the corner of . . ." But my words were drowned out, even in my mind, by a boom across the street. My back hit the fence, breaking my fall before I landed on my butt.

Gabby fell to her knees but stood back up and shakily ran off in the opposite direction from the rest of the kids, as the 911 operator asked me what had happened.

Chapter 22

Firefighters arrived first. Three trucks blocked off the intersection. But while the explosion had been loud, and smoke billowed for a few minutes, there hadn't been much fire. A while back in Northwest Portland a natural gas explosion had leveled an entire building. So we were lucky. Perhaps the destruction was minimal.

Police officers showed up next and roped off the construction site across the street. At least the Rail Yard wasn't taped off and the cart opened only half an hour late. While business wasn't as brisk as usual, a steady number of drinks made their way into the world. Including into the stomachs of the responding police officers.

A voice came to me as I cleaned two pour-over filters. "The worker in the coffee cart, Sage Caplin, called 911. In her interview, she said—"

"I'll talk to her myself," another voice responded.

I took a deep breath. My head still pounded, so I quickly downed another cup of water, hoping hydration would ease the pressure on my temples. Should I call Jackson? But this was, hopefully, about the explosion. If a detective asked about David Stevens, I'd lawyer up.

Harley hissed from behind me, "They're talking about you!"

A woman in a suit, with curly dark hair scraped into a no-nonsense ponytail, walked up to the cart.

"Hi, Detective," I said, and she didn't even blink, although I could tell her hazel eyes were taking my measure. "Coffee?"

"A twelve-ounce drip coffee, black, would be welcome."

I poured a to-go cup of coffee for her, and she put $2 down on the edge of the cart.

As I handed it to her, she said, "Can you come outside and talk with me?"

"Sure." I left the cart in Harley's hands, and we retired to my usual picnic table. After introducing herself as Detective Bennet, she had me recount my morning. Unlike Detective Will, she didn't seem to regard me as a murderer, or bomber, from first glance.

"You're sure you recognized one of the men?" Detective Bennet asked when I told her about Tommy and the teenagers. I had to stop myself from smiling since that sounded like the name of a pop band. Focus, Sage. Focus.

"I volunteered with my friend Manny Rodriguez, who's with ICA, yesterday." I told her about our visit to the camp full of teens, although I left out our reason why.

"You don't know Tommy's last name?"

"No." I described the scar on the back of his hand. Detective Bennet asked me where the camp was set up and took notes.

Visions of Gabby kept flashing through my brain, but I couldn't worry about her right now. Had Gabby vandalized the construction site? New concern filtered through me when I remembered how Tommy had left her behind. Something was off in this whole situation.

"Let's go over the descriptions of the teens." Detective Bennet asked me to describe their clothes and any distinguishing details. I resisted the urge to embellish on what I saw and kept it to the basics. Red T-shirt on one of the guys. Gray belly shirt on the girl who'd climbed the fence. I described Gabby but kept it equally vague, mentioning her dark jeans and long-sleeved black T-shirt.

"I only saw them from across the street, and they ran away, so I didn't see their faces. I only recognized Tommy because he made an impression last night."

"You're doing fine. I wish all witnesses were as observant." She didn't sound like she was blowing smoke my way.

Detective Bennet gave me her card before she left. "Excellent coffee, by the way."

"Thanks, tell your friends!" She laughed and walked away.

A few more customers trickled in throughout the morning. Harley hung out past her usual stopping time but left because we had an order of coffee beans to deliver to the co-op. Our trial with them had turned into a standing order. Thankfully my headache had eased before Harley left, although my body was exhausted. Note to self: no late nights fueled by IPA when I'm scheduled to work the cart at the crack of dawn.

Of all of the cart owners, Diego and Angela showed up first. They were rushing toward Cartography but beelined toward me.

"We heard about the explosion on the radio," Angela said. "Is the Rail Yard okay?"

"The only thing damaged was the construction site across the street."

"We didn't lose power? You're sure?" Angela glanced in my cart like I'd have lava lamps sucking up energy, showing the world, yes, we're fine, in flashes of color.

"Yep, we have power."

"After losing a few days when the police wouldn't let us open, we can't afford to be closed again." Angela leaned against my cart and closed her eyes, while Diego went over to Cartography.

"At least no one was hurt this time," I said. Their callousness toward David's death made me clench my jaw. The kids fleeing the scene, and especially Gabby trailing them, fought with the headache in my brain over which emotion deserved my attention. Both made me feel sick.

"Don't think I'm indifferent to the man dying," Angela said. "If I think about it, I feel nauseous. And unsafe. Our cart's been here for five years. Cartography is our passion."

"Five years is impressive."

"I teach during the school year and keep hoping the cart will make enough so I can quit." Angela's jaw clenched and her look would've been the perfect pose for determination for a sculptor.

"What do you teach?"

"ESL at an elementary school. Diego runs the cart during the school year, although he's also an interpreter, so we're open weekends and dinner two evenings a week once school starts."

Diego locked Cartography and headed our way. "The cart's fine."

Angela let out a deep breath and closed her eyes. "What a relief."

They each bought a macchiato and left to go back to the kitchen space they rented to prepare for today.

The manager of the construction site dropped by before lunchtime. "Thanks for calling 911," he said. "I'm glad you open early."

"What exactly happened?"

"Can I get a round of house coffees for my crew? Seven total. To answer your question, some stupid kids started a fire by a propane tank, which blew. Thankfully it was almost empty, so the explosion wasn't too powerful. We were lucky—the remaining structure could've gone up in flames."

"You were going to take it down regardless, right?"

He chuckled. "Yes, but a fire could've destroyed our tools." As I poured his coffees and loaded them onto two carrier trays, he told me about how they'd deconstructed the building and sent anything salvable to the ReClaimed Goods Center. "Now we're sitting and waiting for the all clear from the fire marshal to demolish what's left of the building."

I handed over the cardboard carriers with the coffees plus an extra cup with cream inside, along with a collection of sugar packets. He paid on the tablet.

"No one was hurt, right?"

"Thankfully, no." He picked up the trays.

I waved as he walked away, and when I glanced at the tablet, I saw he'd tipped me $25. I should call 911 more often.

★ ★ ★

Everyone wanted to talk about the crime scene across the street, although my customers moved on to other issues after hearing the basics. I heard one guy's life story about how he'd moved from San Francisco and bought a house and was raising his two kids here. A woman was frustrated with her high-school-aged daughter who wanted to quit playing in the local youth orchestra. I smiled, happy for any distraction that took me out of my thoughts.

My phone rang, and my pulse spiked as I answered the call.

"Sage? It's Tanner." His voice was too smooth, like the melted caramel I use in our syrups. Warning signs popped up in my brain; he wanted something.

"Oh, hey, Tanner."

"You impressed me during our meeting. I know you're working for Harley on Ground Rules—"

"I'm co-owner."

"Sorry, I know you're in business with Harley. But if you'd be interested in working for me, I'd love to hire you."

"You're seriously trying to poach me from my own business? Besides, Harley and me teaching your staff the basics of coffee brewing is part of our proposal, remember? Annual hours are included for free as long as you commit to serving our coffee for two years."

"Harley's great, but I'd love to have someone around who's more polished. You know the ins and outs of coffee drinks, but you also bring customer-service skills. I can see you being an excellent bartender and trainer."

I forced my jaw to unclench. I kept my voice light with a friendly tone, although I wanted to break out heavy sarcasm. But I didn't want to scuttle the possible relationship between our businesses, so I stayed sweet. "I already work full-time."

"Take a few days and think about it. Even part-time would be a huge help, and I can work with your Ground Rules schedule. Don't say no immediately. Think about it. That's all I'm asking."

The glint of silver hair caught my attention. My body felt lighter.

I'd been waiting for Uncle Jimmy to make another appearance. Maybe this had been his way to give me enough room to get the business up and running on my own after saying hi the first week. If I'd asked for help, he would've shown up. Or sent someone.

"Thanks, Tanner, but I have to go. I'll think about your offer." I hung up, telling myself I was also cutting off the tendrils of annoyance Tanner had caused to creep through my mood. I stepped out of the cart and greeted my uncle as he approached.

"Hey, Bug."

I grinned widely.

But true to form, Uncle Jimmy looked stoic, but his eyes crinkled like they always do when he's in a good mood.

"Want a coffee?"

"Americano, please."

I hustled back to make him one.

Zarek, Emma, and two other cart owners headed to Jimmy like moths to a flame, while Macie followed at a sedate pace. She'd left her apron on like usual, this one bright orange with blue pigeons embroidered on the front. She carried a spool of thread, which she glanced at before dropping it into one of her front pockets. But I couldn't tease her about it since I was still wearing a teal apron that matched the color of my cart. Although compared to hers, mine had a shocking lack of embroidery.

As I carried the Americano over, Zarek asked, "For those of us with leases expiring December thirty-first, when will you start the renewal process?"

"Do you have any plans for the lot, other than keeping it as the Rail Yard?" Emma asked.

"Do you think we can fit another cart in?" Rafael asked.

I handed the coffee over, and Uncle Jimmy said, "Thanks, Bug." Which earned me a few side-eye glances.

"Would you like a slice of pie to go with the coffee?" Macie asked.

"No thanks, Macie. That's a nice apron."

She smiled. "It's my second favorite."

Trust Macie to rank her aprons. But she seemed innocent. Like she deserved protection from the world. The thought of her nephew dealing drugs from her cart made me wary. I should discuss her nephew with Uncle Jimmy later. It'd be terrible if her nephew was caught dealing drugs and Macie lost her food cart.

"As far as your questions, let's talk about leases this autumn. Let's say in October," Uncle Jimmy said. Zarek made a note on his phone. "As far as this lot, I don't have any immediate plans to change things or add more carts."

Uncle Jimmy's words were careful, and from the way Zarek's eyebrows narrowed, he was reading between the lines. Immediate plans didn't preclude long-term development. Zarek needed time to find retail space before renewing, or breaking, his lease. Once again, I realized how lucky I'd been to have some of the difficult business decisions, like where to open, fall into my lap. My spine straightened. Even if I acquired it by luck, no one was going to ruin Ground Rules.

"Have the police told you anything about the murder?" Angela asked. The whole group went silent. A car with a loud muffler drove past, making half of the group jump when it banged.

Uncle Jimmy glanced at the sky for half a second. "I haven't heard a word."

"Surely the police are keeping you informed as the landowner?" Angela asked.

"I've talked to them, but I don't know anything about the investigation."

"Do we need to be worried? Should we pool together and hire a security guard? Especially after the explosion across the street?" Angela's voice went up in pitch.

"I can't afford a security guard," Zarek muttered. Several people agreed.

"The murder sounds like a tragic fluke. But if you're anxious, talk to me, and I'll consider letting you break your lease penalty-free."

"Do you want us to leave?" Rafael asked.

"Not at all. I believe in the Rail Yard and want it to do well. But I won't force anyone to stay here if they feel unsafe." Uncle Jimmy held up his hand. "I have to go, but feel free to email me or call. Bug, walk out with me."

"Sure," I said.

Everyone stared at us as we left, making my skin crawl.

"You've seen the books for Ground Rules. I think we're off to a good start. We've kept the quality of the coffee consistent, even with the murder and today's explosion."

"Tell me about today. I heard a little on the news, but I'd rather hear your take."

Uncle Jimmy leaned against the side of his car, an older, but pristine, BMW he'd bought new once upon a time, as I told him about this morning.

I laughed. "I should start a podcast called *The Saga of Sage* and play it whenever anyone asks about the drama that's turned into my life."

"Buck up, Bug, you've handled everything thrown your way like a champ. Call me if anything else happens."

"For sure."

I waved as he drove away.

My fellow cart owners were standing in a group when I returned to the lot. They stared at me. Diego rubbed Angela's arm. Tears were spilling out of her eyes.

"You're cozy with Jimmy Jones." Zarek eyed me. "Have you known him long?"

"He's family. Does that matter?"

Zarek threw his hands up in exasperation, and when he looked my way, his eyes narrowed. A shiver ran down my spine. But I kept my face still. I stared back, daring him to say something.

"Of course it matters. Think of someone like Foster. Moving here would have meant his business wouldn't have failed. But nepotism won out. You even got the space with plumbed water." Zarek's voice got louder, showing he was on the verge of going from angry to nuclear.

"Six carts lost their lease across the street, not just Foster. All of them would've loved to move here," Emma said.

Zarek took a deep breath and turned away. He crossed his arms over his chest.

"All of them deserved a spot here," Rafael, the owner of the Taco Cat, said. His daughter, about five years old, stood next to him, holding on to the hem of his T-shirt.

Rafael followed my gaze. "C'mon, sweetie," he said to his daughter, and they held hands as they walked back to his cart.

Zarek turned back around to face us. "You should've told us you were related to Jones from the beginning." He dropped his hands to his side, and it looked like every muscle in his body was tense.

Why did my relationship to Uncle Jimmy matter so much to Zarek? Was he trying to hide something?

Emma held her hands in a calming gesture. "Chill, Zarek. Remember how we argued over which cart should move here? Be honest: you only lobbied for Foster because you've been friends for years. You didn't even eat from his cart. So stop being a hypocrite."

"Of course I didn't eat at Foster's cart, I'm vegan," Zarek snapped back. "But it doesn't mean he should go out of business."

"It sucks for Foster. I feel sorry for him, but it's life. We all know we're at risk of losing our space. It's why you're so anxious to renew your lease—"

"Of course I want to renew—"

"Grow up, Zarek, and stop acting like a prick. Or take advantage of your cart being mobile and leave," Emma said, then marched to PDX JoJos.

"I guess Jimmy Jones can't be too worried about crime at the Rail Yard if he's not concerned with your safety," Angela said. She and Diego gave me a final guarded look and returned to Cartography.

Macie stared at me with a befuddled expression, and the pizza cart owner pulled out her phone and looked at it before ambling away, eyes glued to her screen. I clenched my jaw. I wasn't going to apologize. I hadn't done anything wrong, and I hadn't known about the drama here before Ground Rules moved in. It's not like Jimmy had kicked someone out to make room for me. It's not like I'd put another coffee cart out of business.

Whatever. I turned and strode back to my cart.

Chapter 23

As I was getting ready to close Ground Rules, Zarek taped a sign up in the window of his cart, locked the door, and stalked away. He'd never acted angry before, but now I wondered if it was always there, deep inside, ready to explode out. He'd been the last person left in the Rail Yard the night David Stevens died. After I'd biked away, had Zarek returned for some reason? Had he fought with Stevens? Zarek knew about the box cutter in my cart since he'd loaned it to me. I felt sick. Maybe the villain had been in plain sight the whole time at the Rail Yard. Maybe I'd gone out on a date with a murderer.

As I lagged behind Zarek, pushing my bike, I wondered where he was going. Zarek usually kept his cart open all day, and from what I'd seen, his was the busiest. Reviews raved about the zhug sauce he served with his falafel.

Macie also received excellent reviews. Her sea-salt-and-honey pie had a following, along with her marionberry on a naturally gluten-free hazelnut crust. So far, Rafael's taco cart was my favorite, but he made his tortillas from scratch, so he already knew the path to my stomach—I mean, heart.

Zarek power walked like he had somewhere to be. I followed him, letting him get a few blocks ahead, but keeping him in sight. What was he hiding? Was his temper always bubbling away, ready to detonate, or was today special?

After a quarter mile, Zarek turned, and in another half mile, he took another right. A sinking feeling went through me, but I kept up my spy game. After a couple more turns, he was back at the Rail Yard.

Way to go, Harriet the Spy, I told myself. You followed a guy on his daily constitutional. Going for a brisk walk was better than wallowing in anger.

I climbed onto my bike, and as I pedaled across the street, I slowed to a stop. Macie's nephew was skulking on the corner and started to slouch down the street. Clearly, it was time to practice my spy game for the second time in an hour. I inched behind him.

He turned down a residential street and stopped by a bright green Little Lending Library outside a Victorian house. He pulled something from his pocket and left it inside and took out something too small to be a book. He pocketed it. His Chuck Taylors slapped the pavement like he didn't have a care in the world.

After a few minutes, I sauntered to the lending library, holding my bike upright with one hand. I kept my phone to my ear and chatted as if I were talking to someone.

"Oh, look, I found a little library at the same time I need a new book! How fortunate." I scanned the titles. Rather slim pickings, with a couple of philosophy books and two beat-up picture books. But a Cat Winters novel was to the far right. I leaned my bike against my leg.

"Oh, I love Cat Winters!" I said into my phone, and opened the library door. I palmed the small baggie Macie's nephew had left behind before grabbing the book. Sliding both into my messenger bag was easy. I continued down the street, pushing my bike, and pretended to talk until I rounded the corner. I stowed my phone in my bag and took off, wondering what I was carrying. Hopefully, it wasn't too illegal, since I didn't want to be busted for meth.

After a few blocks, I coasted to a stop in a small park and pulled the baggie out and examined it. Four joints, all neatly rolled. Macie's nephew believed in customer service.

Part of me was relieved Macie's nephew was selling pot, which is legal in Oregon if sold from a licensed dispensary or grown for personal use in small amounts. It wasn't as risky as other drugs he could've sold, but he was putting Macie's business at risk. If he was caught dealing out of her cart, she could lose it, and more. Should I tell her?

My phone rang. I answered it even though I didn't recognize the number. A girl's voice made me look up in surprise as if she could see me over the airwaves.

Gabby.

"Can you loan me bus fare? I need to leave town."

"I met your mom the other day. She'd happily pick you up."

"That's not an option." Gabby sounded panicked. Was she in a tight spot, or was the thought of facing her mother scary?

"Gabby, there's a way to get you help, and off of the street, without telling your mom."

Her breath was the only thing I could hear over the phone line for a minute. She finally asked, "How?"

I explained how SKAT and similar organizations can notify social services instead of the minor's legal guardian. "So there's a way. But your mom wants you back."

"No, not anymore."

"She does. But we don't need to argue. Let's get you off of the street, and we can worry about the rest later."

"I don't know."

"My brother is a child advocacy attorney. His office is downtown. You could visit him, and he can help you out."

"What does child advocacy mean?" Her tone shifted to tough, but a helpless note was wobbling in the undercurrent of her voice like she was looking for a lifeline she doubted she'd find. But she was eyeing the bait and starting to bite down. Now I needed to reel her in slowly. Too fast and she'd slip the hook, slide away, and disappear.

"It means he acts in the best interest of the kids he works with," I said, simplifying the concept. "Like in a bad divorce, the court might ask him to represent the interests of the child. He's also worked with kids in foster care and the juvenile court system."

Silence spread over the line, and after a moment I said in a soft voice, "I can meet you at his office."

"Okay."

I made her repeat his address back to me, and we agreed to meet at 4:00 p.m. Now I had to tell Jackson I'd scheduled a meeting with a lost soul at his office. And since she was a kid, I hoped he knew a way to keep her from running off while getting her the help she needed.

Provided she showed up.

An hour later, Jackson glared at me as I explained the situation, including Gabby's connection to David Stevens and the crime scene.

"Her fingerprints were found at the scene?" Jackson asked.

"According to her mom, yes, and remember the detectives showed us her photo." The clock showed it was ten minutes until four, so I went outside to wait for Gabby.

Jackson's office is in an older art deco building in downtown Portland. A coffee shop is in the lobby with a tiny storefront on the sidewalk, and I made a mental note to bring them a sample of coffee beans. I needed to focus on Gabby now and worry about coffee later.

Thirty minutes after four, I was still alone and ready to go inside. But Gabby was walking in my direction. Her steps paused when she saw me. Like she was afraid of me.

She stared at the ground as she walked up. She was in the same black long-sleeved T-shirt from this morning. My breath caught when I saw her face.

"Jackson's office is on the fourth floor. He has snacks and drinks inside if you're hungry," I said, breaking out the same voice as the one I used to coax Bentley to do something scary, like walk past a cat.

As we rode the rickety elevator, which groans like it's not going to make it to the next floor, I tried to examine her without staring at her black eye. Was this why she'd held her face this morning before the explosion? Did I want to know the story of how she'd gotten the injury? She kept pulling the sleeves of her shirt down over her hands, and it was too warm to wear long sleeves. What was she hiding?

Her steps faltered as we stepped out of the elevator. I touched her gently on the upper arm, making her flinch. "It'll be okay."

After I ushered Gabby into Jackson's office, I brought her a can of soda, along with a packet of almonds and dried fruit leather from the stash of client snacks. I'd pocketed one of the chocolate bars in case the situation turned south and I needed ammunition to catch Gabby's attention.

As Gabby tore into the snacks, Jackson looked my way. The meeting was my rodeo. Time to get started.

"Gabby, do you know what happened to David Stevens?"

Gabby stopped chewing and looked at me. She took a swig of soda. She finally asked, "Why do you want to know?"

"I'm concerned."

Gabby stood up. "You said I could get into a shelter without telling my mom. It's the only reason I came."

"We can get you into a shelter," Jackson said. "What, exactly, do you want?"

Gabby looked from Jackson to me and sat down again. "I want to sleep for an entire night."

Jackson's smile made him feel like an oasis of calm. Gabby looked at him warily as he spoke. "I called a friend at a local teen shelter, and she's found a bed for you. She'll be here at five thirty to pick you up. You'll be able to take a shower, eat dinner, and get a good night's sleep. After that, you'll need to work with the counselors on-site to figure out your next steps."

"Can I get eman . . . emack . . ."

"Emancipated? It's unlikely since you don't have a job or the financial ability to care for yourself. But the shelter's counselor will help you navigate your options, whether it's reunification with your parents or foster care."

"David Stevens was my biological father, and he was loaded."

Jackson blinked at the undercurrent of anger in Gabby's voice.

"In your case, provided I have all of the details right, your adoptive parents will most likely become involved."

Gabby's nostrils flared.

"You have the right to be angry with them for not telling you about the adoption," I said. "But I met your mother. She's desperate to find you."

Gabby shook her head. "There's no way she wants me back."

"Why do you think this?"

Gabby covered her eyes. "When I found out Uncle David was my biological father, I stole the emergency fund my parents keep in their bedroom and caught a train here. My friend Becca gave me her driver's license ages ago and claimed she lost it and got a new one, since we look similar, but she's eighteen. When I got to Uncle David's, he wasn't home, so I waited on his front step. When he came home, I asked him if he was my dad, he told me to get lost. I wasn't his daughter. He'd never wanted me. He called me a stupid little girl."

"He didn't invite you inside?" Jackson asked. I read the emotions beneath the surface of his face. He was angry on Gabby's behalf. But he wasn't surprised. Not with what he'd seen over the years. I wished we could both feel shocked. I understood Gabby's sense of betrayal, remembering how shattered I'd felt at thirteen.

"He slammed the door in my face." Gabby narrowed her eyes at the memory.

"What happened next?" I asked.

"I didn't know what to do. I couldn't go back to Seattle. So I checked into a motel I'd seen on the bus ride to David's house."

"Using Becca's ID?" I asked.

"Yes. But I only had enough money for a few nights. I was fig-uring out what to do when I met Tommy, and he said I could stay with him. He acted sweet, at least at first."

"Where'd you stay?"

"We crashed at his friend's house for a while, but we had to move. Some of Tommy's friends had taken over an abandoned ware-

house, and we stayed there for a while. Then we moved to a camp in
a park. The police made us move, and we stayed in a different camp
for a while, then in a van, before we moved back to the first camp."

"Are you still with Tommy?" Jackson asked nonchalantly.

Gabby bit her lip and stared at the ground. "I don't want to be
his girlfriend anymore," she whispered.

Jackson glanced my way and mouthed, *No more Tommy,* and I
nodded. Pushing her, at least now, wouldn't help. But my stomach
felt nauseous as I thought of possible details to fill in the blanks of her
story.

The image of a can of spray paint flashed through my mind.
"Were you part of the crowd protesting the new development across
the street from my coffee cart?"

She nodded. "But I didn't want Uncle David to see me. I hate
him. I want his development to fail."

"Did you start to write something in spray paint in front of it?"

"How did you know?" Gabby's voice went high-pitched, and
her hands fluttered. She twitched in the direction of the door.

"Logical guess. I saw the spray-paint can when I found David's
body, and the police found your fingerprints at the crime scene," I
said, hoping she'd settle down. Stop panicking. Figure out she was
safe.

"I was spray-painting when someone opened the gate to your
lot, so I ducked out of sight. I heard voices, and a scream. I was
scared, but I had to see if I could do something."

"What happened next?"

"Uncle David was lying on the ground. I tried to help him. He
was gurgling and covered in blood. I looked in his pocket for his
phone to call for help. But there was someone behind me. I ran."

"Did you see who was behind you?" I asked, studying Gabby. I
felt like she was mostly telling the truth, but something was off. She
was either lying or leaving out a crucial part of the story.

"I don't know who it was, and after I ran off, I was afraid to go
back to your cart. I didn't want the murderer to come after me. But
I knew it wasn't you. You were nice to me."

My internal meter continued to ping, telling me she was still mixing truth and lies. I didn't know where in her story to start picking to unravel fiction from reality.

"What about the explosion? I saw you running away."

Gabby hunched even more, and her eyes memorized the floor. "I saw you too. Tommy was trying to start the fire. We were getting back at the construction site for displacing people. But I made Tommy mad, and he punched me. It hurt. He lit the fire and punched me again. He ran off. I ditched him, but he's looking for me."

It was hard to breathe as I stared at her. She was too young for any of this.

Gabby turned and looked at Jackson. "What happens now?"

Jackson glanced at his watch. "My social worker friend will be here any minute. You'll be able to clean up and sleep overnight. They'll help you figure out your next steps."

A low voice murmured outside the door, but I couldn't make out the words. The door swung open.

Jackson jumped to his feet immediately. "This is a private meeting."

Detective Will stood in the doorway. He handed over a piece of paper. "I have an arrest warrant for Gabrielle Blake."

Gabby swung to face me. "You gave me up? You promised you'd help me!" she shrieked.

My stomach felt like a horse kicked it. "I didn't give you up. I swear." I kept my gaze level on Gabby, but from the way she glared back she didn't believe me.

The uniformed officer handcuffed Gabby and started patting her down while reciting Gabby's Miranda rights. She pulled something out of Gabby's pocket.

"Detective," the officer said, and held it out. It was a dark leather wallet, way too luxurious for a street kid.

A satisfied look crossed the detective's face after he opened it. He glanced at Jackson. "Is this girl your client too? Care to explain why she has David Stevens's wallet on her?"

Jackson looked at Gabby, and she glared at him.

Jackson took a deep breath. "Gabby, don't say anything to the police. Do you understand? Not one word unless I'm with you. I'll follow you to the police station and be with you while you're questioned."

Gabby glared at me as the police officer marched her out. I felt like I'd ruined her life. Detective Will looked at me straight-faced for a moment before walking out the door, while Jackson grabbed his messenger bag in a rush and furiously power walked behind them.

Chapter 24

My stomach would unravel, dance a jig, and reform itself back into a knot as I waited for Jackson outside the police station. I had a bottle of water, but I couldn't drink anything.

Jackson finally came out. He saw me and headed my way. He sat down on my bench.

"What's happening?"

"She's being held." Jackson bit his lip.

"Could you get her out?" My fingernails bit into my palms, and I forced them to relax.

"But should I? What's her best option here? She doesn't want her parents to know what happened to her on the streets, but she never said her parents mistreated her."

"Do you think Tommy . . ."

"What?" Jackson asked, not making this easy for me.

"Pimped her out."

"Or he let his friends borrow her as a way to get shelter, food, beer, stuff like that. Something bad happened to Gabby. She needs counseling. Her parents need to hire a qualified criminal defense attorney for her because if she's charged with murder, she'll probably be tried as an adult. It looks bad. Her fingerprints are on the murder weapon. She was filmed using his credit card, so she must have stolen his wallet. The police will figure out she was at the construction site explosion."

I shivered, even though the evening was warm. "She said she looked for David's phone. She could've kept his wallet by accident."

"Or she meant to steal it. For now, Gabby will be held in juvenile detention. She'll be safe enough."

"How did the police know where to find her?"

"Good question. Did someone follow you? Or her? She's a murder suspect, after all. In the same crime you're mixed up in. And you dragged her into my office. I have other clients. Other things I needed to do today."

"I'm sorry helping out a teenage girl was too much to ask," I snapped back. My chin jutted out. Too many people had yelled at me today.

"You need to learn to think things through instead of jumping in." Jackson's voice had dropped into low fury. He stood up. "I need time."

Jackson stalked away without looking back.

Adrenaline coursed through me. I didn't want to go back to Jackson's and the room I paid for. Getting my own place should be first on my priority list. Even if it was a shoebox-size studio like Manny and Harley both rented. Everything was too much: my family wanted to treat me like a child they should protect, except when Jackson decided to lecture me about a standard, in his mind, I'd failed to achieve. I'd never be the sweet little sister Jackson could boss around.

Miles's house or the floor of Harley's studio were options since they'd let me crash at their places in the past. But neither sounded right, not today. There were other friends I could call. But there was another option. A better one.

I shoved down my pride and grabbed my phone. Good thing I know a guy.

The next morning, the siren call of coffee convinced me to meet the day. I padded out in bare feet, ready for a leisurely Saturday.

"Good morning, Pumpkin."

"Morning, Dad."

"Coffee is on the counter."

I followed the smell, although I could have found my way into the kitchen with my eyes blindfolded. My dad's bungalow pretty much looks the same as it did when I was thirteen. All pine or blue plaid furniture, like he'd gotten a sweetheart deal on the whole lot. The only thing that had changed over the years was the TV, which was now a flat-screen.

After a brief consideration, I pulled the STATE SPELLING CHIMP coffee cup out of the cupboard, where it sat among an assortment of novelty mugs. The collection of cups were the types given as gag gifts that are donated to Goodwill six months later, with their forever home destined to be my dad's cupboard.

But, in one of the similarities that show we're related, my dad had ditched his drip coffee maker. I'd given him my favorite pour-over cone for Christmas two years ago, and it was sitting in the drying rack, although today he'd used a French press. The basket of the burr grinder I'd given him three years ago was dirty with grounds, so he'd taken to grinding coffee beans fresh.

The care he took with his coffee showed in the taste of the dark French roast, which is another preference we have in common. A few sips and I started to feel like I'd be able to face the day after all. I realized he was using my beans. He'd brewed the Twelve Bridge Racer I'd given him.

"You want to talk?"

I jumped. I hadn't realized my father had followed me into the kitchen. He sat down at the table and put a newspaper in front of him, which he left folded. He looked at me.

I slid into the chair across from him.

"Nothing feels right. Jackson's angry at me. . . ." I told Dad the story. He listened without interrupting, although I could see him tallying up questions from the way he double-blinked a few times.

"Also . . ." I looked down at the table.

"What?"

"My mother called me."

A quick glance showed he was surprised, which quickly slid into a closed-off expression. He shut his eyes for a second. "What does she want?"

"She offered to fund Ground Rules."

He shook his head. "Why'd didn't you hang up when you realized she was on the other side of the call?"

I shook my head, leaving the answer unspoken. Because she's my mother. I long ago recognized there's a small part of me that hopes we could have a relationship. Although I also know there's a higher likelihood I'd turn into a superhero after being struck by lightning. But a small part of me flickers with optimism, and that's the same spot that keeps being devastated, time and time again, so I kept that spot hidden. As if she'd be able to see it through the eyes of strangers and use it to manipulate me. Like she's an evil Santa Claus, always watching.

Gabby must feel the same way about her mom, the deep-seated love, and from what I'd seen, her mother would do anything to get her daughter back. Mary's hope for the future could help her daughter. Fingers crossed that Gabby would be able to see it.

"What are you going to do?" my dad asked

"You mean other than ignore my mother's demands? I'm not stupid."

We sat in quiet for a while as clouds invaded the horizon, elbowing out the morning sun. We were due for rain.

"Call me if your mother contacts you again."

I nodded and took another sip of coffee. "I can do that."

The conversation slid back to normal, and my dad made scrambled eggs.

"I have to ask," my dad said. "Are you seeing anyone? You haven't mentioned dating for a while."

"Don't tell me your grandkid clock is ticking or something. 'Cause that'd freak me out." I eyed my dad, wondering about his game plan.

"I'm curious 'cause I'm going to be amused if you're single, and I have a third date coming up."

Third date? He looked faintly embarrassed as he refilled his coffee mug from the French press. And third? Three? He hadn't mentioned the first two. "You can't complain about me being the dark horse. Go on, spill."

"She's a regular with my weekday cycle group. She's a huge coffee fan, so if you ever meet, you'll have things to talk about."

Other than talking about him. I smothered a smile. "Kids?"

"Two boys, both in college. If that was a backhanded way of asking her age, she's a year older than me."

I hid a smile. "Men older than you have fathered babies."

He winced. "Pretty sure my baby days are over."

A terrifying image of my father and me having kids at the same time passed through my mind, not that I had any immediate plans. This was a subject to never, ever, bring up again. "I hope the date works out."

His last few relationships had slowly fizzled out. But he and this woman sharing his favorite hobby bode well.

"Let's not get ahead of ourselves. Do you think taking her to a stand-up paddleboard class on the Willamette River sounds good? We can check out the new brewery on East Burnside afterward. If she's paddleboarded before, there's a SUP-yoga class we could take instead."

Ah, he'd revealed the real reason for bringing this up: date advice. I hid a smile. "If she bikes with you, I'd guess she's athletic. So SUP or SUP yoga sounds great, as long as she knows how to swim."

"Good point. I should figure out a plan B if she doesn't swim. Like the hike up to Pittock Mansion."

"Consider coming up with a nonexercise-oriented plan too in case she wants to do something more relaxed." And wants an opportunity to show you what she looks like dressed up, and vice versa.

As we discussed date ideas, I realized I hadn't been out on a second, let alone third, date for years. Although something told me a second date with Bax would happen, and the idea both freaked me out and excited me. Although he was scheduling it around when he had custody of his son, so potential land mines were already popping up. But those could be navigated. Knowing my father had a more active dating life made me tempted to bang my head against a table. A desire I'd felt too often in the past few weeks.

The exterior of my father's bungalow reminds me of him. It's straightforward, not flashy, painted a crisp green with white trim. The front yard is cared for, with a few rhododendrons and a lone wisteria, but the backyard, which isn't visible from the street, is a cornucopia of colors. Roses, lilies, azaleas, camellias, plus pots of herbs and three raised vegetable beds fill the space.

I'd left my bike in the detached garage last night, and I headed out with a mission. It was bike heaven in there. He'd mounted his road and mountain bikes on hooks along one wall, with none of them touching the ground, to keep the concrete from drawing moisture out of the tires. I mentally recited my dad's lecture about dry rot and premature tire aging.

He'd dedicated another wall to every sort of tool or product a person could desire when working on a bicycle. After setting my bike on a workstand, I grabbed a rag and can of chain lube from a cubby.

I took a moment to spread lubrication between the side plates and under the center roller of my bike's chain. I tried to remember if there was upkeep I'd meant to do to it. Something told me I needed to be ready for anything.

"I'm glad to see you're keeping up with maintenance," my dad said from the doorway.

I jumped. "As you've pointed out, it's cheaper to keep my bike in good shape than it is to try to fix a problem later."

"This was a good find," Dad said as he looked over my bicycle, which I'd found online for a significant discount. "Are you ready for spur-of-the-moment repairs if you break down on the road?" My father leaned against the workbench on the wall.

"I always carry the multitool you gave me, a spare tube, and a small pump when I ride." The gear took up space in my bag, and I couldn't leave it strapped in a smaller sack on my bike 'cause it would be stolen if left unattended. So I dealt with having half of my messenger bag full of just-in-case tools.

"I'd hate for you to end up stranded on the road."

"Luckily I can always call you."

"There's something we need to talk about." The serious undercurrent in my dad's voice made my hands still. "The more I think about it, the more I'm concerned about your mother contacting you."

"You said so earlier." My eyes went back to my bike, but my hands were still.

"She'll contact you again, and we need to be ready. Do you think it's chance one of the men she scammed ended up dead outside your cart?"

"Uncle Jimmy came to the same conclusion." I made eye contact with my dad. "What do you have in mind?"

We made plans, which helped quiet down some of the uneasiness flowing through me. But stress ate away at me. Something needed to break soon, else I'd end up in a thousand pieces.

Chapter 25

My father left to run errands, and I needed to figure out what to do with my day off. Try to recharge and ignore the weight of David Stevens's death hanging over my life. But my phone dinged.

Text from Zarek: *Someone vandalized your cart. Call me for more details if you want.*

I responded back, *On my way.*

After I wheeled my bike out of the garage, I texted *Thank you* to Zarek and headed to the carts. Even though it was overcast, it hadn't started raining yet.

Most of the carts were open when I rolled to a stop in the Rail Yard, and I wondered again how Zarek managed to work seven days a week. We'd talked about Harley opening Ground Rules on Saturday mornings, or continuing to stay open when a band was on-site, but a weekday-only business made sense while the company was the two of us. If we opened a brick-and-mortar shop, we'd need to hire employees. The thought of managing a staff made my heart pound and my palms feel sweaty.

I told myself to buck up and check out what had happened to Ground Rules, although I wanted to stay at the entrance of the Rail Yard and pretend my only concern was being lucky enough to be able to afford to hire employees.

The cart's door was broken into two pieces, and inside, bags of supplies were sliced open. Spilled coffee beans covered the floor, along with raw and white sugar.

Anger coursed through me, making my hands shake. It took me a few tries, but I dialed the police, then texted Harley and told her what had happened and said I was taking care of everything. I called Uncle Jimmy as a bleak feeling filled me, starting from my toes and working its way upward, infiltrating my hands, and making my eyes burn.

The uniformed police officer who responded didn't take me, or the cart, too seriously and acted as if this were a simple break-in. "Whoever burglarized your cart was probably looking for your cash-box and anything valuable." He looked young, like he'd only been on the force a few years. "I'll get you a copy of the report so you can make an insurance claim."

He told me I could start cleaning up the cart and left. I leaned against a picnic table, not sitting or standing, 'cause that felt like my life right now. Like I was stuck between multiple planes. My phone dinged. Uncle Jimmy. *Miles en route. Stay safe.*

Tell him to bring a new door, I texted back.

One of my regulars stood outside the cart, watching me lug out a garbage bag of debris. On my way back from the dumpster he held up his hand to stop me.

"We'll be open again on Monday," I said.

"What happened?"

"Someone vandalized the cart."

"Stupid tweakers. We can't leave anything outside without some-one stealing it."

"Luckily the damage isn't too bad."

He promised he'd be back on Monday. He walked in the direc-tion of the Déjà Brew beer cart.

When I turned back and looked at my cart, I thought about how we'd only been open for business for a few weeks and been forced to close because of David's death, and now petty vandalism. Although we weren't supposed to be open today, so maybe I was feeling overly dramatic since it was costing me a day off and not a workday. But this couldn't be a good omen. My teeth gritted. The break-in had a personal feel.

Foster walked by, his dreads pulled back in a red bandanna. His glare slid into a gloat.

"What's your problem?" I growled at him.

His upper lip curled up. "As a believer in karma, I love seeing it in action. Maybe you'll be hit by a plague of locusts next."

I wished his plague of locusts would descend and chew off his stupid dreadlocks.

"Did you say that when your cart was forced to close? When friends have personal drama, do you taunt them about karma?"

His eyes narrowed. Foster's nostrils flared as he stepped up to me. "Are you saying my kid deserved to break his arm?"

"Only a monster would say that." I squared my shoulders.

As Foster took a half step back, Adam from the Hangry Hippo cart said, "Everything okay here?"

I kept my gaze level. "Foster was just leaving."

Adam stood with me as Foster marched back to Fala-Awesome. "Foster can be a real jerk. I know we should be sympathetic because he's faced a lot of challenges, but he just rubs me the wrong way."

"Challenges?" I asked as Adam's wife, Carolyn, walked up.

"He was in jail for a while, and someone loaned him money to start his food cart 'cause it's hard for ex-cons to find jobs."

"You talking about Foster?" Carolyn asked.

"What'd he do?" I asked.

"I heard he burglarized houses," Adam said.

My brain froze for a moment. If he'd burglarized houses, he could've picked the lock to my cart, the way someone had done the night David Stevens died.

"That's not what I heard," Carolyn said. "It was some sort of drug charge. Meth, maybe."

More drug deals. I'd have to find out Foster's last name and look him up to see which story, if either, was true.

"What was Foster's cart named?" I asked casually. Between social media and business records, I could figure out his last name if I knew.

"Frankly Good," Carolyn said.

I looked across the street, trying to remember the old carts. "What did he serve? I'm trying to remember it."

"Corn dogs and hot dogs, and he'd expanded into a variety of sausages before he closed," Adam said.

"Plus limeade," Carolyn said.

When I got home, I'd research Foster. But I should embrace the now since Carolyn and Adam were standing with me. Maybe they'd had a reason to hate David Stevens. Maybe their cutesy finish-each-other's-sentences act was a charade.

"How did you decide to open the Hangry Hippo?" Their cart looked sharper than most, with a cartoon hippo holding a fork painted on the shiny black truck.

"It's a passion project for us. We also work for my family's winery," Carolyn said. "After everything that's happened, we'll probably move the cart next to the winery for special events. One of our neighbors owns an estate brewery, and he invited us to serve food on the weekends."

"If we leave after this summer, be ready for the fight about which cart takes our place," Adam said.

Carolyn laced her hands in front of her stomach. "Sometimes I feel guilty that we're here when the other carts lost their leases, but—"

"That's just the way the cookie crumbles," Adam said.

"You don't have anything to apologize for," I said.

"Oh, a customer!" Carolyn darted to the Hangry Hippo. Her flowered skirt swirled around her.

"Let us know if you need anything while you fix this," Adam said. He followed her.

I sat down on the picnic table by my cart and searched for Foster and his cart online. His Yelp reviews were about seventy percent positive.

I read one of the negative reviews: *I ordered a German bratwurst with mustard, and it came with ketchup. I asked for a new bun—I was fine wiping the ketchup off—and the guy with dreads working the cart flipped out on me, saying I'd gotten what I wanted and to leave. I'M NEVER OR-DERING FROM THIS CART AGAIN.*

A negative couple reviews also mentioned Foster's temper. I started to feel cold.

After a few minutes of internet sleuthing, I found out his last name: Armstrong. But Miles showed up with a toolbox and a box of spare parts, including a brand-new lock and dead bolt, so I slid my phone back into my pocket.

Miles gave me a quick hug and then surveyed the damage to the coffee cart. He stepped inside and looked around. "They didn't damage anything, other than the door and doorframe."

I helped him carry the new door over, along with some two-by-fours so we could reframe the doorframe. He'd thought to buy a new dead bolt when he'd picked up the door.

As we dismantled the part of the old door still attached to the cart with hinges, shivers on my back told me someone was watching me. When I glanced behind me, I froze. Detective Will stood in the entrance of the Rail Yard. He motioned me over. I motioned for him to join us and turned back to my construction project.

"The detective investigating David Stevens's murder is here," I told Miles. We worked quietly as the detective walked up, focused on repairing the doorframe.

"Third time something funky has happened here in a week," the detective said.

"Good day to you too, Detective." I glanced at him. He was straight-faced like usual.

I turned back to helping Miles reframe the door. The detective looked past us into the cart.

"Would you like to check out the inside?" I offered. Miles and I quit working and let the detective scope out the interior of the cart.

"Not much damage," he said.

"They sliced into everything packaged, like coffee beans and sugar. I took photos."

"What did you keep in your cart? It sounds like your alleged vandal was looking for something."

The word *alleged* made my spine straighten, but I made my voice sound bored. "As I've told you before, I take the tablet home with me and never leave cash in the cart. Some of the coffee equipment is expensive, but it might not be obvious to someone outside the industry."

"Do you keep drugs or anything illegal in the cart?"

I glared at him. "No."

"Because if David Stevens came here to get proof of an illegal act, you selling drugs out of your cart would be worth setting up a camera to catch."

"If you have questions for me, set up an appointment with my attorney." I turned my back to the detective. But his words made me pause. Someone was selling drugs out of the Rail Yard. I'd stolen one of his drops. Had I been seen at the Little Lending Library? But perhaps they thought I'd hidden them in the cart.

I should talk to Macie. But I had to finish here first.

The detective watched us for a few more minutes. Miles and I worked quietly, only talking when he asked me to hand him a tool or asked me to do something, like hold a two-by-four in place.

Finally, Detective Will walked away.

Miles looked up at me from where he was nailing in the new doorframe. "Bug, I didn't know you were a criminal mastermind."

"According to the detective, I'm all shades of evil. Just wait for the rise of my criminal empire, fueled by dark roasts as black as my soul."

We'd finished replacing the door when Zarek brought over a couple of falafel sandwiches for Miles and me.

"I'm sorry I went off on you yesterday. I was a jerk," Zarek said. "I'm sorry about your door too."

Macie walked past us and waved goodbye, still wearing an apron. Today's was red-and-white-striped with a kitten on the front. Guess this won't be the day I tackle her to discuss her nephew's drug empire.

"This is good," Miles said after downing the first half of his falafel sandwich. I had to agree. Zarek fried the falafel perfectly, but the fresh cabbage slaw and, more important, the zhug sauce—a spicy green mix of cilantro, peppers, garlic, cardamom, olive oil, and a few notes I needed to taste a few more times to identify—made it special.

"The sauce is world-shattering awesome," I added. But my body couldn't relax with Zarek standing nearby. Could he be the villain in this charade? For all I knew, he'd broken into my cart for fun. Or revenge for not telling him I was related to Uncle Jimmy.

"One of my old roommates taught me how to make zhug sauce. I tweaked the recipe a bit," Zarek said.

As we chatted, I wished I could shake today off. But my life felt heavy. Gabby in jail, the cart vandalized, knowing the police weren't any closer to solving David Stevens's murder, fighting with my brother.

Zarek returned to his cart, which Foster had been running while Zarek talked to us.

Foster. He hated Ground Rules in principle. What did he think about the guy who'd shattered his dream? Would he have killed David Stevens for kicking him out of the lot across the street? Did he and David end up at my cart at the same time with tragic consequences?

"I'm driving to the Tav. Want a ride? Uncle Jimmy requests your presence," Miles said after we'd packed the tools we'd used into a locked bin in the back of his truck and cleaned up our impromptu construction site. The new doorframe needed paint, so that'd be a job on my next day off. Or I'd knock it out after work one day.

"Sure, I'll ride with you." After double-checking the coffee cart was secure, I loaded my bike into Miles's truck, and we took off. As we drove away, the rain that had been threatening to pour all day fell from the sky, washing away the summer dust. Maybe it would wash away a few sins as well.

Chapter 26

Miles told the bartender at the Tav to pour me a shot of the new bourbon they'd added to the menu. I sniffed it, the scent of warm caramel and toasted vanilla warming a part of me that felt cold, although I wondered if it was too early in the day to drink. A glance at the clock reminded me it was later than I thought. Drinking at 5:00 p.m. is fine.

Plus it's my day off. I took a sip, the oaky flavor coating my tongue with a lingering note of cherry. It was smooth. I felt compelled to take another sip.

My gaze wandered to the stained-glass windows. The one to the far right has the image of a tiger. Of the windows, it's always felt the least compelling to me.

I paused. The tiger is the demon we all face. We all make choices, like the lady in the center panel motioning to two doors. I froze. The windows showed the Lady and the Tiger. The lady in the center window is a princess, and her lover has been sentenced to open one of two doors as punishment for daring to lift his eyes to her. If he opens the one with the tiger, he'll be mauled. If he opens the door with the girl, he'll be married to her. The princess knows which door has the tiger, and which leads to a beautiful girl. Will she let her lover die so no one else can have him, or will she spare his life and see him married to another?

None of the panels showed the lover. But that's because the viewer is the lover, looking at the scene, determining which door to open. Which choice to make. For most people that come into their bar, they're deciding how long they're going to spend at the temple of Dionysus.

A different set of decisions weighed on me. The rocks glass of bourbon wasn't my dilemma. But most of the choices I'd made since finding David Stevens felt like they had the potential to rip me apart. I'd been poking the tiger for days.

"Good stuff, huh?" Miles slid onto the stool next to me. He held a shot of the same bourbon.

"Don't tell me you guys are going upscale."

"Never. But we can mark this up for the Pearl District residents."

"Pearl-ites?" I offered.

"Pearlians?"

"P-Yuppies?" My body felt heavy as I bantered with Miles. After a few minutes, he left to chat with a friend. I sat at the bar, lost in my thoughts, occasionally talking with a regular who knew I was Uncle Jimmy's niece. Everyone in my life knew me in relation to someone else. No one saw me as the default or the reference point.

If David's death was a message, my family connections might have been responsible. Or perhaps his own actions had inspired his murder if Gabby killed him. She was lying about something that happened when David died, although I couldn't see her as a killer.

My shoulders tensed up when I saw a face heading my way. I turned and looked down at my glass, which held my third shot of bourbon. I should order food. But corn dog nuggets, while the solution for many problems, didn't feel like they'd make a dent in today's troubles.

"Miles said I should give you a lift home." Jackson leaned against the bar next to me. When the bartender came by, he ordered a club soda.

Jackson sipped his water and glanced around the bar. When his gaze traveled back my way, I looked forward again.

"You angry with me?"

"You angry with me?" I echoed back, sounding ten years old. Next, I was going to start making comments about me being rubber, and him being glue.

"I'm sorry I was a prick yesterday. I was tired. Frustrated. Hungry. Bad combo since I went full-on hangry on you. But you didn't have to crash elsewhere. If anything, you should've given me the silent treatment at home."

"Hmm" was all I said.

"Slamming doors was always your favorite. Or you could've taken up tap dancing in the attic."

"Ummm."

"Or you wanted to see your dad for the night."

Of course, he saw one of the truths of the matter. Gabby, and other street kids, always made me wonder what could've happened if I hadn't fallen in with Manny and his mom. I'd been lucky, especially since an older guy had been hassling me when Manny's mom hustled me away and then introduced herself since she'd seen me leaving the shelter when she'd stopped by for breakfast. Or stupid, since I should've known from the beginning my mother hadn't left Uncle Jimmy's business card by chance.

Jackson bumped me gently with his shoulder. "I'll give you a ride home when you're ready to go."

"Must be an exciting Saturday night for you."

Jackson put a page of the local newspaper in front of me. "Not as exciting as your life. How come you didn't tell me you got hitched?"

I groaned, seeing a photo of me in a wedding dress next to a guy in a tux, sporting a mustache that was half-cartoon villain, half–Hercule Poirot. My photographer friend, Erin, hadn't told me these would be in the paper when she'd coaxed me into modeling for her when her professional model canceled last minute. My eyes read the words in the ad: *Portland's Bridal Show.*

"I always think of models as being tall," Jackson said.

"Erin strikes again. She didn't tell me any of the photos would be used for the bridal show."

"They're on a billboard too. I saw one on my way over. I was tempted to stop in the middle of traffic to take a photo."

I wanted to bang my head against the counter at the thought of seeing this version of myself around town. "She told me it was for a local wedding shop's petite wedding-dress line. Erin made it sound like it would be in their look book, not splashed across billboards."

"It's a good photo. Balanced composition. You look beautiful."

"My groom was an absolute douche canoe." I glanced at the black-and-white photo printed in the paper. Me tied to train tracks and him twirling his 'stache would have been a better image, instead of us posed as if we'd tied the knot. I imagined our history: we'd fallen in love at a kombucha bar, bonding over our love of free-range seitan. I glanced up, and a woman walking through the bar made me pause instead of finishing my fake love story. What was Emma doing here?

Jackson followed my gaze. "Who's that?"

"A fellow food cart owner and David Stevens's ex-girlfriend. She claims she was backpacking the night he was murdered."

The woman next to us flinched at my words.

I stared at her. "Want to hear where we buried the body?"

She turned away, and Jackson laughed.

Emma did a lap around the bar and headed toward the door. But she changed courses when she saw me.

"Hi, Sage. Are you a regular here? I guess it's a family hangout for you."

"Something like that."

"Is your uncle here?"

A reflection in the mirror over the bar made me smile. "If you stick around, he's going to show up soon."

She looked at me with raised eyebrows. A voice from behind me said, "Hey, Bug," so she turned. I continued to face forward.

"Mr. Jones," Emma said. "I hoped to find you here."

"Hi, Emma," Uncle Jimmy put his hand on my shoulder. "Miles texted me—"

"Mr. Jones, I've heard about your new micro-restaurant development—"

Uncle Jimmy waved Emma off. "If you're interested in reserving a space, talk to me in six months."

"But that's after I'm supposed to sign a new lease for the Rail Yard. I thought I'd buy you a drink and we could—"

"This is my bar, so I don't need anyone to buy me drinks, and the micro-restaurant development isn't on tonight's agenda. Now, if you'll excuse me . . ." Uncle Jimmy put his hand under my elbow. I stood up, carrying my bourbon. His friends and regulars said hi, but he didn't stop until we were in the dinky office in the back of the bar.

I slouched in the guest seat, and Uncle Jimmy claimed the desk chair. Jackson leaned against the filing cabinet next to me. I wondered if the aroma of bourbon from the shots I'd sipped was infiltrating the room, permeating the air with notes of vanilla.

Maybe I was drunker than I thought.

"Tell me about today," Uncle Jimmy ordered.

"Miles already told you about it in detail." I took a sip of the bourbon.

"But I want to hear your perspective."

After I told my story, I zoned out as he and Jackson talked about the probability the break-in connected back to my mother. It felt unlikely to me, but I didn't bother to explain since they were off and running without my input. My thoughts felt fuzzy. I should tell them about Foster.

"I don't see what breaking into the cart accomplished," Jackson said. "David Stevens might have been a warning to one of us—you, Sage, our mother—but the different elements aren't fitting together."

"We're missing a piece of the puzzle." Uncle Jimmy tapped his fist against the desk.

They debated what happened from the beginning, and I started to nod off. Someone took the now-empty rocks glass from my fingers. I opened my eyes. Jackson.

"C'mon, let's go home."

I stood and followed him in the direction of the back door.

"Be sure to eat something," Uncle Jimmy said.

My words were sleepy. "I'm not a novice."

"Sure, tough girl," Jackson said. "We'll stop for pancakes on the way home."

Jackson's words made me smile because tonight, of any night, called for pancakes.

Sunday was a bust when I woke up with a headache and couldn't be bothered to move until afternoon. Bentley was entirely unsympathetic. I finally consented to take him for a walk around the neighborhood while Jackson was out grocery shopping. Bax checked in a few times by text, recapping his trip to the park with his son. We weren't anywhere close to the "meet a kid" level, but in my down state, I wondered if this was an omen. But I wrote my texts cheerful and with care since I also exchanged a few messages with Zarek and didn't want to mix the two up. All I needed was to make a date with Bax but accidentally text Zarek.

I finally did something I'd needed to do all day: I pulled out my laptop and searched for Foster's criminal record. When I was on the justice department's website, I searched for his name and received several hits. Multiple traffic citations.

Wait a minute. Felony. I clicked the link. Class A felony for delivery of drugs within a thousand feet of a school. I returned to the previous page and found he was convicted of a Class C felony for burglary. Both convictions were about a decade ago. He would've been in his early twenties at the oldest.

Provided it was the right Foster Armstrong.

The records didn't go in depth into details, other than Foster had been released from jail. I searched a couple of newspaper archives but didn't find anything relevant. I'd have to go directly to the source and ask.

In the late afternoon, I met Harley on a street away from the Rail Yard. The back seat of her car held bags of coffee beans and sugar. I gave her a new key to the cart since we'd changed the lock.

"I can't believe someone broke in." Harley clenched her hands as she looked at the new door. The unpainted wood of the doorframe stood out next to the teal cart.

Looking at it made me feel angry all over again like I'd been attacked, not just our cart.

Diego walked by, carrying plates. "We were sorry to hear about your cart!" he hollered.

The noise made my head ache again. I rubbed my forehead.

"You okay?" Harley asked.

"I'm not jazzed about working tonight."

"Go home. I've got this. I don't have anything important planned."

"You sure?"

"Of course. This is our joint business, and you're not the only one with barista skills. Besides, based on last week's take, it'll be slow. As we talked about, it's not worth opening for the music nights."

"If we're open all weekend, it might work." Something to think about when I didn't feel weighed down by 80 million other decisions. I leaned over to pick up my bag. When I straightened up, taking a moment to stretch, I noticed Emma talking with an older man in a black bowling shirt. Her hand was on his arm. Emma looked my way, and when she caught my eye, she turned away. The man glanced at Ground Rules, but followed Emma as she retreated back into her chicken-and-jojos cart.

Zarek walked over as I started to leave. "You doing okay? You look off." Zarek stood close to me. He'd been nice yesterday, but I couldn't forget his yelling at me about Uncle Jimmy. What game was he playing?

"My head's killing me. I'm heading home."

"That's too bad. I was going to ask if you wanted to hang out tonight. Foster can close the cart."

Was Zarek asking because he was interested in me, or because he saw me as a route into one of Uncle Jimmy's developments? But I kept the smile on my face from faltering. Foster glanced our way, and when we made eye contact, he pulled his head back into the cart.

"I've heard sketchy stuff about Foster. Like he was in prison."

Zarek's mouth scrunched to the side. "Who's been gossiping about Foster?"

"People. Is it true? You're protective of him, so I figured if anyone knew the truth, it'd be you."

Zarek looked at the ground. He rubbed the toe of his sneaker against a small hole in the blacktop. "Foster and I were friends growing up. We played soccer together on the same club team, and he was offered a scholarship to play for UCLA. But he was arrested for selling pot not long after high school graduation. He lost his scholarship. His parents kicked him out, and he was arrested for breaking into their house to get his stuff. They pressed charges."

"That's rough."

"I've always felt bad for him 'cause he lost everything. He's still bitter about it. His food cart was doing well, but being thrown back into the job market again has been terrible. I'd help him more if I could, 'cause he's feeling hopeless right now. His girlfriend's been amazing through this, thankfully."

Being in Foster's situation would be terrible, but suspicion continued to build in me. Did Foster see David Stevens as ruining his life again? Was Foster angry enough to have killed David?

"So, about tonight?" Zarek grinned at me. But the tinge of sadness in his grin spoke to me. It was hard to be happy after talking about something so dark.

"Rain check."

"I'll hold you to that." Zarek grinned again for a second before trotting back to his cart.

Harley stepped out of Ground Rules. "You have all of the luck."

"The jury's out."

I split. I needed to figure out what was going on before I got tired and blew up all of my friendships.

Chapter 27

A typical Monday morning was a relief after yesterday. Harley showed up with supplies and helped during the rush. She left to drop off samples at a few shops, including the one in Jackson's building. Since it was quiet, I called Gabby's mother, Mary Stevens Blake, and asked if she would add me to her daughter's list of approved visitors at juvenile hall.

"Jackson is your brother, correct?" Mary asked. "I met him yesterday morning when I drove down. He's doing a good job for Gabby."

"I'm sorry she's in juvie."

"At least I know where she is. I know our reunion isn't going to be easy."

"I remember being an angry teen. Just be there, no matter how much she pushes you away." I stopped myself from adding, *And, hopefully, I'm right and Gabby didn't kill her biological father.* Because Gabby knew something, even if she was innocent.

"That's what I'm planning to do. I'm already researching therapists in Seattle."

After a few minutes, we hung up. I geared up for the lunchtime coffee rush. Several people had recognized me from the billboard and online ads for the bridal show and assumed I knew all about it.

"Honestly, I have no idea which vendors will be there." I took a drink order from a woman who'd gotten engaged yesterday. "But check out their website. My friend Erin's an awesome photographer if you need photos."

Bax walked up while I was making a mocha, and my heart rate sped up a few beats, but my hands didn't waver even though they felt shaky. He chuckled as he listened in on my bridal-shower conversation with the customer. The woman finally walked away, carrying her skinny mocha, after I'd written down Erin's website for her.

Bax said, "I asked if you were married and you said no."

"Ha ha ha," I said sarcastically. I smiled in spite of myself.

"Do you model often?"

"Just when my friend needs a short blond girl. Although if I'd known the photos were going to be splashed everywhere, I would've upped my rates. I did the shoot with the wedding dress in exchange for lunch."

"Sounds like a reasonable rate to me."

I laughed. "The original model came down with chicken pox, so the photographer begged me. She's been a good friend for years so I couldn't say no."

"Would you be up for posing for referential sketches? I'm working on a rough idea for a video game. Your rates sound reasonable and I'll happily buy you dinner in exchange."

I laughed. "What type of dinner are we talking about?"

"Something special, obviously."

Zarek walked into the Rail Yard, pushing a couple of boxes on a handcart. Zarek's eyes narrowed when he glanced at Bax, but he powered by. Bax didn't notice.

All I needed was boy drama at work. But I told myself to focus on the charmer who'd ordered a pour-over, which I took extra care to make.

"Seriously, take this." He tried to shove a $5 bill my direction.

"Nope. On the house."

He studied my face, still holding the five. "How about I buy you dinner later this week? My son goes back to his mom tomorrow, so I'll have more free time. How about Thursday evening?"

"Works for me."

Bax slid the money into his pocket. "Tell you what. I'll pick you up at seven on Thursday."

"Any details I should know? Do I need any special shoes?" All I needed was for him to take us on a romantic outing through Forest Park while I tottered around on adorable sandals impossible to walk in due to their sky-high wedge.

"Look cute."

"Nothing more?"

Two men walked up, so Bax shot me a knowing grin and picked up his coffee. He sauntered off. I laughed and made a couple more coffee drinks.

By the time I'd finished at the cart, checked in at the warehouse, and worked with Harley for a while, it was about time for the visiting hours at the local juvenile hall.

True to her word, Mary had added me to Gabby's approved visitor list. A juvenile hall guard led me to a room filled with tables. I sat, waiting for Gabby to be brought out.

Gabby's footsteps slowed when a guard brought her into the room. She stared at me like I was a coiled snake, ready to strike. But her eyes looked more spirited than before. Her brown hair was shiny and clean, as was her orange jumpsuit. She sat down across from me.

"How are you doing?"

"Why do you want to know? You put me here." I realized what was different: she'd lost her aura of defeat. She was ready to do battle once she decided which direction to charge.

"I swear I didn't tell the police where you were."

"Why are you here?" Gabby's eyes were fixated on the table between us. She crossed her arms over her chest.

"I know you're not telling me something about what happened the night your biological father died. I promise I'll help you get out of here if you stop holding back."

She looked at the table for a minute before making eye contact with me. "Uncle David was arguing with a woman. I didn't see her and couldn't hear the words, but the voice was female."

Pieces fell into place in the puzzle in my mind, although I was still trying to make out the pattern. Gabby had been afraid I was the woman. It was logical, considering where David had died, and how I'd gone looking for Gabby afterward. This would clear Foster, although he still felt like the best suspect to me.

But who would have visited the Rail Yard that late at night, after Zarek and I had locked it up? Emma? She'd been dating David Stevens. Did she kill him and split town? Take off for a few days to settle her nerves until she came back to play the grieving ex?

"Are you going to go now? You've gotten what you wanted." Gabby crossed her arms over her chest and slumped back in her chair.

"Do you want me to leave? Or you can tell me about your day. Your choice." The signs said no touching else I would have patted her hand. All I could do was layer an understanding note into my voice.

"I don't know what to do. Should I agree to go back to Seattle if I'm not charged with a crime here?" Confusion and despair were written all over her face, but a tiny flicker of hope was behind her eyes. She looked stronger now, even if she was trapped in juvie.

"Why would you refuse to go back to Seattle?"

"I can't imagine walking back into my old school as if I'd been on vacation for a few months. Pretend I'm the same person I was. Try to be happy."

"I don't know Seattle well, but I'm positive there's more than one high school."

Gabby's eyes focused on my face. "What do you mean?"

"Ask your parents if they'll enroll you in a different school.

Maybe there's a private school you'd like. Or a magnet school or different public high school."

"Do you think my parents would let me do that?" The look of hope was stronger in Gabby's eyes. She started to look more like the girl in the photos her mother had shown me.

"It never hurts to ask."

As we talked, I thought about how I needed to solve David's murder to get Gabby out of here.

All of the signs pointed one way.

I needed to talk to Emma.

Working the coffee cart the next day felt wrong since Gabby was in jail and I had a lead to free her. I went about my usual life even if I wanted everything to come to a stop. I wanted to find the answers I was searching for.

When it was quitting time, I locked up the coffee cart. The Rail Yard was nearly deserted now, after a brisk lunch rush. An entire busload of tourists had shown up, excited to try their first Portland food carts. Emma sprinted by, yelling she was going to the grocery store since she'd run out of potatoes, which is fatal when your specialty is jojos.

Emma's leaving made me tighten my fingers and want to pummel something. I hadn't had a chance to talk to her about David Stevens. I'd been debating my approach, how I'd coax her into talking. She was a mom. Bringing up David's biological daughter sitting in the local juvenile hall might make her confess the truth.

Since I couldn't confront Emma, although I was going to pin her down as soon as she returned, now was as good of a time as any to talk with Macie about her nephew. I took a deep breath and squared my shoulders. I marched to 4 and 20 Blackbirds.

"Macie?" I climbed the three steps to her cart and poked my head in the entrance. She was sitting in the corner, next to the door. She held a dark pink cloth printed with pies and rolling pins, and she was embroidering something.

"Yes, dear?"

"Okay if I come in?" I walked in before she had a chance to respond. I leaned against the counter. "There's something I want to talk about with you, and, well, it's difficult."

"Okay." Macie continued to embroider, pulling a navy thread through the fabric. But I couldn't make out the shape of the image yet.

I took a deep breath. Now that I was here, I wished I were anywhere else. But she could lose her whole business if the police found out. "I saw your nephew selling drugs out of your cart."

Macie's hands paused. She looked at me with wide eyes. "For real? It's about time the kid showed some initiative."

"You . . ." My brain didn't know what words to form. Macie was okay with her nephew dealing drugs?

"This is the first time he's been proactive in his life. I'm proud."

"Well, as long as you know, I guess we're good." I took a step backward. My foot kicked a box of fabric squares, knocking it over.

Macie started to stand, but I waved her away. I knelt and picked up the box. I put the squares back inside, looking at the one on top. An embroidered slice of cherry pie. She'd worn this on an apron the first time I met her. She'd said it was her favorite.

"Are you making a new apron?"

"Oh, yes. My favorite used to be the cherry pie one you're holding, but it got too stained to wear. Thankfully I was able to salvage the best part, and it will look lovely on this new apron."

I looked back at the fabric square and noticed dark brown flecks staining the edges. I gave it a second look as a feeling of horror started to grow within me. The stains looked like dried blood. The puzzle pieces in my brain clicked together, creating a cohesive pattern, although I was still missing a few pieces from around the edges. Macie's button store had been displaced by one of David Stevens's developments, and now she thought the Rail Yard was at risk.

"You know, I think I left the kettle on in my cart." I should leave. Call the detective. Or maybe I was wrong and the stains were just cherry pie, or something. But my heart thumped.

"Oh, dear. Did I not cut all of it off? I did so hope to salvage part of the apron."

My mouth was open, and I forced it to close. My breath felt shaky. "You killed David Stevens."

"I'm sorry you figured that out, dear. Although I'm not as sorry as I would have been since you're related to Jimmy Jones."

Chapter 28

Macie held a pair of sewing scissors as she advanced my way. I backed up. My foot stepped on another box on the floor. I slipped and flung my arms out as I tried not to fall.

"Did you want the police to think I'd killed David? Is that why you left his body by my cart?" I'd realized how tall she was compared to me.

"Oh, not at all, that was luck. I caught David breaking into your cart when I was bringing a new mixing bowl. I'd dropped my favorite bowl earlier that day and it broke into a million pieces. It's been a rough summer."

"How did you jump from catching David breaking into my cart to killing him?" My thoughts were spinning in circles, looking for a way out of this.

"We talked. Did you know his new building is going to have electronic hawk noises? He's going to scare away all of my babies! And he wanted to find blackmail material to force your uncle to sell this lot to him. I couldn't let him destroy my pie cart. Not after losing my button store."

I froze when I stared at Macie. Blackmail? Me?

"You know, I didn't understand why David thought putting a camera in your cart would force Jimmy Jones to sell out to him. But I didn't know you were related. Now it all makes sense."

"What did David think he'd catch me doing? Singing off-key to the radio?" I wanted to glance around Macie's cart but instead searched my memory while eyeing her, keeping a safe distance between us. What had been in here when I entered? A rolling pin was a few feet behind me. I edged backward.

"David had a nice spy camera, so I took it home with me. I synced it with my tablet so I can watch my babies at home while I'm at work. I should've known you'd be a problem. After all, you let your dog drink the pigeons' water."

"Bentley was only here one day. I didn't know how important the water was to you." I edged back another inch. "Why did you use the box cutter from my cart?"

"When I hit David, he was only stunned. Zarek borrowed my extra box knife to loan to you, so I knew it would be in your cart, and David had already unlocked your door. Zarek likes you, you know, but you don't make it easy on him."

She talked about my love life as if this situation were normal. Like she always hunted down people for fun. I swallowed hard. My foot slid backward a half inch.

"This was my chance to protect my business, as I need this cart, you know, and to save my babies. So I took it."

I shivered. Macie was so nonchalant about killing a living, breathing man. Macie the human-game hunter. I edged back another quarter of an inch.

"You were wearing your apron, weren't you? You always forget and wear them home."

"I like my aprons. They have pockets. It's too bad my favorite ended up soaked in David's blood. At least I was able to salvage the patch from the chest. There's always a silver lining."

"What's your end goal here? If you hurt me, people will get suspicious."

"Oh, you came in to rob me. You're part of the Portland Mafia, so people will believe me. That's what people call Jimmy, you know. The Portland Mafia."

"Bobby Kennedy took down the Portland mob back in the 1960s," I said, remembering a book review from the local paper as I grasped at any topic that would distract her. She needed to focus on my face, not my hands. I was there. I reached behind me, feeling for the rolling pin. But my skills were rusty. I'd miscalculated and brushed the rolling pin just enough to make it spin away from the edge of my fingers.

"Stop that." Macie stalked forward.

There was only one option. I crouched and sprung toward the customer window. Macie rushed after me. Something sliced my calf as I threw myself outside. The cutesy tin buckets holding plastic forks and knives on the edge of the ordering window crashed down to the pavement with me.

Chapter 29

I'd balanced on the window's wide ledge enough to get my feet under me, so I didn't land headfirst. But the ground hurt as I hit and rolled, scraping up my arms and legs.

A woman's voice yelled from the direction of my cart. "Sage, are you okay?"

I looked up and saw Emma. At the same time, Macie stumbled down the stairs of her cart, huffing angrily. She held sewing scissors in one hand and a rolling pin in the other.

"Emma, call 911!" I yelled.

Zarek rushed out of his cart as I tried to stand up. My legs worked, although my right calf stung. I felt like I'd downed eighty shots of bourbon in an hour.

Zarek ran in my direction.

"Watch out!" I screamed as Macie swung the rolling pin at him. Zarek jumped back. Macie lost her balance and stumbled. He circled around her. Emma held her mobile phone to her ear, and she was talking. She had better be on the phone with 911, or we'd have a serious conversation about priorities later.

Zarek wrapped his arm around me, helping me feel steady. "What's going on?"

Macie stood up and faced us. She held up her scissors. "Sage tried to rob me."

"Tell the truth, Macie." Adrenaline still pumped through my body, but it was going to fade. But I made my voice sound tough like I was in control. I straightened my shoulders, playing the part of someone unflappable. Someone strong. Like an Amazon. Zarek's hands had shifted downward, steadying me. I drew strength from his presence. "Everyone will find out. Do you want them to hear rumors or the truth from you?"

Sirens in the distance made me hope this would end before anyone else got hurt. More hurt, anyway, as my calf screamed at me.

"Truth, what is truth?" Macie flicked her head, showing she was a vulture in the body of a pigeon.

"Truth is telling the world why you killed David Stevens instead of letting others take the blame. Did you know the police are holding his teenage daughter? She was here. She saw her father die."

"The only kid here was a gutter punk who begs for food."

Part of me rejoiced. Jackson and I had heard Gabby's side of the story, but Macie could only have known Gabby had been here if she'd done it.

"Macie killed David Stevens? For real?" Zarek asked. His arm around my waist twitched. If Macie rushed us, we might get in each other's way. Zarek could get hurt. But I couldn't step to the side to put distance between us.

"Yes, Macie killed David," I said as two police officers ran into the lot.

"Put the knife down!" one of them ordered.

The last of my adrenaline fled. My legs shook. Zarek lowered me to the ground, although we both kept our eyes on Macie.

Macie brandished her scissors in my direction, which, from a distance, looked like a knife. "I want that girl arrested!" she screamed.

"Ma'am, put the knife down," one of the police officers repeated. Both officers had their guns drawn but held low.

"Listen to them, Macie. You've already killed David Stevens. We don't need a second death here," I said.

Macie tried to run at me, but one of the officers tripped her.

Within seconds, he'd kicked the scissors away and wrestled her arms behind her back. She squirmed, trying to fight. I breathed out in relief when the officer clicked handcuffs into place. Her rolling pin rolled away from them, slowly making its way to the fence along the side of the Rail Yard.

Emma came rushing over with towels. She knelt by me. "Your leg."

I looked down and saw a gash where Macie had cut me as I was jumping out of the window.

"Sharp scissors," I said, feeling sick to my stomach. My brain felt faint.

Emma held a towel to my leg. "Stay focused."

I focused on her concerned eyes, wondering how I could've suspected her of murder. Zarek grabbed one of the towels and put it on top of the first, which was already turning pink.

One of the officers joined us.

"Macie confessed she killed David Stevens. She tried to kill me too. There's a fabric square in her cart with an image of a slice of cherry pie on it. David Stevens's bloodstains are on it."

"An ambulance is on its way," the officer said.

Both Zarek and Emma focused on holding towels to my leg. I looked at the scrapes on my hands, but no one was worried about them.

"Did you hear me about the fabric square? It's proof," I said.

"I heard you," the officer said. "Now calm down."

"Macie hurt David?" Emma asked me. Her hands trembled on my leg.

"Yes, I'm sorry."

"May she rot in . . ." Emma's voice broke off. Tears streamed down her face.

"I'm sorry," I whispered.

Within a few minutes, an ambulance arrived. A short while later, I was on my way to the hospital.

*   *   *

"Knock knock."

I smiled 'cause I recognized the voice from the doorway of my hospital room. "Hi, Dad."

"Pumpkin." He walked in, a gold shield clipped to his hip.

"You at work?"

"Taking my lunch. So you're going to live?" He commandeered one of the chairs next to my bed.

"Looks like it. I have stitches in my leg, though. I didn't need surgery." My calf was going to ache for a while. But no tendons or ligaments had been hurt in the making of this film, so it was all good.

We chatted for a few minutes before another person showed up at my door.

"Hey, Jackson, come join the party," I said.

"You okay?" He handed me a bear holding a crutch with its leg in a white cast. I snorted.

"A pie maker with a thirst for murder can't keep me down for long." I winced. "Okay, I need to work on my delivery and word choice."

"I hope the pain meds are helping your leg and not just affecting your brain," Jackson said.

"At least I was wearing shorts, so my favorite jeans weren't ruined."

"Jeans might have kept you from needing stitches."

"Look at you, throwing logic around."

But my humor faded when my next gentleman caller showed up. Jackson and my dad followed the direction of my gaze.

"Detective Will," Jackson said. My father nodded hello.

"I need to get your statement about the events of today." Detective Will walked over and leaned against the wall, where he had a view of my face. He held up his phone, showing me he was going to record our conversation.

"What do you say, lawyer?" I asked my brother.

"Let's hear it. Try not to babble."

So I told my story, which felt too bizarre to be real. But I'd always said Macie was doing her best to keep Portland weird. I hadn't realized how far she'd go.

"It ended with me vaulting out of a pie cart. Solid eight for effort, but I didn't stick the landing."

"Back up. What's this about her nephew dealing drugs?" Detective Will asked.

"David Stevens didn't know about that," I said, and waved my hand. "Macie told me she took one of David's cameras home, so I bet it has a serial number or something you can tie back to the Stevens company account. Arthur said they buy the cameras for use on their construction sites."

"Back to the drugs."

"Macie's nephew sells joints when he works at the cart. Another time, he left a couple of joints in a Little Lending Library around the corner. I saw him do it, so I pretended I was taking a book but palmed the joints. To think I was worried about Macie getting into trouble because of her nephew. I threw the pot away, in case you're wondering. Say no to drugs and all. Especially when your dad's a police officer."

Jackson was trying not to laugh, but he sobered up. "When did this happen? Before or after your cart was broken into?"

"Before. Since Macie was the killer, her nephew must have broken into my cart, looking for the baggie. I can't think of any other reason why someone would break in but not take anything. Unless Foster was just being a jerk." Now that I knew who'd killed David Stevens, the final puzzle pieces had clicked into place. Uncle Jimmy had been wrong. David's body wasn't a message to my mother. We'd jumped at ghosts, although my mother had inadvertently caused David's death. David saw me and assumed I'd do something blackmailworthy. But the steps he took turned fatal. I frowned.

Detective Will asked me more questions, going through my conversation with Macie in depth.

"I told one of the officers about the fabric square," I said.

"We found it and will analyze the stains to see if it's blood."

"You're always the optimist."

Jackson snorted.

My father glanced at his watch. "I need to go back to work." He patted my leg that hadn't been slashed by a baker obsessed with pigeons.

"See you later."

"I'll stop by Jackson's house when I get off work."

Hmm, how many stairs can I handle with stitches? At least Jackson's living room couch is comfortable if I couldn't get up to the attic. Or I could take over Bentley's extra-large dog bed, even though it smelled like Eau de Australian Shepherd.

My dad left. Detective Will straightened up from where he'd been leaning against the wall.

"I told you from the beginning you were wasting time investigating me."

"Perhaps, although you ended up in the thick of the soup."

"More like the filling of the pie." I hadn't been the spider in the middle of the web, but I'd been the wrecking ball that smashed everything. "What about Gabby? Macie admitted Gabby was there when David died, and there's only one way she knew that. Because Macie is a murderer. Which are words I never thought I'd say."

"You know, I might've heard something similar from Zarek Costas and Emma Dennison," Detective Will said. "In the course of doing my job and interviewing them."

"I could've saved you time." I frowned, seeing one puzzle piece that didn't seem to fit into this picture. "How'd you know Gabby went to Jackson's office?"

"Police work. Plus a bit of luck when one of the parking enforcers saw Gabby and recognized her from the photo we showed all of them. Once I saw the list of businesses in the building, I made an educated guess where she'd gone."

"Meter maids are only around when you don't want them. Do you ever see one when some jerk's parked blocking your driveway? No." My brain felt as if it were starting to float above my body.

"Take care, Sage. Stay out of trouble." Detective Will was smiling for once as he walked out.

Chapter 30

After a few days, the stitches on the back of my leg shifted to annoying versus painful. But I appreciated Harley taking over the cart full-time for a few days, since standing was uncomfortable. The flowers Zarek dropped by the day after my showdown with Macie were beautiful, and Emma stopped by with Thai peanut butter cups from a local chocolatier. Manny and Harley had come by and played *Settlers of Catan* with Jackson and me, and from the way Harley kept looking at Manny, I saw a few dates in their future. Bax had biked over daily at lunchtime with takeout, plus he'd come over a few evenings. He was running the risk of developing a bromance with Jackson, showing there's a first time for everything. Part of me was tempted to do a Harley and tell my brother I had first dibs.

I took Bentley for a slow walk, enjoying the relatively cold seventy-five-degree weather. My life felt peaceful, especially since I'd heard from Gabby. She'd agreed to move home. Her parents had found her a therapist and promised to enroll her in a new school so she could make a fresh start in more ways than one. She wasn't facing charges for the construction-site vandalism since she'd agreed to testify against both Tommy and Macie.

As Bentley and I walked, I remembered the words from a poem one of my professors had quoted in class: *Like the air around me, I al-*

ways rise. But I'm more like bread dough than air. Kneading makes the protein structure of the yeast form bonds that allow bread to rise. Going through the past few weeks had only made me stronger. I hoped someday Gabby would be able to say the same thing.

My phone dinged. Unknown sender.

I heard you solved the murder of one of my old boyfriends. Good job.

My mother. I took a deep breath and shoved my phone back into my pocket. Bentley leaned against my leg. I reached down and caressed the back of his head.

"You know what will fix my mood?" I asked him. "Coffee. Coffee makes everything better."

So we went out for coffee and let the future take care of itself.

RECIPES

Kopi Jahe

You can make kopi jahe the traditional way—cowboy-style—by mixing the ginger, water, and grounds all in the same saucepan and bringing it to a boil, which is how Sage first came across the drink while staying at a surf camp in Indonesia. But if you want an easy way to filter the coffee, Ground Rules recommends using a French press.

Note the 1 tablespoon to 1 cup of water ratio below; you can make a smaller or larger serving of kopi jahe by decreasing both the water and number of tablespoons of coffee grounds, or increasing them, as long as you keep to the 1:1 ratio.

Ingredients
6 tablespoons of coarse-ground coffee
6 cups of water
¼ cup sugar; Ground Rules recommends turbinado
A piece of fresh ginger about three inches long, crushed or
    chopped finely. A garlic press can be helpful here.
Coconut milk

Optional Add-Ins
Lemongrass (one stalk, cut into thin rounds)
2 cinnamon sticks
3–4 whole cardamom pods, crushed with the back of a spoon or
    with a mortar and pestle

Special Equipment Needed
French press (able to hold at least six cups of hot liquid)

Preparation
Mix the water, sugar, ginger, and any (or all) optional add-ins into the saucepan. Bring it to a boil. Reduce heat to a simmer and stir until the sugar is dissolved. Simmer for 2–3 minutes.

Meanwhile, add your coffee grounds to your French press. When the water-ginger-sugar mixture is done simmering, pour it into the French press and stir. Let the coffee steep for four minutes, then plunge the coffee. Pour into cups and add coconut milk to taste.

Mason Jar Cold Brew Coffee

Kyoto coffee—aka cold brew—has been popular in Japan since the 1600s, and legend has it that Dutch coffee traders brought the practice with them from Indonesia. Nowadays, you can buy premade cold brew concentrate, but making your own is simple. You only need to mix coffee grounds and cold water together and let them sit in the fridge for 12–24 hours.

Cold brew is sweeter and less acidic than coffee made with hot water. You can buy fancy pitchers to make cold brew, but you can also make it in mason jars or a simple French press.

Making coffee is all about the proper ratio of coffee grounds to water. To make a cold brew concentrate, you'll need ¾ cup of coarse-ground coffee to 4 cups of water.

You can double, triple, quadruple, etc., this recipe, just keep the ¾ cup grounds to 4 cups of water ratio intact.

Ingredients

4 cups of water
¾ cup of coarse coffee grounds

Preparation

Mix four cups of water and the ¾ cup of coffee grounds in an appropriately sized mason jar and screw on the lid. Place in the refrigerator for 12–24 hours.

When the coffee has brewed to your liking, strain it into a clean pitcher or mason jar.

Serve over ice and dilute with water or milk at a 1:1 ratio, or to taste. To sweeten, add in simple syrup.

Sage Simple Syrup

Use this simple syrup with an herbal note in cold brew, hot coffee, tea, cocktails, etc.

Ingredients

2 cups of water
2 cups turbinado sugar★
20 fresh sage leaves★★

Preparation

Bring the water to a boil in a saucepan; add the sugar and stir until it melts. Add the sage leaves and simmer for about one minute, then turn off the heat and let the sugar-water-sage mixture seep for 45 minutes. Strain the mixture through a sieve into a bottle, jar, or other closable (and airtight) container.

The sage simple syrup will last up to two weeks in the refrigerator.

Tip from Ground Rules: English mesh tea strainers, especially the ones with long handles meant for loose-leaf tea, can be great for straining syrups, especially if you use mason jars with reusable lids at home.

★You can substitute any type of sugar, including brown or granulated. Turbinado has a rich, molasses-like flavor, which makes a visually dark syrup, while granulated sugar will create a visually lighter syrup.
★★You can add more sage leaves if you'd like a stronger flavor, or use fewer to make a milder syrup.

Sage Coffee Soda

A coffee soda is a refreshing afternoon drink on a hot summer's day. This version uses sage simple syrup, which gives the soda an herbal note.

Ingredients
¾ cup of cold brew concentrate
1 tablespoon of sage simple syrup (or to taste)
Ice
¾ cup of club soda

Preparation
Mix the cold brew concentrate and simple syrup in a wide-mouth, pint-size mason jar (or glass of your choosing). Add ice to the top of the glass, then slowly pour in the club soda. Lightly mix, and you're ready to rumble with your coffee soda.

Sage Tea Soda

If you're not a coffee fan, you can still make your own soda, but using tea! You'll replace the coffee concentrate with tea brewed extra-strong (e.g., with a higher ratio of tea leaves to water than usual).

Ingredients
Tea of your choosing (black, green, white, rooibos)
1 tablespoon of sage simple syrup
Ice
¾ cup of club soda

Preparation
First, you'll make your tea concentrate. You'll want to dramatically up your ratio of tea leaves to water. If you're using a teabag, instead of one tea bag to one mug of water, you'll just add maybe an inch of water in your usual cup.

Brew the tea for the usual amount of time (30 seconds to 1 minute for green, 3–4 minutes for black, 6 minutes for rooibos). Do not brew the tea for longer than usual—that will make it bitter. We want to make the tea stronger, not over-brewed.

Once your tea concentrate is done and you've strained it and/or removed the bag, you're ready for the fun part!

Mix the tea concentrate and sage simple syrup in a wide-mouth, pint-size mason jar (or glass of your choosing). Add ice to the top of the glass, then slowly pour in the club soda. Lightly mix, and voilà! You have a tea soda.

Sage Cold Brew Cocktail

Ingredients
1½ ounces of cold brew coffee★
1 ounce of bourbon
1 ounce of half-and-half or nondairy alternative (coconut milk or Oatly Barista work well)
½ ounce sage simple syrup
Ice
Cinnamon stick

Preparation
Add all of the ingredients except the cinnamon stick to a cocktail shaker and shake for about ten seconds. Pour into a coupe glass and garnish with a cinnamon stick.

★One fluid ounce is equal to two tablespoons.

Sage's Favorite Brunch Cocktail

Cold brew coffee, berries, and fresh grapefruit juice pair with gin and Chambord to make a fresh cocktail perfect for starting—or ending—the day.

Ingredients
6 blackberries or raspberries
1 ounce Chambord
½ ounce sage simple syrup
1 ounce gin
1 tablespoon grapefruit juice
Ice cubes
2 ounces of cold brew

Equipment
Cocktail shaker
Coupe glass

Preparation
Crush five of the berries with the Chambord, then mix them with the sage simple syrup in the cocktail shaker. Add 1 ounce of gin and the tablespoon of grapefruit juice. Add the ice to the cocktail shaker, then pour the cold brew over the ice. Shake well and then strain into the coupe glass. Garnish with the sixth berry.

This cocktail goes well with Oregon French toast for an extra special brunch.

Oregon French Toast

Fun fact: Oregon produces about ninety-nine percent of the USA's hazelnut crop, and it's been the official state nut since 1989. Although Oregonians tend to call the nut a *filbert*.

Serves 2 people.

Ingredients

2 large eggs, beaten
1 cup of milk (or Oatly works well as a nondairy substitute!)
2 teaspoons of sugar
½ teaspoon vanilla extract
½ teaspoon cinnamon
⅛ teaspoon salt
1 cup of coarsely chopped hazelnuts
4 slices of day-old challah bread, cut thickly (brioche or French bread also works)
Butter or canola oil

Preparation

Whisk together all of the ingredients except the nuts, bread, and butter or oil in a mixing bowl. Put the nuts in their own wide-mouth bowl.

Prepare the griddle or skillet by either melting the butter in the pan or rubbing canola oil across the surface.

Dip the bread slices in the egg mixture, taking care to soak both sides, then dredge the bread in the hazelnuts.

Cook the bread slices in the skillet until brown, about 2 minutes per side.

If you want to up your Oregon cred, serve your French toast with marionberry jam! Or serve it with maple syrup, other jam, butter, fresh fruit, etc.

Zarek's PNW Zhug Sauce

While Zarek prefers to serve zhug sauce on falafel, it's also excellent on eggs, grilled meat, and more. Since it's easier to find fresh jalapeños in Oregon, Zarek started using them, although some people use serranos or Thai bird chilies.

For brunch, consider serving zhug sauce on poached eggs and pairing with espresso or Turkish coffee.

Ingredients

3 cardamom pods (internal seeds only—remove the seeds from
  the exterior pods)
1 teaspoon black peppercorns
¼ teaspoon whole coriander seeds
½ teaspoon whole cumin seeds
3–5 fresh jalapeños, chopped (note: swap in a habanero or two if
  you want to make this spicier)
4 garlic cloves, chopped
Juice from one lemon (about 2–3 tablespoons)
1 teaspoon kosher salt, or to taste
½ cup olive oil (extra-virgin is best)
1 cup fresh parsley
1 cup fresh cilantro

Preparation

Put the cardamom seeds (remember, internal seeds only), peppercorns, coriander seeds, and cumin seeds in a dry skillet over medium-high heat, swirling often, until they turn fragrant. This should take about two minutes. Remove from heat and put the seeds in either your mortar and pestle or food processor to cool.

Once cool, grind the seeds into a powder. Don't over-grind—you want this to remain chunky. Add the chilies, garlic, lemon, salt, cilantro, and parsley and combine them into a rough paste. Slowly drizzle olive oil in until the oil is emulsified; season with additional salt if desired. The sauce should be thick and chunky versus smooth. It can be served immediately or stored in the refrigerator for several weeks.

Acknowledgments

Fresh Brewed Murder wouldn't be in your hands today if not for my agent, Joshua Bilmes, and my editor, John Scognamiglio, and his team at Kensington. So grande, no, venti, thanks for all your sage advice.

My early readers and critiquers deserve an endless number of lattes for giving me feedback on *Fresh Brewed Murder,* so let me know when you want them, Nevin, Miriam, Robin, and Peter. Ester went above and beyond the call of duty by reading an early draft and answering law-related questions. Thanks to Bill Cameron for designing my website and for being a writing-related sounding board.

All mistakes are my own. As always, thanks to Jim, who is the cream . . . err, oat milk . . . in my coffee.

If you like the idea of suspended coffees, please know it's a real movement embraced by cafés worldwide. The concept of suspended coffees—or caffè sospeso—originated in Naples, Italy, at the turn of the twentieth century. I first became aware of the movement thanks to Todd and his Ole Latte coffee cart in Portland, Oregon. So next time you buy a cup of coffee, consider paying one forward.

Finally, I'd like to thank the hardworking food cart owners in Portland, Oregon. Food carts are emblematic of Portland, with their mix of independence, passion, creativity, and quality. I hope I've represented them well in *Fresh Brewed Murder!*